"Don't you l..."

"Don't give me that hope. Please. I'd rather be a lifelong friend, but I don't want either of us to think that we could be more. Not on a part-time basis."

Scott was breathing hard. Amelia remained silent as he walked to the edge of the ocean. He turned, looked at her and came back. Gently he lifted her into an embrace and whispered against her hair.

"Ah, Amelia. Hell, you make me crazy. I just found you, and now I'm going to lose you."

"No, you're not. I promise." Her lips kissed the tender skin behind his ear, and his head moved into the caress.

"Let's go home," Scott whispered. "There isn't much time left. An afternoon and a night. It isn't much, and I need so much from you."

ABOUT THE AUTHOR

Rebecca Bond holds an M.B.A. in marketing and has worked as an advertising copywriter, as well as an account executive. Her passion is traveling, which she feels gives her new story ideas; she has been all over the world, including China and Japan. A native Californian, Rebecca lives in Los Angeles with her husband, a federal prosecutor, and her young son, Alexander.

Books by Rebecca Bond

HARLEQUIN AMERICAN ROMANCE
92–IN PASSION'S DEFENSE
109–BED AND BOARD

HARLEQUIN INTRIGUE
31–THE MATTHIAS RING

Open Channels
Rebecca Bond

Harlequin Books

TORONTO • NEW YORK • LONDON
AMSTERDAM • PARIS • SYDNEY • HAMBURG
STOCKHOLM • ATHENS • TOKYO • MILAN

Published October 1986

First printing August 1986

ISBN 0-373-16172-7

Printed in Canada

Chapter One

Sounds of laughter were everywhere. The children ran to bushes, trash cans and park benches. Their little hands searched out every conceivable hiding place, pinching and grasping, looking for the colored eggs and bags of candy that had been hidden throughout the park.

For the most part, the eyes that shone with antici- pation were bright and black. These were the children of the ghettos, children who had seldom, if ever, hunted for an Easter egg in all their short little lives, children who lived in tall, run-down apartment build- ings where a lawn was unheard of and extra money for an Easter basket, much less anything to put in it, was a luxury beyond comprehension.

But that day, under the glorious Los Angeles sun, in the week before Easter, these children did not feel underprivileged. The excitement of the event wiped out, for a moment, their dreary days and nights. They became like children anywhere who are suddenly thrust into a wonderland of color and candy.

There, shading their eyes from the bright spring sunlight, visitors would have taken in the scene, and a smile would have crept to their lips as their gaze wandered. But then they would have focused on the one person who did not belong. They would linger for a minute, looking at the tall woman in the beige suit, wheat-colored, like her hair. They would think her a social worker as they watched her bending over the raven-braided little girl, helping her pull a purple egg from the crotch of a small tree. Perhaps, if they were close enough when she turned, they would notice the people who stood near her, waiting, watching. And, if they were closer still, they would hear her speak into the microphone she raised to her wide, full lips.

"... and, so, this is Amelia Jenkins reporting live from the third annual Easter egg hunt sponsored by the city of Los Angeles."

Still holding the little girl's hand, Amelia looked down, then back to the camera, and smiled a smile so dazzling that the cameraman instinctively lingered longer than he should.

"That's perfect, Amelia." Tom lowered the Mini-cam from his shoulder and spoke as he walked toward her. Amelia had released the little girl and was ready to go on to the next assignment, but the child still stood looking up at the tall woman with the porcelain skin as if expecting her to continue the hunt. She was unaware that Amelia's high heels would have precluded such a venture even if she had been inclined to participate.

"Thanks, Tom." Amelia sighed, raising her slender fingers to her forehead. She could feel beads of sweat forming just below the perfectly straight part in her hair and behind the low chignon, which still looked impeccable despite the ninety-degree weather. She wondered if her makeup would last through the day. There were still three interviews to do and it was already one o'clock in the afternoon.

She lowered the cordless microphone to her side and knit her brow as she considered her schedule. There was the Olympic track champion who had come to Los Angeles to make his film debut, the newly re-elected mayor who would be serving an unprecedented fourth term and...and...

"Tom, who have I got scheduled at four? For the life of me, I can't remember." Her eyes squinted at the handsome man who came to a halt beside her. She was so preoccupied with what seemed to be her failing memory that she didn't notice his smile brighten as he looked into her robin-egg-blue eyes.

Usually, she would draw her lips into a tight line when his attention became too evident in public, but on that day she hardly realized he was there. She could have been talking to her appointment calendar, flipping casually through the pages, for all she knew. For, if there was one thing Amelia Jenkins was, it was professional. More than professional. Some called her driven, some a workaholic.

"You were going to Redondo Beach to check out that guy who made a million making surfboards or Windsurfers, something like that...." Tom Creighton's voice trailed off with practiced restraint.

He knew that look on her face; it meant only one thing—business. It was one of the qualities he loved most about her. Amelia Jenkins was a consummate professional, a woman who had worked her way up to be one of the most respected talk-show hosts and newswomen in Los Angeles. Not only did she manage to do her interviews for the nightly news, but she was always supremely prepared for her weeknight half-hour in-depth news show. Amelia usually knew more about her guests than they knew about themselves.

"Oh, yes," she mused aloud. "That's not one I'm looking forward to. The guy is obviously a fluke."

Amelia handed her microphone to one of the assistants as casually as she would have laid her purse on a table, and moved to begin the walk back to the van. Her mouth started to form words, but they were never spoken. She felt a tug at the hem of her skirt. She almost didn't notice, so engrossed was she in her thoughts, but the insistent tugging finally caught her attention. She shook her head as though fighting off sleep, looking toward the offending sensation and thinking that she had caught her skirt on a tree, ready to be miffed that she wouldn't look perfect for the remaining interviews.

Instead, she found herself looking down into the upturned face of the little girl who had been on camera with her. The girl's pudgy little hand was caked with dirt, and Amelia noticed the imprint of four little fingers on the golden silk of her suit.

She gave a sigh of disappointment as she stared at the dirt, but then, seeing the expectant look on the little girl's face, she bent down, balancing herself on the balls of her feet, and carefully took the girl's hands in her own.

"I have to go now," she said, forming her words carefully as though that would help the child understand. "I can't stay." She tried again, and again was given a look of such hope that it seemed it would melt her heart. She quickly glanced at Tom and, seeing that look of unutterable delight on his face, she pulled back from the girl. Amelia didn't want Tom to see how much the child's action had affected her. In front of her crew, and especially Tom, Amelia wanted to remain professionally aloof. It was the only way to command the respect she needed.

"Tom, get someone to explain to her that she has to hunt on her own now.... Please," she said, as she unwound herself and brushed at her skirt.

Quickly he moved toward one of the city proctors, who explained in rapid Spanish that the blond-haired woman had to go. The little girl smiled sadly, then reached into her basket and offered Amelia the purple egg.

Forgetting Tom and her crew, Amelia took the egg, bent down once again and kissed the little girl on the cheek before she watched her scamper away, already forgetting Amelia. Watching her go, Amelia felt that all-too-familiar pain in her heart, the tug that signaled another intruding thought of personal loneliness. Would she ever watch her own child skip away from her? It hardly seemed likely, since there had been little time for romance as she worked her way up the newsroom ladder, and now, perhaps, it was too late. But, efficiently controlled as always, Amelia put such thoughts out of her mind, fighting them back until they were hardly more troubling than an annoying gnat. Turning to Tom, she spoke again. "Now, where were we?"

They began to walk toward the van slowly, since the ground was soft and Amelia's shoes were of cream-colored kid. For once the Parks Department had done its job and watered the ground. The only problem was that they had done it only two hours before the hunt was scheduled to begin. *How inefficient,* Amelia thought to herself before she turned her attention to the dark-haired man beside her.

"Scott Alexander." Tom simply refreshed her memory with his hint, and Amelia took it from there.

"Oh, yes, the wunderkind of Windsurfers. He's scheduled for the show Tuesday night. I can tell you I'm not looking forward to this at all." Amelia slipped a pair of sunglasses over her eyes and climbed into the back of the van, talking the entire time. "I know his type. Surfer boy makes good just because the current fashion is windsurfing. The old 'right place at the right time' and presto... millions. Did you see that promotional photo he sent? I mean, it has all the professionalism of a potato!"

Tom fell back into his usual seat beside her. He knew that tone of voice and waited for her to get it out of her system. Amelia was a fighter, and he knew that her assessment of people was usually right on target. In this case, he had no reason to think any differently. He, too, had seen the photo.

"If he was such a hotshot businessman, don't you think he would have the knowledge, if not the courtesy, to send us something we could use on the air? The office is always very specific about that. People on the show are told that their photos will be used in the intro portion before we actually get to the taped interviews. But this jerk sends a photo that belongs in a family album. Did you see it?"

Amelia turned to Tom, demanding an answer this time. She looked confused. When it came to business, anything other than complete perfection baffled her. It was incomprehensible that anyone concerned about his image would not do everything in his power to create the proper aura about himself. After all, she had gotten to the top of her profession by doing everything by the book, which proved that it paid.

"Yeah, I saw it. Cute, if you like that kind of thing." Tom shrugged, remembering the snapshot of the man standing beside the gleaming Windsurfer.

He wasn't dressed in a business suit, which would have been the norm. He wasn't dressed at all, so to speak. Instead, he leaned casually toward the colorful sail, his arms crossed over a bronzed, almost hairless chest, his long legs planted in the sand. His only covering was a pair of baggy shorts that looked as though they had seen better days. Yes, Tom had seen it.

The face of Scott Alexander was still clear in his memory. Alexander seemed to be exactly what Amelia made of him . . . at least from his photo. The man's eyes danced as though suddenly amused. His smile was crooked and would be considered charming by the majority of women under twenty-five, Tom imagined. He wasn't handsome in the strict sense of the word, or maybe the picture didn't do him justice, for in it he lounged as though he were the most desirable male in the world.

"Well, I'm not bowled over by that kind of thing," Amelia said, bursting into Tom's thoughts. "It's strictly high school. The kind of publicity picture you'd use if you were running for campus hunk." Amelia lowered her eyes and inspected her mauve-tipped nails. Tom glanced at her. She was definitely hot on the subject, and he almost felt sorry for the guy. He wouldn't want to be interviewed by Amelia if he were Scott Alexander. She had no mercy for people who simply floated through life.

"Yep, you're right. I know the information package we have on him makes him seem less than substantial. College in Hawaii . . . probably majored in surfing. His father gave him the money to start this business. I stopped counting the number of other jobs he had. Never married. Almost seems like a drifter, considering the traveling he does. His only saving grace is his Vietnam record. Funny, he volunteered for his tour of duty. You wouldn't expect a guy who seems to have a minimal attention span to do that kind of thing. Not only that, he did two tours as a lieutenant flying choppers. I guess that counts for something."

"I suppose," Amelia said, shrugging, "but I still don't understand why the station was so anxious to include him in this piece on local entrepreneurs, unless they're trying to raise the ratings with the under-twenty-five demographic. Sure his company is succesful, but I think we should only have those people who really struggled with a new idea...." Amelia's voice trailed off, and she turned her head to look out the window and watch the park filled with children fade into oblivion. "Someone who really busted his butt..." she mused to herself, remembering again how hard she had worked for what she had.

"MAMA," AMELIA SAID. She was twirling the thin layer of dust on the windowsill into fanciful rings, examining each of them as she did so, just before her mother's dust cloth swooped down to wipe the entire sill spotlessly clean. Amelia backed away and leaned against the wall, watching her mother dreamily.

She was a beautiful woman, thought twelve-year-old Amelia. Beautiful and strong. A proud German woman who took tight-lipped pride in the fact that even though she had come to the United States when she was nineteen she had learned English so well that she had no trace of an accent. Amelia's mother was a woman who could survive, as she put it, anything.

But Amelia had been too young to really appreciate what that meant in terms of the war. It wasn't until her father died when she was eleven that she understood that strength was of spirit and mind. This was the strength her mother imbued in her. For a year now she had had to be strong, too. It was confusing. It was hard to do. But, following her mother's quietly determined example, Amelia was learning to find strength in herself. Sometimes, though, like today, she wanted something else. She wanted to be a child.

"Ja," her mother answered, never breaking stride as she moved about the apartment putting things in order. While one hand dusted, the other fluffed pillows, straightened pictures and smoothed tablecloths. Her feet pushed the rug into a perfect rectangle as she passed by on her way to clean the bathroom. Amelia smiled, knowing her mother did not realize that she sometimes lapsed into the all-too-familiar German when her mind was elsewhere.

"Mama, can't you slow down for a minute? I've already done the bathroom." Amelia followed her mother, flipping her long blond braids over her shoulder. She hated her braids, but it seemed to give her mother such pleasure to plait them each morning that Amelia didn't have the heart to suggest cutting them—at least not that year.

"Ah, that's a good girl." Her mother shot a small, lovely smile over her shoulder but forged ahead to the bathroom anyway. "I'll just check it one more time."

"But, Mama, I thought since I did all my work and the rest of the house looks great, maybe we could go to the beach. It's going to be such a hot day and . . .''

Amelia stood in the bathroom doorway, watching her mother check for any spot of dirt. She liked things so clean! Work, work. Her mother's hands were never idle except in church.

Suddenly, Martha Jenkins stopped and straightened her back, turning toward her towheaded daughter. For a moment, Amelia thought her mother was going to reach for her, hug her, but then she saw that that was not the case. She smiled anyway. She had learned long ago that her mother was not the kind who hugged and kissed the way some mothers did. No, her mother loved her in a much different way.

She was always there when Amelia came home from school; she baked the things Amelia liked; she taught Amelia how to be a good, decent, strong person. But sometimes Amelia wished they could have just one day to laugh and do silly things. Now, as she watched, her mother perched on the edge of the tub and motioned Amelia toward her. Amelia stood before her and let her hands be captured.

"Amelia, there is so much to do here. Closets to be cleaned, furniture to be moved, and I promised Mr. Gleason I would have his books done by Monday," her mother explained patiently. Amelia nodded but her words raced ahead anyway.

"But today is Saturday. You have all day Sunday, and I promise we won't stay long. I could clean out the cabinets tomorrow while you work on those old books...." Amelia used her most persuasive smile and spoke so quickly that her mother actually broke out into an unaccustomed laugh.

"Ah, lamb," she said, releasing Amelia's hands and throwing up her own, "life is so boring for you alone with me. Why don't you call up some nice friend and go to the beach?''

"No, Mama, I want to go with you. And life isn't boring. Not all the time anyway." Amelia didn't want to tell her mother that she felt uncomfortable with the girls in her class at school. They were so . . . so . . . *silly* all the time. She had been silly like that once, before her father died. But now she knew there were other things she had to do. She had to work hard so that she and her mother would be comfortable. Nothing was more important than paying her mother back for this past year and all those years ahead when she would take care of Amelia alone. Every day Amelia's need to be a flighty little girl lessened, and her mother seemed to be proud of her. Oh, if only the mood hadn't grabbed her with such force today!

"All right, just this once we'll have a holiday like we used to when your papa was alive." For an instant Amelia thought she saw tears in her mother's eyes, but in a moment they were gone and her mother was preparing for their outing as efficiently as she had been cleaning the house moments before.

They spoke little as they waited for the bus. They walked with measured steps to the high, grassy bluff above the beach, four blocks from where the bus let them off. Amelia breathed deeply, the smell of sea and sand tickling her nose. The warm West breeze enveloped her, so that she hardly noticed her mother spread the blanket and motion for her to sit down.

"Someday, Mama, I'm going to be rich and buy you a house by the sea and we'll live there and you won't have to work anymore. I'll even hire a cleaning woman and you won't have to dust anymore. . . ." Amelia lowered her coltish frame onto the blanket and stretched her body, which was just now pushing toward womanhood.

"Then what would I do with myself?" her mother asked, setting out sandwiches and juice.

"Why, whatever you wanted," Amelia answered, shading her eyes from the sun, surprised that her mother would ask such a question.

"But without good honest work there is nothing. There is only time to grow old." The silence descended once again as Amelia lay back on the blanket, slowly eating a sandwich as she considered what her mother had said.

Only time to grow old. How awful, she mused to herself, turning the phrase about in her mind, keeping rhythm with it as she munched her food. She stole a glance at her mother, whose proud head was tipped to watch the people playing on the beach. Her mother would never be old. Oh, Amelia would work hard and buy her a house on the beach and she would never let her mother grow old. And neither would she let herself grow old. Her mother was right. Work. She would work hard, and together she and her mother would stay young forever. Amelia listened well to her mother. Perhaps too well.

"WE'RE HERE," Tom said, nudging Amelia's arm and pulling her back from the remembrances of her fight—some would say flight—to the top and how it began.

"I thought we were doing the mayor first." Amelia's statement was a question although she tried to disguise it. She prided herself on her memory, knowing where every minute of every day went.

"I guess I forgot to tell you. Her office called and switched her appointment to the later spot. We're doing the Olympian first." Tom spoke as he hopped from the van, knowing full well that he had informed Amelia of the change but admiring her too much to call her on it in front of the rest of the crew. He knew how hard she would be on herself if she thought she was in error, but he also knew how gentle she was when others were. Still, it was unlike her to be wrong. Her mind had been elsewhere for weeks now. She seemed to be struggling with something but she had not offered to share her problem with him.

"Oh, that's okay." Amelia's lips parted in a relieved smile. "I've got today's interviews almost memorized, so it doesn't really matter who's first."

She stepped down from the van after Tom, straightened her skirt, and strode on ahead toward a small crowd at the entrance to Mann's Chinese Theatre in Hollywood, leaving Tom pleased that he knew her so well.

The ornate old theater was one of Hollywood's most prized attractions. Sightseers never failed to be in awe of the outrageously oversized pagoda that was one of that city's first movie houses. Here, klieg lights had once pierced the night sky while stars of a golden era stepped delicately from their limousines to drink in the adoration of crowds roped off just far enough away so that they could not reach out and touch a mink or pull at a satin gown or a pleat-panted tuxedo.

Now, in the hazy afternoon light, the pagoda theater looked garishly old. It had been eons since Hollywood turned out for a premiere. The tourists still came to gaze but now even they seemed sadder, tattered. There were no longer any gods or goddesses of the silver screen, and Hollywood Boulevard seemed tarnished in their absence.

Yet, that day a small crowd had gathered around the lesser deity who was Amelia's target. A brash young man, known for his extraordinary power as a high-jump athlete, and for his even more extraordinary power to talk about himself to a fault, was already awaiting her crew. Heaving a sigh, Amelia strode resolutely through the crowd, introduced herself and began the tedious task of getting a word in edgewise while the young athlete plugged his new, and destined to be short, career in the movies.

It was almost four when Amelia and her entourage finished with the mayor. The Olympian's interview was in the can, and the heavily loaded van was heading away from the concrete forest of the city toward the edge of the world, the city of Redondo Beach, which looked out on one of the most beautiful stretches of beach in southern California.

"Perhaps we should call ahead and tell Mr. Alexander we'll be late. He may want to reschedule this interview for another day, Tom. After all, I can't imagine he'll take too long. His business did not exactly involve revolutionary marketing theories so far as I can tell."

Amelia was tired. Her golden head rested against the unforgiving seat of the van. The athlete had tried her patience at every turn and she had left the mayor's office wondering how the woman had ever been elected. Not that the mayor wasn't a charming lady, but she was a less-than-aggressive politician, and Amelia wondered if she really earned the salary she commanded. Now the thought of having to deal with

the half-naked surfer she had seen in the picture ran-
kled her.

She could understand his attraction. He looked like
everyone's idea of a southern Californian success. She
imagined that he commanded quite a coterie of ador-
ing little beauties at the beach. But she wasn't interested in him as an attractive man. Amelia only wanted
a strong show for her piece on local entrepreneurs and
she didn't think Scott Alexander would be the strong-
est link in the chain.

"Already had someone call, Amelia. He said come
ahead," Tom answered while he fiddled with the daily
log.

"Okay," she sighed, never opening her eyes, "we
might as well get it over with. But I want to make this
one quick."

"You got it. Just set the pace and we'll follow suit."

Amelia nodded and didn't stir again until she heard
the driver curse the deplorable parking situation he
found in the beach town.

"Double park, Sam," Amelia ordered as she sat up
and tapped the burly man on the shoulder. "We'll all
jump out and you can find a space at your leisure."

"You got it, Ms Jenkins," he said as the van veered
precariously close to a row of compact foreign cars
and came to a halt.

"Everybody out!" Tom ordered. "And thank God
for Minicams!" A tired chuckle rippled through the
vehicle as Amelia and her crew of four scampered out
of the van.

"It's down these steps and to the right," Tom said,
indicating the way to Scott Alexander's business
headquarters. But Amelia wasn't listening. All those
old feelings were overwhelming her... brought on by

the sea air with the sticky feel of salt in it. She was home. This was the home she had always promised herself but never quite managed to find. How many years ago was it that she had stopped looking at houses by the beach? Three? Five? She didn't know. She had meant to keep up the search. But, like her mother, she never seemed to have the time for leisure. She had to keep working.

"Amelia, this way." Tom had taken her elbow and was steering her toward the steep steps. Amelia shook her head to clear it so she could attend to the matters at hand. The last of the crew was already on the walk that separated the beach and the buildings.

"Sorry, Tom. Don't know what got into me." Gently she removed her arm from his grasp. She had been adamant that no one at the station know they dated occasionally, and Tom had adhered to the rule as though it were one of the Ten Commandments. Yet it still surprised him that even an innocent gesture in public could make her pull away as though the world would think he was propositioning her. Even though he believed he was in love with Amelia Jenkins, even though he knew he admired her greatly, Tom still thought she was wound a little tight at times.

"No problem. I just know how much you want to get this day over with," he said as she preceded him down the steps, unaware that he was admiring the way her skirt swayed against the back of her knees, the way her hips moved underneath the perfectly tailored cloth.

She picked her way slowly down the ancient stairs. Redondo Beach was one of the oldest settlements on the Pacific coast and that feeling of decrepitude one would find in most cities became charm here.

Though she tried to tame them, her clear blue eyes roamed beyond the concrete walk and the white sands to rest now and again on the pier. It looked weathered and strong like an ancient, wooden-legged seaman. It looked as though it found it strange having to bear upon its back the slick new restaurants and arcades. To her left she could see the great lighted sign arching over the entrance to the pier. King Harbor, it announced in huge letters that hung in the blue sky as though they were a message from heaven. Her ears perked up at the sound of the high tide crashing onto the shore and dancing its pagan dance around the pilings.

"Tomorrow..." she promised herself, "...tomorrow I'm going to start looking for that house again." And with that promise Amelia felt her heart give way to a gentleness she sometimes forgot existed in her. With it came a swell of loneliness great enough to match any wave the ocean's depths could muster.

But then, as she followed her crew, another sound invaded her mind, assaulting her ears. It was the sound of music, loud and raucous—and of laughter. How on earth were they going to conduct an interview with a party going on? This was going to be impossible, and she wouldn't put up with such unprofessional behavior no matter what the station manager said. If she couldn't get Mr. Alexander to stop partying and treat this interview seriously, then he was out of the segment. Period.

She strode resolutely through the door that Tom held open for her, her chin tilted as though for battle, her lips trembling for the first words she would speak when she encountered the Prince Royal of Windsurfers. But before she could speak she felt an arm around her waist and she was being twirled into the room.

"Just what we needed," cried a deep voice tinged with the pure joy of living. "Another beautiful lady to help us celebrate!" Amelia's head snapped toward the voice, the breath almost knocked out of her by the pressure of the man's muscular arm.

"Stop it!" Amelia commanded without thinking, her voice cold and biting enough to break through even the heavy rock music that blared in the room. Exhaustion had set in an hour ago and she didn't feel like playing. She stared at the hand on her waist and, with great deliberation, reached down to remove it before she turned to face her happy attacker.

"I'm here to see..." she began as she straightened her broad shoulders and turned her eyes toward him. The man was very young, a boy actually, and at her harsh words he released her, backing off, unsure of what he had done to anger her so. As he turned, Amelia saw another man, his face hidden by the boy. She heard him speak despite the roaring music.

"It's okay Jeff, but I think we better tone it down a bit," the man said. It was lovely, this easy, friendly, lilting assurance that came from the man who now moved toward her. And it was then that the world dropped away and only she and the soft-spoken man were left facing each other. The music, the noise, the people, were gone for an instant.

Surprise and anger were quelled by a feeling much more powerful—the raw sense of her womanhood. It tugged at her like a winter wind pulling delicate drapery through a window foolishly left open before a storm. Hard as she tried, for a moment Amelia could not shut that window. She was caught by the wind, pulled by it, until she thought there was nothing left but to leave the window open and succumb to the insistent wind.

Amelia Jenkins faced Scott Alexander and was left speechless by what she saw in his face. It was a nameless something that she had always been afraid she would find one day, though she had been unaware of the fear until now, because it was so deeply seated. Unwilling to give in so easily, she struggled with her surprising emotions until they were shut off in favor of the ones she could understand.

The man was as he had appeared in the picture, but different somehow. The eyes were so brown they were almost black, but instead of giving off the hazy glow of a man playing at business they were hard as flint underneath the light brows that almost softened them. The nose was not hawklike as she had first imagined. Rather it was chiseled, Roman, a work of art. And his lips, smiling now despite her displeasure, could easily soften and close about her own with surprising swiftness and delicacy. She knew it instinctively.

Yet, Amelia also knew what she expected of him and she would not be put off. Amelia thought she understood him all too well, and her initial assessment of him was proving to be true. Here was not a businessman of unique proportions. Here was a little boy, despite his age—which she guessed to be close to her own thirty-three years. Perhaps, like a little boy, he could be delightful and just as instantly cruel. He had gotten too much too easily. She knew what he was like.

"Sorry, ma'am." His strong, callused hand flew to his T-shirted chest in mock embarrassment. Amelia watched that hand, wondering why the combination

of calluses and manicured nails should be so enthrall-
ing. She barely heard his apology but was well aware
of the teasing tone of his voice.

"You must understand that when you walk into
Original Windsurfers you take your chances of being
swept away by some of the most handsome and lov-
able rakes this side of Marina del Ray. Especially when
we have just been awarded one of the biggest con-
tracts in our history."

"I don't mind taking chances, Mr. Alexander.
That's my job. But I don't classify walking in here as
a chance. It was a calculated risk. Are your employees this jubilant when they work for a living?" The
voice with which she spoke was reserved. She was not
here to judge, no matter what her personal feelings
were. She was here to report and report she would, if
she could keep herself from feeling electrified each
time Scott Alexander looked at her.

Amelia straightened her jacket and adjusted the
eggshell-colored silk tie at her neck. Her hands fluttered more than usual as she attended to her clothes.
She needed a moment to recover her senses, to recu-
perate from the surprising effect he had had on her.

"We're always happy." Scott moved in closer, tilt-
ing his head so that she could feel the warmth of his
breath brushing her cheek. "That's half the reason for
my success. Happy employees, profitable business. I
believe people should let their hair down as much as
possible." His hand reached up and almost touched
the heavy chignon at the nape of her neck as though
to illustrate the point. Amelia watched, fascinated,
then jerked away.

"Look, I'm here to do a job," Amelia began in an
effort to take command of the situation. It wouldn't

do to alienate him before the interview but he was making it very difficult.

"What? You mean you're not here for a custom-made Windsurfer? I thought you were probably some beauty queen being followed by the press! Why, it would only take a moment to determine your stance and get your measurements...." His face had relaxed into seriousness, and Amelia almost thought he believed what he said until she saw his eyes roaming over her, taking stock of her as he murmured the word "measurements."

Her face burned with the blood that boiled up from every part of her body. He was throwing her off balance and in a moment she would not be able to regain it. Suddenly she was aware of her crew, standing close, watching carefully to see how Amelia Jenkins would handle this sandy-haired beach god. Strangely, she thought she felt them pulling for him—not her. But she knew she was misreading the vibes. They all respected her and wouldn't want to see her done in by such a man.

"No, I'm Amelia Jenkins from KNXT-TV. Perhaps you've forgotten that you were due to be interviewed today?" *There,* Amelia thought, as she spoke in her most condescending tone, *that ought to put him in his place.*

"No way, pretty lady. I couldn't forget something as important as that. I'm one of your biggest fans. I've been looking forward to this for a long time. I guess it was just wishful thinking that you might want something more." He raised an eyebrow toward the group behind her and Amelia was shamed by the titters that erupted from her crew.

"I assure you that isn't the case. Now, I realize how valuable your time must be," she went on crisply, most professionally, her smile frozen on her lips, "so I promise we'll make this short and sweet and then my crew and I will leave you to your party."

"I see. Of course. I'm sure you've already had a long, hard day." He moved away, his voice no longer playful, his smile melted. A hint of disappointment, perhaps? For some reason Amelia found herself hoping that was the case. Unable to help herself, she noted his slim hips encased in tight jeans. She sensed the strength of his legs. She shuddered and closed her eyes momentarily, only to open them as he spoke.

"This is a celebration, but it is not far off our normal mark. You see, we have a philosophy here: happy hands are busy hands. I know it's backwards," he said turning to face her again, "but happiness is very important to me."

"I see," Amelia said simply, even though she felt his words were meant to somehow pierce her in some hidden place. They were words that stripped her soul before him. She motioned for a microphone and hid her confusion behind it. "I gather you're ready to start?"

"Yes," he answered in a low voice. "I've been ready for a very long time."

He swept his hand before him. Amelia's spine tightened. He seemed to be enveloping her with that unnameable something that made up Scott Alexander.

Raising her hand she signaled to the crew, and Tom hoisted the Minicam. She saw the surprise, the anticipation in the faces of her crew. She looked toward Scott Alexander, who stood ramrod straight yet inexplicably relaxed. The music now became a buzz saw cutting through the tension emanating from her. For a minute everyone stood without speaking. Then a smile spread across Amelia's face, and she turned toward the camera.

"Good afternoon. This is Amelia Jenkins here with Scott Alexander, president and founder of Original Windsurfers. An amazing success story with some unusual twists." She turned her dazzling smile on the tall man beside her and he smiled back, and their eyes were locked together in some unspoken promise.

"HOW'D IT GO, BOSS?" The man who spoke was bent over a piece of hard foam, his gnarled hands laying sheets of colorful fiberglass delicately over the mold before he applied the resin that would harden the board, bonding the mold and the fiberglass together.

"Okay I guess. Good public relations if nothing else." Scott shrugged and hunkered down next to Sailor. The man had been his friend ever since they served together in Vietnam. He was a straggly character, a far cry from the proper soldier he had been. But then they were all a far cry from what they had been then, thank God.

They had been drawn together during their basic training in the oddest manner, and Scott still remembered how it had happened as though it were only moments ago.

Until that night they had paid little attention to each other. Scott, charmingly lamenting the loss of his long golden locks, had captured the imagination of the others in his troop. Most had been drafted, but here was a handsome young man, full of life, his number not even called in the draft, who had actually chosen to be there. And the best part of all, he wasn't a fanatic.

Immediately the rest of the men relaxed. He didn't strut up and down spouting platitudes about the righteousness of their mission like some ROTC recruit. He wasn't a weirdo bent on adventure and living out a James Bond fantasy. He was simply a guy who, in that nervous mix of men, seemed as calm as a lake in the morning.

His quick wit and willingness to help out when he was needed was exactly the reason people liked him. He was an enigma. They could make of him what they would, because he never cornered them to spill out his life story. Instead, he let them talk and talk and talk. Everyone loved Scott Alexander.

Everyone, that was, except Sailor. Only he wasn't called Sailor then. He was Ted Lapides, a straight-and-narrow kind of guy. In a way he wasn't that different from Scott. He didn't pour out his life story; he didn't corner anyone and tell them how deeply he felt about the rightness of what they were about to do. But then, he didn't have to say a word. What he felt emanated from him like heat from the sun. He wore his convictions like a heavy cloak about him. Ted measured his life very carefully. Each step he took was calculated to get to the top of the heap, not through conniving or politicking, but on his own merits. He was, in short, dedicated to whatever task was at hand, and that was why he didn't like Scott Alexander. Ted Lapides didn't care for someone who eased himself into a picture. Where Scott was a watercolor, Ted was a paint-by-numbers picture.

It was mere chance that brought them together and bound them together.

Ted was having difficulty on the obstacle course. It cut him to the core not to be able to finish the course in record time. It was those damn ropes that he had to climb in order to scale a wall. He couldn't seem to get his momentum up.

Each night he would sneak out of the barracks and attempt the feat once again, and each time success eluded him. One night Scott, unable to sleep, saw him leave. For a moment he considered closing his eyes and pretending he had never seen Ted. Then, realizing that the MPs could bust Ted for being out past lights-out, he slipped into his fatigues and followed.

When he finally reached the obstacle course, Ted was already working. Scott saw the determination and frustration of the man. It was a suffering Scott didn't like to witness. It made him uncomfortable to realize that, for this guy, there was nothing else in the world but those ropes. In the few minutes he watched he discovered what the problem was. His natural instinct to help came to the forefront, and he walked from the dark of his hiding place to stand beneath the rope from which Ted dangled, halfway up, breathing hard and cursing.

"I see the problem," Scott said nonchalantly.

Ted, surprised and frightened by the voice, lost his tentative hold and fell to the ground at Scott's feet. When he looked up, his lips were curled in anger. He would have preferred the MPs to this golden boy.

"There's no problem here," he muttered, and pulled himself up, ready to take the rope again.

"There must be if you need to sneak out just to have a rendezvous with a rope," Scott said as he moved past Ted and grabbed the rope.

"If there is, it's none of your concern. Just go back and play father confessor to all those others," Ted snarled. Scott ignored him.

"You know," he said, as he pulled on the rope and dangled with it a few feet above the ground, "life isn't meant to be lived alone. Sometimes people need help. It's no big thing. I mean, that's what we're here to do, right? Help those people far across the sea. Maybe some of us aren't, but most of us are."

Ted relaxed, surprised at what he was hearing. This surfer from California was saying the same things he felt. And the way he said them may have lacked Ted's intensity, but the sincerity couldn't be missed. Ted thought, perhaps, he had misjudged the guy.

"Anyway, if we're going to help them we should start by helping each other. Now look," Scott said, looking upward, "don't attack the rope. Save that for later. If you do, you'll be at odds. Attack always puts you at odds with something. Like a girl. You wouldn't attack a girl, would you?"

Ted shook his head even though Scott couldn't see him through the night.

"Okay, then, just go with it, with what it wants to do. See, swing with it, sail with it. Man, it feels good and it works. You miss too much being so single-minded. You miss the feeling."

Suddenly Scott was scurrying up the rope, swaying with it as if he were in some GI ballet. And, as quickly, he was down again, grinning his gorgeous grin as Ted approached. Silently the rope passed between them, and as Ted began to climb Scott urged him on.

"That's it, sail with it, just like catching a big wave, just like a big wind catching the sail…that's it…. It's the sense of life in everything.... Even that rope...a sense of life..."

The big man hesitated, then climbed. He hesitated once more, then climbed all the way to the top. He felt it, that wind. He was sailing. Seconds later he shimmied to the ground and stood face to face with Scott. Neither spoke for a long time. Then Ted rubbed his hands together.

"It worked," he admitted almost sheepishly.

"Yep, you were definitely sailing," Scott answered, as they turned to walk back to the barracks together.

They never spoke of the incident again. And when Scott tagged him Sailor, Ted didn't object. It seemed appropriate. Others picked up the name as Ted Lapides sailed through Vietnam, never missing a step.

That had been a long time ago. Scott reached out with the memories and patted Sailor's back. They had come such a long way. It was a pity that Sailor hadn't remembered that simple lesson when he returned to the States. But at least Scott had been there to help teach it again. Maybe someday Sailor's life would be what he wanted it to be again.

Sailor didn't look at Scott, knowing full well that the man had been lost somewhere in the past for a moment. Still, he had to say what was on his mind.

"That dame was really a buster." Scott nodded, pulled back into the present and happy to be there. "Okay if we turn the music back up now?" The sandy-haired man nodded again.

"Sure, go ahead," he said.

Sailor rose, muttering all the while to himself as he left. "Some people ain't got no sense of life...." Scott heard Sailor say. Then all voices were drowned out by the rising music, and the shop returned to normal.

But Scott's thoughts were not on the happy work environment he had so painstakingly created, nor were they on the respect he showed his workers or his understanding of their personal lives. His mind was on Amelia Jenkins.

No, Scott thought, some people have no sense of life, but he would bet his new contract that Ms Jenkins did. She just didn't know it and that was a waste. He should have... His thoughts trailed off. It was time to get back to work. He knew that he and Amelia would meet again.

AMELIA'S LOG

March 22

Long day. Didn't get a chance to call Mama. I'm sure she didn't miss the call. No matter how hard I work she seems to work harder. Wish she could find a good man to share these years with. She's still so beautiful.

Beautiful. Funny word to remind me of the worst part of the day... meeting Scott Alexander. We didn't hit it off. Have to admit I had a bit more respect for him at the end of the interview than the beginning. He knows how to turn a profit with an albeit unorthodox way of doing business. Don't think the respect was returned in kind. Didn't expect it to be. Things come too easily to a man like that. In business one year, a success the next. He didn't talk much about the how of it, only the success of it.

Amelia's prediction? Easy come easy go for Mr. S. A. of the windsurf set.

Late. Tired. Call Mama in the morning. Get Mr. S. A.'s face out of my brain. I'm getting soft!

Chapter Two

Some days are so wonderful in southern California that it's impossible to tell Los Angeles from its suburbs. The big, bold globe of a sun blankets the land until one city melts into another in a glorious celebration of bright white heat. But this March day had not been like that.

Amelia had risen late, tired from her weekend work the day before. She donned a faded gray jogging suit and her well-worn tennis shoes, tied her hair back in a bright pink sweatband and jogged out the door into the strangely overcast day. The air temperature was not easily discernable. She felt warm and muggy in her sweat suit as she moved, yet the moment she stopped running her spine spasmed with chill. The weatherman would call it overcast but warm. To Amelia, days like this felt like limbo—neither here nor there. It was earthquake weather to southern Californians, tornado weather to Midwesterners. She smiled without mirth. She could use an earthquake. It might shake her out of the doldrums she'd been in the last two days.

Her breath came in measured puffs as her long legs carried her down the steps of her building, the one she had taken an apartment in when her mother insisted she stand on her own two feet and live her own life. But Amelia knew that it had been her mother who desired a little space, a little independence.

The streets of her neighborhood were as familiar to her as the back of her hand, yet she stumbled over cracks she could navigate in the dark. She veered onto Mrs. Taylor's lawn and thanked her lucky stars that the old woman was not around to yell at her. Finally, before she had gone half a mile, she missed her step and fell onto the side of her foot, sending a stab of pain up her right leg.

"Damn," she muttered under her breath, "this isn't going to be my day."

Leaning back against one of the large olive trees that lined the avenue like silent sentries, Amelia looked up into the sky as she rubbed her ankle. She wished for clouds. Big, white, fluffy clouds to drift by and uplift her spirits. But she knew none would be forthcoming. Her mother would say she felt antsy. It was a good word. She had that skin-crawling feeling that something was going to happen. A sudden downpour? A broken bone? It was that kind of day.

Pushing herself away from the tree, Amelia hopped up and down, gingerly testing her injured ankle. There was nothing wrong with it, thank God, but the morning jog was over. Her heart just wasn't in it. She might as well go back to bed.

Smiling wryly, Amelia began to slowly walk in the direction of her apartment, wondering as she did so where her heart was. There was a void deep inside her like this day of perpetual nothingness. Even her work seemed to lack the thrill it had once held for her. She was in a rut. She had climbed to the top of the ladder in Los Angeles and there was only one place left to go—and that was to a national show.

She kicked at a stone. The idea excited her; still, it was not the soul-shattering objective she had once thought it to be. But then, that could be because no one had approached her with such an offer. Perhaps if it were a reality, she could recapture her momentum, get the mind fires burning once again.

"Amelia, you idiot, get yourself together," she commanded softly under her breath as her building came into view. Forcing herself to a burst of energy in order to rid herself of her lethargy, she trotted up the steps and down the hall, continuing to bounce from one foot to another while she inserted her key into the door. She was feeling better... by a bit.

Pulling the sweatband from her head, she let her waist-length tresses loose and unzipped her sweatshirt, rubbing the beads of perspiration from between her breasts. The pink terry-cloth band was tossed onto the dining room table, which was still littered with the Sunday paper.

Amelia grabbed the phone and collapsed onto one of the chairs, propping her feet on another chair while she dialed her mother's number. Cradling the phone on her shoulder, she picked up the real estate section of the *Times* and began to peruse its contents while she listened to the ringing.

She was so immersed in her daydreams that she waited five minutes before she realized her mother wasn't home. The pictures of the three million-dollar homes overlooking the wild beaches of Malibu had caught her fancy, and she was swept away to a world beyond ringing phones and faded sweat suits.

Finally, regaining her senses, she glanced at the kitchen clock, noting the early hour. Her mother would be at church or serving at the weekly pancake breakfast at St. Martin's.

She poured herself a cup of coffee and ambled back to her chair. This time she went through the listings in earnest, knowing now what she needed. A change. Something to really throw herself into. A project. A place of her own where she could exhaust these nagging feelings of emptiness, work them into the ground as she painted and papered and made herself a nest. She had been in this one-bedroom apartment too long, Amelia decided, running her long-nailed finger down the beach listings. Manhattan, Redondo, Playa del Ray. She chewed her bottom lip in excitement. There were a hundred listings that sounded interesting and were in her price range.

Two bedroom, one and three quarter bath, newly refurbished. $210,000.

One bedroom, fam. room, garage. Two blocks from beach. $198,000.

Three bedroom, needs work, big yard, $185,000.

Carefully, Amelia folded back the paper and began to circle those listings that interested her. She had an hour and a half before the open houses would be available for viewing, but now, her energy returned, she could hardly wait. Putting aside the paper after circling more houses than she could possibly see in one afternoon, she went to shower, a smile now playing about her lips. She felt revived and ready to take on the world.

"DID YOU GET a set-up sheet?" Amelia was barely in the door before the real estate agent was upon her. God, they were all so cheery! As though buying a house was no more than a whim of the moment.

"Not yet," she answered, trying to summon up the excitement she had felt earlier in the day when she had begun her hunt.

"Well, here you go. Copper plumbing, kitchen's just been retiled and the owner will carry paper," the agent stated with a broad grin, handing Amelia a sheet filled with facts and figures about the small house before turning his attention to the young couple who had entered on Amelia's heels. Obviously he felt secure with the house. This wasn't going to be a hard sell.

Amelia added the paper to the ten others in her purse, knowing she would need peace and quiet to consider them properly. Now she just wanted to get a feel for the house.

This one was the best so far. The rooms were small, but someone had lovingly decorated each and every one of them. The master bedroom was the palest rose. The bathroom was papered in tiny roses. The kitchen was bright with white tile and, standing at the sink, you could see the long strip of beach below. In the living room there was a Spanish fireplace and a high-vaulted ceiling. There was even a two-car garage, something almost unheard of this close to the water.

Behind her Amelia could hear the young couple asking questions and she smiled. They really couldn't afford the house. She could hear it in their voices. But she could. She stood in front of the French doors in the bedroom and looked out into the small yard. Turning, she looked at the room itself, then closed her eyes. Yes. Her king-size bed would fit. She imagined a plant over the dressing table, imagined waking up to a yard filled with flowers, waking up in this charming house alone.

Amelia started. The thought had come so quickly, out of the blue, that it shook her sensibilities. Was she really that lonely? Of course not. She had a few close friends and there was Tom for an occasional date when she wasn't busy with the show. She had her mother. But there really was no one just for her.

She had made her own world and been very selective about whom she let in. It wasn't a crime not to be in love. Yet it was somehow sad that there wouldn't be someone to twirl her about in each room of her new home, if she should decide to buy one. There would be no one to carry her over the threshold or sit with her among the boxes sipping wine the first night. But that's all it was, just a little sadness, she convinced herself.

"How do you like it?" The real estate man was old and paunchy, and Amelia smiled. Yes, it was better to wait for just the right person, she decided, silently wondering if this man's wife still thought he was as nifty as he was the day they married.

"I love it." There was no hesitation as she ran her hand over the panes of the French doors. "How motivated is the seller?"

"Very. They say the price is fairly firm, but I happen to know that they need to sell. You won't find a better buy in all of Redondo Beach...." The man continued talking. She had stopped listening and let her mind drift back to the last time she had been in

Redondo. Just one day ago. Twenty-four hours ago she was being twirled about, a boy's hand on her waist and another handsome face looking into hers. But . . .

"I said, do you have an agent?" The man had moved closer, startling Amelia.

"No, not yet. I'll want to think about it a bit." She moved toward the door and the man followed her down the small hall and out onto the porch.

"Well, if you're serious you better put in an offer soon. It's only been listed for a week and already I've got three or four people who are seriously interested."

"I'll keep that in mind," Amelia called as she went down the walk.

"Hey," he yelled after her, "I love ya on the news!"

Amelia chuckled at the notoriety her job brought. It was nice to know people appreciated her hard work. She waved her hand behind her head, sure that the man was still looking after her. He was quite a salesman, but luckily she had the presence of mind to know when to leave. There was more to being happy in a house than the house itself. She checked her watch. It was already half past three. She stood back and looked at the house she might decide to call home. Yes, she loved it—the little brick walk, the wrought-iron work over the small window in the heavy wooden door. Even the roof was wonderful, dipping and climbing like some elfen structure into peaks and valleys.

But now for the big test . . . the neighborhood. Casually, she walked about the streets, noting the local groceries, the cleaning establishments. Then, saving the best for last, she made her way to the beach.

The weather had not cleared and the grayness of it was becoming deeper with the approaching evening.

Yet, as she stood just off the sand, the ocean beckoned and the grayness became soft, a filtered twilight
that made her feel calm and safe. To her left she could
see the curve of the land, the Palos Verdes hills dotted
with Spanish-style mansions. She saw the pier, quiet
on this Sunday afternoon, with a few people moving
up and down its concourse. There was a spattering of
surf fishermen packing up their gear to her right and,
far out on the ocean, near the breakwater, she could
see the sails of two Windsurfers. One was yellow, the
other red and black. They bobbed on the water,
sometimes disappearing as a gust of wind pulled their
sails down, forcing their riders to pull back against the
wind, righting their boards. Were they Original
Windsurfers, Amelia wondered, two of Scott Alexander's creations spinning over the sea?

Pulled to stand at the water's edge, Amelia removed her shoes, rolled up her gabardine slacks and
moved across the beach. The sand felt cool and silky,
and her toes dug deeply into it as she pushed herself
forward. Now and again she would turn and find the
house. The third time she did so she found herself
thinking of it as her house. That was a good omen.
Walking backward, she considered it, already feeling
herself become a part of it and the land around it. She
could be very happy there.

Finally, reaching the last bit of dry sand, she settled herself in, moving about until she had made a
comfortable little place for herself.

Amelia pulled the set-up sheets from her purse and
found the one she sought. The house was perfect.
Lifting her eyes to stare out to sea, she attempted to
calculate her monthly payments if she got it for ten
thousand under the list price. She stared at the sails of

the Windsurfers, hoping it would help her concentrate. They were closer now, coming in to shore.

But instead of keeping her mind on the numbers she found herself wondering if the wind wasn't too strong for one of the surfers. The black and red sail continued to bend toward the water. It jerked, pulled up and once again dipped back into the water. The tide was coming in. The waves were not dangerous but they were getting bigger. The piece of paper she held in her hand fluttered to the ground, and Amelia leaned forward to watch as the yellow-sailed board seemed to try to reach its companion.

Then she was on her feet. She could hear voices out in the ocean, the two men yelling at each other. The yellow sail turned toward her and, catching a stiff gust of wind, flew toward the beach and then turned sharply as though to wait. The other board dipped, pulled up and sailed toward the sand. Amelia strained to see what was happening. Instinctively, she moved toward the water. It lapped, frigid, against her bare feet but she didn't notice.

The red and black sail went down again. They were much closer now. She could almost see the two men. But each time she tried to focus on their figures a wave blocked them from view. Suddenly, just as she was getting a clear idea of what was happening, the red and black sail dipped for the last time and the swells threw the surfer from his board. The board reared under the motion, breaking in two as it crashed into the sea. Amelia stifled a scream. Should she run for help? She couldn't see the rider. His friend must surely be picking him up. Yet when she turned her attention to the other board she saw that it was heading to shore, moving closer, the big, burly man riding it to a perfect landing.

"Are you crazy?" Amelia yelled, running toward him, splashing through the waves, hollering and waving her arms. The man didn't seem to hear as he lowered his sail.

"You!" she screamed again. "Your friend is still out there. Go help him!" She was frantic now, her long hair whipping around her face as she ran, catching in her mouth, pulling through her lips and making it difficult for her to talk. The man looked up, watching her run. *He must be crazy,* she thought.

As she came closer she saw that perhaps he was. His hair fell in long wet strings almost to his shoulders. His body was bare save for cut-off jeans, yet he didn't seem to be affected by the cold water.

"You!" Amelia was upon him now. He was a giant, and even her tall frame was diminished by his height. She saw that he wore dog tags around his neck. Certainly, though, he could not be in the army. His hair was too long, his stance too casual.

"Me?" He looked at her and pointed to his chest. *The man must be an imbecile,* Amelia thought, her heart pounding hard and fast as her eyes continued to dart out to sea. The broken board was now being carried out, away from the beach. She didn't see the surfer.

"Of course you. Do you see anyone else on the beach?" She didn't wait for an answer. "Your friend. His board's gone. Go help him. Are you deaf? Didn't you see what happened? Your friend is—"

"Perfectly all right." The voice that finished her sentence came from behind her. She whirled to face its owner. Confusion, relief and anger all flooded in on her. She had been so sure the man was dead. And now he stood before her, wet, calm, his face plastered with a gorgeous smile even while his breathing was heavy from the exertion of swimming in. The smile was Scott Alexander's. Amelia's mouth fell open. Her face burned with embarrassment and her eyes flew from one man to the other.

"You're . . . you're . . ." she stammered.

"Let me help. You want to say: 'You're all right' or 'you're Scott Alexander' or 'you're Scott Alexander and you're all right.'" His dark eyes were laughing. He found her fright intriguing. Scott shook his wet head, sending a spray of water from him. Both hands pushed it back from his broad, clear forehead. He wouldn't have expected it from her. No, he would have expected Amelia Jenkins to cover the story and then go home, if their first meeting had been any indication of her makeup. But, actually, he was delighted simply by the fact that she was there.

"Any one of those sentences would do just fine." He spread his legs firmly in the sand while one hand slowly drew the zipper of his wet suit down until the top of his chest was clearly visible. Amelia's breath stopped. He looked gorgeous in the fading light. He was not merely on the beach but a part of it. He was health and freedom and strength.

"I . . ." Amelia's knees felt weak. She had felt sure that the surfer had been lost to the waves, sure that she had just witnessed a death. She felt her legs buckle, and all she could do was think how weak she must appear. She was falling toward the sand and there was nothing she could do about it.

But she never felt the sand on her legs. Instead, four arms reached out for her and pulled her upright. Two of them were large and hairy, connected to hands that could easily palm a basketball. The other two were sinewy and covered with a fine light down, the hands callused but manicured. The hands of Scott Alexander pulled her up, and the other man stepped back to let him hold her close.

"Whoa." His lips were close to her ear, his breath warm, and she could smell the salt water on his body. Water dripped from his hair, darker now with the wetness than she remembered, and fell on the shoulder of her thin blouse, the drops rolling down until she could feel the moisture on her breast. She shivered against the sensations. The weakness she felt now was from more than the shock of the accident. She looked up into his eyes. They glittered with concern even though he still smiled.

"You're really shaky." His voice soothed her nerves, calmed her for a moment, only to pull her up again with anticipation.

"I'm all right, really." Her protest was useless. He tightened his hold about her as though that might prove what he said, but it only added to her distress.

"I'm fine. Truly I am. I just thought that you had been lost out there." She pulled away. She didn't want him holding her like that. She hated her body for betraying what her mind struggled to control. She wasn't weak. Between the two of them she was probably the stronger. But the chemistry of the man was almost overwhelming.

His arms released her, yet his eyes remained on her, wary. Amelia's own arms flew about her body, hugging it as though to hide her breasts, the tears of salt water clinging to her blouse, making it transparent and

offering a glimpse of the French lace bra she had in-
dulged herself with.

"I thought I had been, too, for a minute there."
Scott backed up a step or two, looking ready to spring
back, as though he was unsure that her own legs would
hold her.

"Well, now that I know you're okay, I'll go."
Amelia turned, then hesitated. She could still feel the
tingling in her knees. Would they hold her so she could
make a dignified exit? But before she could answer her
own question he was beside her again.

"Look, I think you might be better off if you rest
for a minute. You're soaking wet and it's getting dark.
Come back to the shop with me and I'll get you fixed
up. Sailor, stow the board, then you can take off. We'll
figure out what went wrong tomorrow. I'll take Ms
Jenkins with me." Scott Alexander spoke to the large
man who was his friend, but his eyes never left Amelia as he moved to take her arm.

"But, boss . . ." The man's protest was simultane-
ous with, and almost as vehement as, Amelia's.

"No, I'm fine." Amelia fairly shouted her objection. "I'm fine." The words poured out, her voice
shaking. Whether this was a delayed reaction to her
fright, or apprehension about accompanying Scott
Alexander, or a response to the shock of his touch, she
wasn't sure. But her words cut off any further conversation between the two men. Both of them simply
stood and watched as she continued to back away
from them, bending to retrieve her purse, trying to roll
down her soppy pant legs.

"I'm just fine. I'm glad you are. I've got to go. . . ."
With one pant leg rolled down and her purse and shoes
clutched to her chest, Amelia looked at the duo once

again. Just as she was about to take her leave, just as she turned her bare feet toward the high ground and the safety of her car, the ankle she had turned that morning gave out.

"Ahhh..." Her cry seemed to bring the two men to life, but this time neither was fast enough to catch her as she crumpled to the ground. She felt the sand adhere to her wet clothing as if it were magnetized. For a minute she simply sat there, looking as though she couldn't figure out what had happened. Then she was on her feet again.

The tears welled up in her eyes. They were tears of frustration and pain. She didn't want to be here with these two men, one looking like an escapee from a mental institution and the other like an overgrown teenager. It was humiliating. Why didn't they just go away and leave her alone? Why hadn't this day ended on a high note? She had needed that so much.

"Hey, are you hurt?" Scott had taken a step toward her but came no closer.

"No. I...I turned my ankle this morning jogging. That's all. I stepped on it wrong." Amelia hated the catch in her voice. God, she was tired. Turning her back on him, she picked up her purse again. "I better be going."

The fight had gone out of her. She didn't care what either of them thought. She looked ridiculous, wet, bedraggled, like a hag. She had been on the go all day and she was cold. Amelia couldn't even react to Scott's nearness as he touched her arm.

"Look," he said gently, "I insist you come with me. I'm sure I gave you quite a start and you look as though you could use some warming up."

Amelia raised her eyes to glare at him but it wasn't in her. He smiled softly.

"No double entendre." He held up his hand in an innocent gesture. "I'm cold and tired, too. How about a cup of coffee, then I'll let you go on your way?"

Amelia nodded. Why not? It was a long ride back to her apartment, and he was right. She was cold. She felt sticky with salt and whipped by the breeze. A cup of coffee couldn't hurt.

"Sailor, just take the board," Scott said to his friend. Amelia watched, noting the disapproval in the other man's face. Was it of her? Or was he just jealous of his friend in general? It didn't matter. The gorilla of a man Scott spoke to shrugged his shoulders and began folding the sail of his board quickly, tensely, expertly. He didn't say a word.

"Now," Scott went on, "is your ankle okay? Then come on with me. It's not a long walk, but the sand is tricky so be careful." Scott had released her elbow but his hands still hovered near her arm. Amelia looked down at them but could only see the length of his muscular thighs. That same strange feeling engulfed her again—that tingling warmth that neither started nor ended in a particular part of her body. Then she looked at his hands. They really were beautiful: well formed, strong, exciting—as exciting as the flesh of his legs, the curling light hair that disappeared under the latex of his short, black wet suit. He was a good-looking man.

"I'll be all right, thanks," she said, turning away so that he wouldn't realize how closely she had assessed his body. "I can do very well on my own."

"All right. Let's go." Misunderstanding her clipped tone, he strode on, faster than she. Perhaps he had made a mistake making overtures to this woman. When their eyes met she turned away. It was not a terribly polite thing to do. Maybe she was as full of herself as Sailor seemed to think. Well, nothing to do about it now but make the best of it. He slowed slightly and let her catch up. They walked on in silence.

Amelia's mind raced. She didn't like the silence. It gave her too much room to think, to observe him. She felt uncomfortable in its folds, so she started to speak, quickly, without thinking what the words were that came out.

"You know your friend doesn't seem to have a brain in his head. I can't understand why he didn't go back for you and then when I hollered at him he looked at me like I was crazy. Does he work for you? Why would you keep someone like that on? He seems so surly...."

"Wait a minute." Scott turned, stopping abruptly and forcing her to do the same. The new, harsh tone in his voice made her look directly into his eyes. What she saw amazed her. It was anger. Deep and dark. It had appeared so suddenly in those happy eyes that her mouth opened slightly as though to protest the sudden change.

"Look, lady, I know you're supposed to be a hotshot reporter...able to discern the indiscernible...and maybe you are in front of the camera. I can take your high-and-mighty attitude when it's directed at me like it was during that interview, but don't you ever insult someone you don't know." Scott was in motion again before she realized it. He strode over the sand as though it were a manicured lawn. Then, regaining her senses, she hurried after him. Her ankle truly hurt now, and she could feel the tight pain crawling farther up her leg with every step. But she had to catch him. It was so necessary because she understood what she had done. Without actually putting a name on it, she realized that her words had attacked someone he loved. It was funny that she knew that, since the only person she would ever feel so strongly about was her mother. But know it she did.

"Scott! Hey, Scott Alexander, wait a minute. I'm really sorry. I didn't mean it the way it sounded," she called as she hurried after him as best she could.

He didn't stop, but his steps slowed. She could see that. Amelia tried to imagine his face. Was it softening again, falling back into that devil-may-care look she had seen when she turned to find him behind her? He stopped for just an instant, turned a bit, then went on through the doorway of the plant. Amelia followed him into the building she had entered only yesterday as a cool and resourceful newswoman.

He was standing just inside the door, pulling the wet suit from his body. She leaned against the doorjamb, tired and contrite. She understood deep friendship, though she had never experienced it herself. Other than her mother there was no one she would defend so adamantly. That was something to admire. She admired his gentleness, too. He had been truly concerned for her out there on the beach. She had seen it in his face, in the way he moved toward her when he thought she was hurt. That concern, which she had at first thought was a lame excuse to get close to her and flirt like a beachboy, was only the normal concern of one person for another. It was an interesting combination, an intriguing one.

"I..." Amelia began softly but the words came out clipped and cold. "I'm sorry about what I said." She hadn't meant it to sound that way.

"Don't do me any favors. I don't need them." He threw his wet suit into a corner and ran his hands over his smooth chest as though to warm it. Then he turned and looked directly at her. She felt his eyes range over her face; she saw them soften as he saw her sincerity.

"Thanks" was all he said before he walked toward the back of the long building and disappeared. Amelia looked around her. Boards in every stage of construction were strewn about the huge, cold building. There was a rickety table and a chair in one corner and she went to it. Amelia sat down heavily and raised her ankle, gingerly placing it on her knee. She massaged it, so engrossed in the effort to relieve some of the soreness that she didn't hear him return.

"You can put this on." He tossed a robe into her lap and she looked up. His eyes slid away from hers, but she felt a gentleness in his manner that made her want to reach out and put the robe around his shoulders.

"It's okay. I don't think that's necessary," she answered, lowering her eyes so that he could not see the real reason for her refusal. The thought of sitting before him in nothing but a robe was almost as dangerous as doing it. She could imagine those hawklike eyes sweeping over her, determining without really trying which curves were the folds of the robe and which were the natural contours of her body. Self-consciously, she plucked at her blouse, which now clung to her like a second skin.

"Suit yourself," he answered, unwilling to let go of the last little bit of anger he felt toward Amelia. He moved about the room with such familiarity that he

looked as though he were performing a choreographed dance. Amelia watched him.

His normally tan flesh was still pale from the pressure of the rubber wet suit he had worn. It needed to
be rubbed and warmed back to normalcy but Scott
Alexander ignored the need, turning quickly instead
to find Amelia's aquamarine eyes raking his body, not
clinically, as he would have imagined, but softly and
curiously. It stirred in him memories of long ago, when
he hadn't known women so well, when he had enjoyed the shyness of first love or the brashness of desire, when barriers had to be broken slowly or hurdled
like a gate in front of a champion jumper. He smiled
as she turned away. The lady was not made of iron, as
she appeared.

"Now." His tone was gentler, almost understanding, though he still didn't know if he wanted to understand this woman who sat before him. "Let's take
a look at that ankle. And don't tell me it's nothing.
You wouldn't be rubbing it like that if it were."

Bending on one knee before her, he took her foot in
his hands. His skin was surprisingly warm despite his
late-afternoon romp in the ocean, and Amelia steeled
herself against it. This man was not for her. She must
remember that. She was not a one-night stand. She
was an intelligent woman. Too intelligent to be taken
in by charm and good looks, for certainly that was all
Scott Alexander possessed. The rest of him, his psy-
che, his soul, was flippant. He was a dilettante, and
that quality was evident in the way he conducted his
business, the way he took risks in the sea. Still, she
couldn't deny her attraction to him. She couldn't
shake the feeling of pure desire she felt every time he

touched her. And those times were becoming all too frequent, albeit unintentional.

"It doesn't look too bad," Scott mused aloud, as he gently poked the ankle. Amelia remained silent, her long fingernails digging into the sides of the chair. "There's no swelling." He squeezed her slender ankle. "Strong lady." He raised his eyes momentarily. "I know this hurts. You don't give an inch, do you?"

"Not if I can help it." The words were torn from between clenched teeth and Amelia fought the tearing of her eyes. Maybe there wasn't any swelling, but her ankle had stiffened as she sat there and it hurt like hell.

"That's no way to live, you know." He was talking slowly, saying personal things in a very impersonal way. Amelia had never met anyone who could do that. It was disarming and, had she not been on her guard, it would have been so easy to be drawn into the deception.

"It's the way I live and I find it perfectly suitable.... Ouch!" Her foot jerked out of his hand. Her eyes narrowed as she held her foot, wondering if he had pressed a little too hard on purpose.

"Sorry," Scott said, the glint of humor returning to his eyes as he grabbed her bare foot once more. For a moment he worked in silence, gently massaging her ankle. His fingers were serious on her skin but she could sense the amusement inside of him. Then he laid her foot in his lap, holding her leg by the ankle, his thumbs slowly working up and down.

Amelia thought she would surely die from the delight his effort caused. Strings of fire climbed from her ankle up her leg and exploded in the pit of her stomach. Her head fell back slightly, her long hair brushing the seat of the chair. Her breath caught. Had he heard it?

"It's fine," she breathed, pulling her foot back without much conviction. But he held on.

"Not yet. This will help. There might be swelling later. These are the arteries that run down into the foot...." One long finger traced the blue, pulsating vein as he continued, "That's why you're probably feeling a throbbing...." The finger continued on its course, circled the ball of her foot, then rested gently on the instep, "...Right here."

Amelia licked her lips. Throbbing. Yes, that was the word for it. Hot, insistent throbbing. But in her ankle? She wasn't sure. She only had to stop it wherever it was.

"Yes, I do feel it. I think it'll be better if I go home and put it up." Amelia's statement was a whisper and her words hung in the air between them. An invitation.

"Would you like me to take you? Or you could pretend you're home here. I could order a pizza or barbecue some steaks. I could..." His fingers had begun the rhythmic massage once again, and this time Amelia was certain it was not for medicinal reasons. He had leaned closer, turning his eyes up to hers, his lips precariously close to her skin. He kissed her leg just below the knee where her slacks were rolled up.

"What in the hell do you think you're doing?" This time Amelia jerked her leg away from him, the force of her action sending him falling back onto the floor.

Scott Alexander looked stunned for a moment, splayed out as he was on the cold concrete floor. His hands were behind him. They had broken his short fall. Then, slowly, he lowered himself onto his back, and his taut stomach heaved with a laugh so deep that Amelia could feel the vibrations deep in her own body, coursing through it as though the sound itself had become part of her blood.

From her throat came the sound made only by a word strangulated by frustration. Instantly, Amelia was attacking her slacks, rolling down the still-soggy legs. She grabbed her shoes and winced with pain as she tried to fasten the straps of her sandal over her foot. She felt so stupid, not because she had rebuffed him but because she hadn't done it sooner. Was this man some magician, that he could make her forget who she was? Make her forget the qualities of abandon that seemed to be a part of his working life and now his personal life? Oh, he was insufferable. She could not be seduced by some playboy beach bum, not with a little massage and a kiss, no matter how sweet the sensations had felt.

Giving up the effort to put on her shoe, Amelia stood up, clutched her purse and hobbled, one shoe off, one on, toward the door. But his voice stopped her before she reached it. He was still laughing.

"Come back here, Amelia Jenkins." She looked back. He was flat on his back, his head tilted at a crazy angle so that he could look at her. Even through her haze of indignation Amelia could not miss the softness she saw in the eyes that looked at her, gently baiting her.

"Come back and be with me," he said once again as he raised his hand toward her, beckoning her.

"I am not one of your insipid little beach bunnies, Mr. Alexander," Amelia said, her voice low and controlled. "I don't appreciate familiarity."

"You could have fooled me," Scott shot back. "I thought I felt a tremor of appreciation. Well, at least your gorgeous legs appreciated me." He chuckled again.

"You're insufferable. You're a boy playing a man's game. You may be lucky with this business. You may be lucky with all the half-clothed young girls on the beach. But I play in the big leagues, where people work for what they want whether it's success or love."

"And how often have you worked at love?" He challenged her, rolling over to cradle his head on his hand, his chiseled face narrowing almost perceptibly before her eyes.

"That's none of your business," she snapped, not wishing to even consider the answer to his question.

"You're right, it's not. And just for the record, neither my life nor my business revolves around people who have to work for love." He threw the word "love" back at her just as she turned on her heels and left him.

AMELIA'S FINGERS SHOOK just as they had when she tried to put the key in the ignition of the car. Now she could hardly dial the phone. She needed to talk, to hear someone speak to her kindly. Her thick skin had been thinned suddenly and expertly by a man she hardly knew, and Amelia longed for reassurance.

The phone rang, a bell jangling happily in an apartment not so far away. Amelia had wanted to run to that apartment but somehow felt ashamed. In the state she was in she would not and could not face anyone, least of all her.

Finally, the ringing stopped and Amelia pressed her cheek into the phone and managed a bright greeting.

"Mama?" she said, and even she heard the tension in her own voice. "I just wanted to make sure everything was all right. I hadn't talked to you in so long. Is everything okay?"

AMELIA'S LOG

March 30

DAMN! DAMN! DAMN!

Chapter Three

Two things happened on that Monday morning that warned Amelia to simply go back to bed and call in sick. First, her ankle was swollen and throbbed so badly that she could not get into her heels and was forced to put on a pair of soft sandals with her new peach-colored linen suit. She looked ridiculous.

Then the hair dryer broke, leaving her to deal with her long tresses as best she could. She tried turning on the oven but the blast of heat seared her neck. She then considered simply putting her head in the oven and having done with it. Instead, she toweled her head until it hurt and wrapped her still-damp locks in an uncomfortable chignon at the base of her neck, all the while going over the conversation she had had with her mother the night before.

There had been no mention of Scott Alexander. But somehow her mother knew that Amelia's agitation was not simply due to a twisted ankle and a quiet Sunday, as Amelia had protested.

"How is Tom these days?" her mother had asked out of the blue.

Amelia knew the older woman would never flatly ask how her love life was. It was something they had never discussed. Her mother either preferred to remain aloof, feeling that it was only her daughter's business or, perhaps, believing her daughter didn't have a love life at all. Amelia was never sure. She thought of it once in a while and considered discussing such things with her mother, but Martha was always very busy. And, deep inside, there was a small part of Amelia that didn't want to admit defeat in the eyes of her mother. Her love life wasn't a defeat, although she sometimes felt that way. It was only that she hadn't set her mind to changing the circumstances of it. If she worked at it, certainly things would be different. Still, discuss it with her mother? No, it just wouldn't seem natural.

"Fine," Amelia answered, surprised. "Why do you ask?"

"I just thought perhaps you had seen him today." A statement, not a leading question.

"No, not Tom." The negative answer swung in the air like a pendulum, implying that she had seen someone else, but when no explanation was forthcoming Amelia's mother went on to other things.

"So, you were looking for a house?" The conversation swung back to real estate, and Amelia lay back on the couch with her eyes closed. She could almost see that pendulum above her, but instead of marking the minutes of an hour it marked the fleeting moments of her life. "Scott, Scott," each imaginary swish seemed to whisper. Amelia blocked out the image.

"Yes," she said, thankful for the opportunity to put her mind back on the little house on the beach. "Mama, it would be perfect for both of us. Remember how I always said I'd buy you a house on the beach? Well, this may be it." She put a happy note into her voice. It would be nice if her mother moved in with her just like they had planned so many years ago.

"No, Amelia. That's sweet, but no. I'm perfectly happy where I am, and I think it's time you think about sharing a house with someone else if you don't want to live alone."

Amelia's eyes shut tighter. She wanted to cry. *With whom, Mother,* she desperately wanted to ask. *Are you suggesting a man? A live-in lover? A woman? A roommate? Tell me, Mother, what I should do. I've never had to think in these terms before, never wanted to. It was always you and me working against the world. Tell me what to do.*

But none of the questions were ever spoken, the pleas weren't uttered. It had always been that way with them. They loved each other, respected each other, but had never shared such intimacies. Now the comfortable, unassuming closeness Amelia had always felt fled, leaving a deep chasm she could not cross because neither of them knew how. They were such private women.

IT SEEMED SO LONG AGO, last night's conversation. It had been just as well that she hadn't spoken of what was truly on her mind—Scott Alexander. Her billowing attraction to him as a physical man was something she didn't want to admit to herself much less to her mother. She wanted to put the entire incident, and the man, out of her mind.

She would have preferred walking on a bed of hot coals to being reminded of the pain he had inflicted on her. The pain of feeling less than adequate. All night she had dreamed. All night she had been assaulted by images of empty spaces: her studio, her apartment, even the beach. They were empty save for her, and everywhere she looked she saw signs. Big white signs with black lettering. And only one word was written on them: WORK. In the empty spaces she heard laughter. Deep, warm laughter. And no matter how long she searched these wide open spaces, no matter how many corners she turned, she still couldn't find the person whose laugh promised comfort, companionship and love. The stupid, idiotic, romantic dreams left her shaken.

"Amelia, they need you on the set." Tom stuck his head into her dressing room, pulling her out of her reminiscing. He was about to turn back to the hall when he hesitated. "What happened to your foot, or is this a new style?"

"Very funny," Amelia answered, her voice tired. "I hurt my ankle jogging."

"Hope it's nothing serious." Tom was gone before she could answer.

She would have liked to explain to him what happened, talk with him for a minute. Surprisingly, he didn't seem interested in commiserating with her. But then, Tom wasn't the kind to get all mushy over something as insignificant as a turned ankle. Actually, Tom had never really made any advances at all, even though he kissed her when they went out and held her hand during a movie. But he was always at a distance, as though he thought she might turn into stone if he tried anything. Scott Alexander didn't think she was stone. He had liked touching her. She had felt it.

Pulling herself out of her chair, Amelia picked up her script and walked into the studio, favoring her ankle only slightly. The aspirin had helped the pain and the swelling seemed to have gone down. She was sure it would be fine by the next day, but this day still stretched ahead of her.

"Sam?" she called loudly into the darkened abyss beyond the stage, shielding her eyes against the glare of the lights directed at her.

"Yo!" came a voice from the great beyond. Amelia turned her head in the general direction of the cameraman's voice.

"Try to keep me in three-quarters, okay? I haven't got the right shoes on."

"Sure thing, Ms Jenkins," the man responded, and she heard the whir of the camera motor as he moved the lens up a bit farther.

"Here you go, Ms Jenkins." A young girl, the set stylist, appeared from nowhere and moved the small coffee table to cover Amelia's feet. "This should help in case there's any difficulty with the camera."

"Thanks..." Amelia's appreciation, while sincere, seemed laconic because she had forgotten the girl's name. But it didn't matter, since the girl disappeared almost as fast as she had materialized.

"My hair look okay?" she asked into the darkness around her, fingers fidgeting with her now dry, tight chignon. She had done the best she could with it but she still felt uncomfortable.

"Sure, fine," came a voice of undetermined direction. It sounded less than convincing.

"Ten seconds," came another voice. This time she recognized it as the director's. Amelia straightened her shoulders, closed her eyes and imagined a plumb line pulling through her body, inching her up until she was stretched to the limit, her bones creaking with the effort, her skin tingling with the concentration. It was an exercise that took a moment but one that carried her with grace and style through each show. It was part of the way she worked. It allowed her to forget her hair, her shoes, anything that had seemed amiss.

As the director gave the cue Amelia's eyes opened. A calm strength had come over her features; her skin had taken on a luster that had not previously been there. Her voice was lowered by a tone, soft but forceful, and she was in her element.

"Good morning from all of us here at KNXT. I'm Amelia Jenkins, and this is *L.A. In Depth*." She smiled at camera one and then, seemingly without effort, her face floated into view of camera three.

"Today we are going to take a look at the men and women who are turning the business world on its head here in Los Angeles. They are our own breed of entrepreneurs who have done things their own way, tackled not only our marketplace but sometimes the nation's and the world's. People whose undying beliefs in their worth, and that of their product or service, have provided jobs for the community and, in most cases, wealth for themselves.

"What makes people like this tick? What makes them give up a secure existence and plunge all their resources including, at times, years of their lives, into achieving one dream? Where do they come from? We'll answer these questions and more when we return in just a moment."

The monitor cut to a commercial, and for thirty seconds Amelia watched as an animated computer ran through a warehouse solving every single problem it encountered. Out of the corner of her eye she saw two men standing almost outside the darkened studio but close enough to her stage and pool of light that she felt invaded. She could hear them whispering but couldn't make out the words. The voices sounded familiar. Amelia identified one as the station manager's voice. The other one? She couldn't quite put her finger on it yet. Then she turned back to the camera, dispelling the itch of familiarity that the second voice had left tickling at the back of her mind.

"Mary Carney is a housewife of grand proportions. She is not married, nor does she have children. Yet Mary spends her days shopping for baby clothes, straightening houses, going out for groceries, paying bills and just about any other task you can imagine that would fall to a housewife. But Mary doesn't do these chores at her own home. She has over five hundred homes to contend with and over twenty 'professional housewives' on her staff at Rent-A-Wife.

"Let's look now at how Mary created her successful business and at the struggle she was faced with as a young, single woman without great financial resources, as she set off to become her own boss while providing a much-needed service in our busy everyday lives."

Amelia's face faded from the screen only to be replaced by a taped vision of herself. She watched the monitor as the interview began, but her concentration was interrupted as she sensed someone moving toward her.

Swiveling in her chair, her pen tapping at her lips, she looked toward the gloom. There was a glimpse of sandy hair but the man's face was backlit; he was only a silhouette. She could see the shine of a light suit. His stance was casual but she sensed the power behind it. She stared at him for a long time, but he didn't move, didn't acknowledge her interest in him. Yet, she sensed him watching her, taking her apart piece by piece. She sensed she knew him.

She swiveled again; her uninjured foot began to tap. His presence bothered her. The manager should have known better than to let someone she didn't know on the set. It was his station but it was still her show. But then, he probably had enough faith in her professionalism to know that one extra body on the set wouldn't unnerve her.

The segment ended. She was back on camera, ready to introduce the next part of the show. They had split the tape into two shows. Three interviews that day, three the next. It was a good show.

Twenty minutes later she was wrapping up.

"Thank you for joining us today. We hope you've enjoyed this glimpse into the lives of some of those who have done it their way. Tune in tomorrow when we'll talk to Marge Bonner of the Women's Bank, Todd Lungren of Tomorrow's Software, and Scott Alexander of Original Windsurfers. Until tomorrow, this is Amelia Jenkins wishing you a good day." She smiled, held it and waited.

"That's it, Amelia," the director called and she relaxed. Suddenly the studio was alive. People were talking, machinery was moving, the next show was being set up and Amelia was left on her own.

Gathering her papers, she stood up carefully and tested her ankle. It was already feeling better. Yes, she'd be able to get into her shoes tomorrow. She took two steps down from the platform that served as her stage and waited while a camera was rolled by her. Then, just as the huge piece of equipment cleared her view, Amelia looked up, prepared to find her way to her dressing room as soon as possible. But she never took the first step. Her feet were grounded to the scarred linoleum as her eyes locked with those of Scott Alexander.

"Surprise," came his greeting. The inflection the word carried was confusing. There was a bit of a question, a hint of a statement and a little tad of mischievousness. But the latter was so minimal that Amelia only heard the question.

"Yes, as a matter of fact I am surprised," Amelia answered, lingering only long enough so that she would not appear rude. She clutched her script tighter, her eyes dropped to her shoes and suddenly she wished she looked better. Not that it mattered if he thought her attractive, of course, but she was always more confident when she was put together properly. That extra edge that made her a top professional in her field was certainly needed now.

"Are you here for another interview, or just on a publicity jaunt through all the stations in the city?" Though she hadn't meant it, the words sounded sarcastic. He did seem to bring out the worst in her, but the tall man before her ignored the tone.

"Actually, I was hoping to get an interview today. With you...." He let the invitation hang above them in the air.

"Well, I'm afraid that would be impossible, Mr. Alexander." Amelia's heart was racing. He had somehow moved closer to her, inhibiting her personal space until she felt it closing around her like a vise. He smelled of the sea and sand and sun and she became too aware that she smelled of makeup and hair spray. "My day is booked and, truthfully, I don't think there is anything you could add to the interview we did earlier. I think I found out everything there is to know about you. Now, if you'll excuse me.''

Amelia tried to walk around him, but he moved sideways to stop her progress, splaying the fingers of his lean hand on the wall. She looked first at his hand, framed by a starched white cuff. It surprised her. His shirt was beautifully tailored and his cuff links were gold, tasteful. Then she let her eyes slide back to his, challenging him, daring him to continue to block her path. Keeping her distance from him had become a personal contest. She did not want what he had to offer. It was dangerous to Amelia . . . her profession and her sanity.

"I really doubt that you found out everything about me. As a matter of fact, I know for certain that, while your questions were insightful, you only touched the tip of the iceberg,'' he insisted charmingly.

"That may be, but I think the tip is all I want to touch at this point. So, if you'll . . .'' Amelia knew then that she had to get away from this man.

She knew he was right. There was much more to him than met the eye. He had proved that on the beach, in his shop. One moment he was carefree, the next angry as he defended his friend, the next gentle as a lamb as he tended her ankle. And finally, finally, when he kissed her . . . She knew enough to realize that such a man could steer her so far off the straight and narrow that she would never find her way back. Amelia didn't want to detour. Her course had been laid years ago and she wanted to sail through her open channel to success and security.

"I must insist.'' He stepped back, allowing her to move forward only an inch. "Just ask me one question. Just one and I'll go. I feel that our first interview lacked the personal touch." His insistence would have been sweet were his physical presence not so annoying, like an itch that touched something deep inside her that had never been touched so strongly before. He was grinning at her, aware, she knew, of the effect his presence had on her.

"All right, Mr. Alexander." Amelia drew back, hugging her notebook to her chest as though that might keep his eyes from roaming over her so audaciously. He was like any one of the hundreds of teenagers on the beach—full of himself and of the fun he liked to make. But he wasn't a teenager and she would remind him of that fact.

"Exactly what are you doing here, playing games, when a man of your stature should be attending to business?" Amelia set her lips in a thin smile, feeling sure that he would get the message. But he only threw back his head and laughed. It was a short but pure laugh, and it surprised her because it made her want to smile.

"Good question," he answered, looking down at her, "and one I would like to answer over lunch." He raised his hand when he saw she was going to object. "I only suggest lunch because I have a feeling you wouldn't be caught dead with me after dark, Ms Jenkins, so dinner is out. Am I right?" Amelia tilted her head sideways, neither confirming nor denying what he said, but Scott didn't miss the smile that had come unbidden to her lips. "Well, in any case, I'm not playing games. I came here today to apologize for my behavior yesterday. I believe I offended you and I am truly sorry. I'd like to answer the second part of your question, about my business stature, in a more relaxed setting, if you don't mind. I feel you don't like me or my way of doing business, and perhaps if I could talk to you again I might be able to rectify that.''

''Why is it so important that I understand your business—or you, for that matter?'' Amelia was curious now. She had not expected an apology, had never considered that he might have the manners to admit that he had done something to apologize for.

''You know, Amelia. You don't mind if I call you Amelia, do you?'' She shook her head. ''I thought about that all the way over here. I couldn't for the life of me figure out why you were worth putting on a suit on a beautiful day like today, getting in my car and driving into this pit they call downtown. But the longer I drove the more I remembered the look on your face yesterday when you thought I had been hurt.''

''But, I didn't know it was you,'' she protested, immediately wanting to reassure him that she would have been concerned for anyone in such a situation. He must realize he shouldn't take her concern personally. But he never let her finish.

''That beautiful hair was streaming around you like a mermaid's tresses. Those very blue eyes were frantic. You were quite the charmer yesterday, so different from the prim and proper Ms Jenkins who showed up at my shop to do her duty of keeping the public informed. Anyway, I figured a woman who can be two women at once is definitely worth the drive—and the suit.'' He tugged at his tie as though uncomfortable, but Amelia could see that he was just as at home in the gorgeous blue silk suit he wore as he had been in the black wet suit of the day before. She chuckled. He was pleased.

''And I just wanted to prove to the Amelia of yesterday that I'm not the cad playboy of Redondo Beach

she thought I was. And, maybe, I want to prove to Ms
Jenkins that I'm not the nitwit businessman she
thought I was.''

"I never said anything of the sort about your business." Her face was on fire, embarrassment coursing
through every nerve of her body. How had he read her
so well?

"I know you didn't, but I'm not an idiot. In fact, I
read people rather well and—'' he moved closer, his
hand sliding across the wall so that now his arm almost surrounded her, holding her prisoner without a
touch "—I read faces and bodies, and the stories
yours tell are very interesting. I'm curious about the
two Amelias, and my sixth sense tells me that at least
one of them is just a tad curious about me, too." His
slightly arched eyebrow rose a bit, in a silent question.

Amelia watched him watching her for a reaction.
She kept her face impassive, her body straight and
proud. Yet she felt that he saw into her and was pulling from her every secret desire, all those young-
woman dreams that had been buried because they in-
terfered with life's realities. She felt her heart tug as
those dreams slowly came to the surface one by one,
as painful as a million tiny splinters she hadn't even
known were there. Why not? a little voice inside her
demanded. Demanded so strongly, in fact, that it
forced itself to the surface of her consciousness, and
she heard her own thoughts echoing its words. *Why
not?* she wondered.

For a long moment they stood staring at each other,
struggling in a contest of wills. Finally, in an utterly
feminine gesture, Amelia lowered her eyes. But it was
not the flirtatious action it seemed. She looked away

because she felt her soul fly out from her as she looked deep into his brown eyes, and she knew that he saw things in her she never knew existed. Yet, Amelia could not perform the same magic with him, and she felt small and helpless in front of him.

"There's nothing to be afraid of, my lady," he said softly, bending his head and whispering into her ear. She felt the warmth of his breath on her neck, prickling at her skin so that she longed for his touch to calm her. "There's only life and it's meant to be lived."

"That's exactly what I do." Amelia's head snapped up as his words reminded her of exactly why she should not get involved with him. His living was fragmented, disjointed. He seemed to have no path to an objective. He would have his fun trying to figure out who she was and then he would be off on another adventure. He seemed to think her way of life was not living at all.

Well, she would keep her objectives clear in her mind. She would be the one to simply enjoy the lunch, listen to him and then go on living her life. Somehow, though, that thought didn't have as much strength behind it as it usually did.

Scott Alexander straightened and put out his arm. Amelia ignored it and they left the studio together, walking side by side. Equals, Amelia thought. Scared, Scott decided.

"YOU KNOW, I'M GLAD you finally dropped the 'Mr. Alexander.' Standing here, crunched in this line for almost half an hour, it would have seemed silly to keep it up. Under these rather intimate conditions it's better to be on a first-name basis, isn't it?"

Amelia tipped her head to look up at him, then bent from the waist to look at the line, which stretched before and behind them.

"I never should have let you talk me into this." She looked up again smiling, so that he knew her reprimand was only halfhearted.

"That's more like it," he said softly, his body moving ever closer to hers until she could feel one hard, muscular thigh rub against her own.

"What is?" Amelia asked, wanting desperately to keep the conversation going in an effort to ignore the physical contact. It was nothing more than cause and effect. The crowd caused him to move closer, she had nowhere to go and the effect was a meeting of bodies...nothing more. Yet, how much more it felt to her. No other man's touch had ever caused so much excitement in her as did this casual contact. It was ludicrous, but she felt as though everyone in the lunchtime crowd at El Tepiac's was watching. She felt as though they were on the verge of cheering her on, knowing that all Amelia could think about was how it would feel to wrap her slim legs around Scott's long tan ones.

"The smile. That's more like it. It makes your face light up like sunrise over the ocean." Scott offered the compliment and then eased over it as smoothly as a swell at dawn. She liked that. He didn't wait for the impact of his words or actions to cause discomfort.

"As for talking you into coming here... Well, when was the last time you took a long lunch? Or any lunch for that matter?" He raised his eyebrow at her. "I have a feeling it's been longer than a month of Sundays. Let me see." He put his fingers to his forehead like a cockeyed fortune-teller. "I believe that Amelia

Jenkins spends most of her lunch hours slaving over a hot typewriter or tape recorder, going over her interviews and schedules and questions. I see a strand of hair falling over her face. She pushes it back just long enough to take a bite of one of those horrible mystery-meat sandwiches she sent her assistant out to the lunch wagon for. I see, rain or shine, long, lonely, tedious lunch hours." He opened his eyes and lowered his hand, offering her a smile as open as a little boy's. "How'd I do?"

"Pretty good," Amelia conceded, laughing. "I have to admit that you've basically hit the nail on the head. It's not quite the dire situation you make it out to be, but I do stay in a lot. And I'm not going to apologize for that. It may not seem like fun, but hard work is the only way I know to get ahead."

"Did I ask you to apologize?" he bantered back, his smile broadening. "I happen to agree with you. I think hard work is extremely important. I just think you have to pepper it with a little bit of fun now and again. And now happens a lot more often than again in my book."

"You mean like the way you handle your business?" Amelia countered, remembering the blaring music, the employees who looked like meal applicants at a soup kitchen.

"Yes." He defended himself without being defensive. "Just like the way I run my business. Believe it or not, what you saw the other day was hard work. Have you ever tried to lay fiberglass over coreform all day? Resin it, sand it, resin it again, sand it again?" She shook her head as they moved to the head of the line. The ten people in front of them all moved into the small Mexican restaurant at once. Amelia was glad.

She was getting hungry, but she was also getting interested.

"Well, until you do, don't knock the little extras that make the work go faster. The people I employ are artists. They mold those boards to each customer's weight and height. To the way he or she stands on the board. They lay the fiberglass like an artist puts on paint. Look." He held up his hands and now, at close range, she could see the spider webs of cuts on his palms. She wanted to touch them, see if they hurt. And if they did she wanted to ease the pain. He was mesmerizing now, more so than he had been in their interview. But then, she wasn't asking the questions, leading him. He was speaking from the heart and she was touched.

"See these hands? The fiberglass splinters bite into them every time I make a board, and I don't do that very often now. Maybe I've gotten soft with success. I still work beside my crew, but not the fourteen hours a day I used to." Amelia's eyes widened, asking a silent question.

"What? You think I've never worked a fourteen-hour day in my life? Oh, Amelia, I've worked days a lot longer than that and at a lot tougher jobs." His face softened, almost saddened, and Amelia leaned forward, waiting for him to go on. This was a surprise.

"I worked on the pipeline in Alaska. The days weren't only long, they were cold. Then I put in a couple of more hours a day studying, so I would understand how business really worked. Oh, I may not have a fancy degree. But I remembered what I learned and then I tempered that with what I wanted. I always loved working with my hands. I was a construction worker once—you know, those guys who love to whistle at pretty office girls on their lunch hour? And there were so many other jobs. All of them gave me ammunition for doing what I really wanted to do. Don't you see? Everything is a learning experience for me. Just because that experience hasn't been gained in an office, or in one place for ten years, doesn't mean it's any less valuable."

He paused for breath. Amelia was intrigued with the seriousness of this monologue. The free-sailing wind-surfer king had turned the tables on her. Here was substance. But before he could speak again his good humor returned, and the mood was broken as the door of the restaurant opened and they were beckoned in.

Scott's hand was on her back, gently pushing her forward, and Amelia found herself in a small room. Quickly she scanned it, all her reporter's senses quickening.

The noise was deafening because twelve round tables were squashed into the same space that held the kitchen and a bar with ten stools. On the smoke-stained wall at the back of the room, a statue of Our Lady of Guadalupe stood on a small platform, her chipped arms reaching out as though to bless the diners. Flowers, in various stages of life, were strewn about the plaster statue's feet. Over the kitchen door were photographs of weddings, baptisms and graduations.

"The owner's children. Nice, isn't it?" Scott said, following her gaze as they wended their way through the closely knit tables of the happy lunch crowd.

"It's interesting," Amelia conceded.

"Not impressed by sharing your happiness with the world? Amelia, I would have sworn there was a soul in there somewhere!" He held out a chair for her and she slid into it, glancing up quickly to see the ready smile on his face.

"Oh, there is. It's just a bit more private than that." She smiled, too. He was a nice man. There wasn't a trace of the haughty creature who had kissed her damp leg a day ago. He didn't seem to be making fun of her, just making a friendly observation.

"A soul can be too private, you know. If it is, it takes all the joy out of living." He took his own seat and leaned back, watching her.

"Joy comes in many forms, doesn't it, Mr. Alexander?" Amelia placed her purse on the table and laced her fingers under her chin. He was an interesting man. Perhaps she would find out something she could use the next day when the time came for his segment on the show.

"I agree. And for me the joys of life are simple. Like having a beautiful woman call me by my first name. Which is Scott, in case you've forgotten."

"Oh, I don't forget the who of a story, Scott," she answered, deferring to his request with a smile on her lips. It was fun bantering with him. "Joys of life are simple for me, too. They come from knowing that I have done my best, been my best, each day of my life. One must have goals, otherwise life is just living for the moment."

"And you find that objectionable?" Scott raised an eyebrow.

"Not objectionable, just unsuitable." Amelia's smile broadened as she reminded him of their earlier conversation.

"Well put, madam reporter." He chuckled and the sound washed over her with a warmth that rivaled that of the close, busy family restaurant. "But don't you consider the shortness of life when you look for suitability? There are so many things to see and do. I can't imagine you aren't a bit of a dreamer. After all, wasn't it yesterday that I found you sitting on the beach with your daydreams? You can't deny that you were reveling in the wonder of the world just then."

"No, I won't deny it. But I was not daydreaming. I had a purpose." Amelia leaned back, confident of the rightness of her stance, enjoying the opportunity to give Scott Alexander a lesson in how those without luck work for what they get.

"You see, Scott, I'm considering buying a house. I had spent hours yesterday looking at beachfront property because I adore the ocean. But just because I love it doesn't mean that I am going to go out on a limb for it. If and when I buy a place it will be because I earned it.

"When you found me I was going over the spec sheets on the property I had seen. This isn't a whim, it's what I would call a well-earned indulgence." Amelia watched him, wondering if he would understand now how different their thinking appeared to be.

"But it should be," he said slowly, considering his words carefully, "an indulgence, period. Like the way I run my factory to make work fun. Don't you think work should be fun?"

"I never considered it so," Amelia said truthfully, and Scott was amazed at the openness of her statement. Could it be that someone with her energy, her brains, her looks, had never done anything for the sheer joy of it? She needed shaking up.

"Then I'm sorry for you, Amelia," Scott said in all seriousness. He waited, anxious to see her reaction.

Her eyes widened at first, then narrowed with what could have been construed as anger, but in his heart he knew it was hurt.

"I don't need strangers to feel sorry for me. We all live as we see fit. There are plenty of people who would trade places with me any day." Amelia's voice shook as she spoke in her own defense. His words had hurt and she was surprised. Surprised because, upon a quick reflection of her adult life, she couldn't readily recall one incident that had been done for the sheer fun of it.

"Perhaps you need one less stranger in your life, Amelia." Scott reached out and touched her hand, which was resting on the table. His touch was light, quick, barely perceptible, but she shivered against it.

"I don't think I need anything of the sort," she whispered, the words sounding strangled as they escaped from her tightened throat.

"Well, perhaps not, but we shall see...." He smiled now, drawing her back into the world, which seemed so nonthreatening. He was a magician. He could pull from her feelings she had never stopped to consider and then put them back into his imaginary black hat, to be used again at some later date. It unnerved her, this way he had of segueing through a conversation the same way he seemed to go through life.

"Now," he went on, seemingly oblivious of her discomfort, "I know there is one thing you need right now and that is something to eat. I won't stand for any objections; I'm doing the ordering. We are going to start the education and relaxation of Amelia Jenkins right now."

Again the magician took over, and a waitress materialized from out of nowhere to take their order.

"I COULDN'T EAT another bite!" Amelia collapsed against the back of the chair, staring at her plate, still half full. "I wish you had listened to me when I told you I only wanted a salad." Scott grinned at her. Her face was flushed with the effort of conversation combined with the task of trying to eat a Hollenbeck burrito.

"No. No one comes to El Tepiac for the first time and doesn't at least attempt to finish off a Hollenbeck. I've never been able to do it." He nodded toward his plate, and she looked at the remains of his meal.

"But you certainly did a better job than I," she answered, happily exasperated.

"Well, if there weren't some differences between men and women just think how boring life would be. Men just happen to have a greater capacity for Hollenbecks, that's all." He shrugged his shoulders, turning his palms skyward.

"Is that a fact of life, sir? Can I use it on the record?" Amelia teased, feeling feminine and wonderful for the first time in a long time.

"Definitely on the record. And I have it from the best scientific authorities that a woman cannot finish a Hollenbeck burrito." His lecture seemed so serious that Amelia chuckled.

"Is that so?" Amelia pushed back her hair, shot him a look of challenge, and attacked her burrito once again. But Scott's hand captured hers.

"Amelia, you'll burst!" Scott said, restraining her as he laughed delightedly. "This isn't a contest, you know. I think it's wonderful there are differences between men and women, at least outside of the workplace."

"That's better," Amelia said, putting down her fork and sliding her hand from his grasp. Unconsciously, she rubbed the place where his fingers had held her. The place was warm, still showing the imprint of his hold. He was strong in ways she wasn't, possessing a physical strength that excited her. "You admit that your thinking isn't all chauvinistic?"

"My thinking isn't chauvinistic at all. I'm just repeating what I had heard. You know, this burrito was named for the Hollenbeck police division right here in East Los Angeles, and it was the policemen of that division who offered that tidbit of insight. So you see, I'm only repeating what I heard. Don't construe that as my pattern of thinking. I just figure, who am I to argue with the law?"

"You amaze me, Scott." Amelia looked at him thoughtfully for the first time.

"Why, thank you. I almost hesitate to ask, but what is it about me that amazes you?"

"The way you speak. I mean, your vocabulary, the easy way you have with words. I—"

"Wouldn't have expected it from a beachboy, right?" Scott finished her thought for her.

"Well, as a matter of fact, yes." She tilted her head in embarrassed agreement. "I didn't catch a scholarly drift in your words during our interview the other day."

"That's because the other day I didn't feel scholarly. I was talking about my business, and as you saw, there isn't anything terribly intellectual about it. It's manual, an art form. I was in my art-form mode that day."

"Do you have a different mode for every day?" Amelia asked.

"Sometimes for every minute. But my favorite mode is complete thoughtlessness when I'm on my board. It's like being in a sailboat without the boat. I can challenge each wave or float free if I want to. I control where I go and what I do with that sailing board. It's more than surfing, less cumbersome than sailing.... It's pure physical sensation—my favorite mode to be in," Scott bantered.

Amelia could see the truth of what he said behind his eyes and she felt sad. Sad because she had actually enjoyed her lunch with him. She had found him to be intelligent and bright and witty, found him to be a man of great physical desirability who could be gentle as well as forceful. Yet, the crux of the matter was that he was not someone she could ever hope to have a meaningful relationship with, because as he himself admitted, he did not travel a road she could identify with. For Amelia there was always the single-mindedness of work, the goal of security and a meaningful existence at the end of her road. For Scott it seemed that there was only the moment, the short range. The sigh that welled up in her chest was expelled from her lips.

"Is that sigh a sign of contentment because of the company, or because you managed to wade through half a Hollenbeck?" Scott had leaned toward her across the small table, waiting for her to lift the fringe of dark lashes that hooded her light eyes.

"The Hollenbeck," she lied, guarding against the tug of desire deep in the pit of her stomach that urged her to pursue this newfound friend. She would like Scott Alexander to be her friend, but to allow that was to tread on dangerous ground. She could so easily want him to be more.

"Sorry to hear that." He seemed sincerely disappointed. "Maybe next time."

"I don't think there will be a next time." Quickly Amelia dispelled any plans he might have had.

"Didn't your mother ever tell you that you should think before you speak?" Scott asked lightheartedly. He was taking her statement far too lightly, and Amelia felt a tad miffed.

"She didn't have to. I was born cautious and industrious just like her."

"And beautiful?" Scott queried playfully. But the mood for playing had passed, and Amelia answered seriously.

"Yes, she is beautiful. But not strictly, in the way you mean. There's more to beauty than what the eye beholds."

They had left the restaurant, moving out into a gorgeous Los Angeles day. The sun was shining, but a breeze blew through the city and softened the heat to warmth. Amelia turned as she spoke and slipped her sunglasses on. For a moment she waited for Scott to respond. But when he didn't she felt her eyes questioning him, even though she knew they were hidden behind the dark lenses of her glasses.

Finally he made a move. With casual purpose he reached out and tipped her glasses down her nose, holding them between two fingers as his eyes met hers, reading the questions there.

"Madam reporter, you haven't even begun to unearth the real Scott Alexander, so I would caution you not to jump to conclusions about what I mean and what I don't." Carefully, he pushed her glasses back up to shield her eyes, took her elbow and guided her to the lean, black Datsun sports car that had whisked her to this place in the heart of the city.

Settling back in the seat, which surrounded her like a cocoon, Amelia watched as Scott got into the car, turned the ignition and expertly swung the car into the flow of traffic. Soon she turned her head and let her mind roam free while they rode in silence to the studio.

"Don't get out." Amelia put her hand on his arm, restraining him as he moved to leave the car, surprising herself as she did so. Without realizing it, she had imagined touching him from the moment she saw him. He was that kind of man, the kind that invited touching and closeness. She wouldn't have been a woman if she didn't feel it. And now her flesh made contact with him. He felt good. She could feel the sinewy muscle under the suit coat. Had it tensed at her light touch? Amelia withdrew her hand as quickly as she had placed it on his arm. Scott began to protest but she stopped him.

"The traffic is bad and I really have to rush now. Thank you for everything. The lunch, the apology, everything." Amelia's eyes lingered on him for a moment. Surprisingly, she didn't want to leave him but she knew she must. She reached for the door, but before she felt the handle she felt something else. It was his body heat surrounding her and then it was his hand on top of hers. Amelia whirled as best she could in the small car to face him, an objection springing to her lips, a demand that he let her out.

She saw that smile again, the same one she had seen as he ministered to her ankle in his plant. It danced on his face—a smile of delight, whether in himself or her she didn't know. And before she could protest, his lips were on hers, soft and warm, gently insistent. It was the kind of kiss to melt into, and for an instant she did until, regaining her senses, she yanked away, taking her hand from under his.

The air crackled with emotion. Desire. Surprise. Confusion. Worst of all, indecision. His arms remained around her, his eyes gently questioning, and Amelia gazed into them for a long time, trying to read what was hidden there. If there was a chance, even only a slim possibility, that they could come together on a plane of mutual understanding, she owed it to herself to find out. Amelia now knew that she longed for the closeness of a man who would share her ambitions, share her life and her love, which she knew would be all-encompassing when it was finally given. But Scott Alexander? Was he the man she had been waiting for? It was all too confusing. One minute they were in sync, the next she was being reminded of the frivolous side of his nature.

Slowly Amelia lowered her eyes, looking away from those dark orbs that seemed to draw her to him instinctively. Pensive in the now-quiet car, she turned and flipped the door handle, swinging her long, lean legs out of the car, feeling his eyes on her all the while. The door swung shut behind her, but as she walked away she heard the whir of the electric window being lowered.

Then there was only silence. Scott watched as Amelia hesitated, waiting for him to speak, then walked on, her back straight, her hair glistening in the sunlight, her shoes out of place and incongruous with her outfit. It touched his heart to watch the proud lady in the soft shoes. He knew that she needed time for herself, so he did not call out to her. He only watched until she disappeared through the doors of the station building.

"There will be another time, Amelia. Many more times. But, for now, time is yours." He smiled, righted himself and started the long drive back to Redondo Beach, knowing that, in the end, she would see how right they were for each other.

AMELIA'S LOG

March 24

Had the most interesting lunch with S. Alexander today. He looked like a fashion plate but took me to the smallest, most homespun Mexican restaurant I've ever seen. We looked like escapees from *Vogue*! At least until someone noticed my shoes!

Funny that I didn't feel uncomfortable in the least...in dress, that is. The man has the most amazing way of making me feel uncomfortable in other ways. Have to admit, I don't really mind it. If only he were a little more serious about the world. Strike that—a lot more serious. Or less serious about me. Strike that—about my body. Oh, strike it all. I don't know about that man. Maybe I'll decide about him when he calls. I know he'll call. He's that kind. At least he has perserverance. That's not enough for a relationship. Still, you never know, do you?

March 28

Mom called tonight wanting to know if I was

going to church with her on Easter Sunday. Naturally, I told her I would. We'll probably have breakfast out. Mom always said that without little children fixing breakfast and dying eggs seemed sort of sad. I think it's just too much work for her. She's not really old but I think she's slowing down. Her house is still neat as a pin but there is something different about her. I can't imagine her ever not working. Still, who knows what I'll be doing when I get to be that age?

Haven't heard from Scott. Really thought he would call. I'm sure he enjoyed the lunch the other day as much as I did. Not that there is any hope for a deep and permanent relationship. I'm sure he understood that. Funny, this silence, though. Seems out of character for him. Then again, what do I really know about his character? Enough.

How did I leave it? I'm not sure, this week's been so busy. I don't think I was rude. I'm sure I didn't exactly encourage him, but still . . .

God, Amelia, this sounds like a sixteen-year-old's diary. Don't be so stupid! If the man doesn't want to see you again that's all there is to it. What's the big deal?

The big deal is I can't seem to get him out of my mind. He's so different than I initially expected him to be. Hard to discount the fact that he is intelligent, witty, charming, not to mention very sexy. Too bad he's also flighty, a clown, and his first love is windsurfing.

Enough. I'm tired. Big day tomorrow. Time to close. Still, I have to wonder why hasn't he called?

April 3

Easter was very nice. Mom looked great. Unfortunately, the brunch at the Hilton started off badly. The glasses were spotted and it drove Mother crazy. She is such a perfectionist! Am I that bad? Probably. But for good reason. At least I don't worry about spotty glasses. Energy is better spent on the important things like interviews.

Funny, how sad I feel that the telephone hasn't rung yet . . . except for Mom and Tom. Going out to dinner with Tom on Wednesday. Strange how I never noticed that he is just a tad boring. Not like Scott, who never seems at a loss for words. Still, it will be nice to have a break. The apartment suddenly seems very lonely.

Put an offer in on that house on the beach. Hope they accept it. If they do that will cure my blues. I might even throw my first party. A housewarming. I'll invite the entire crew. I might even invite Scott Alexander. After all, he might be waiting for me to make the first move. He's probably used to women doing that. Well, the hell with him, then, if that's the case. This is it. Two weeks is enough.

Time to close. I seem to be going to bed earlier and earlier. Have I been working that much harder?

One last note: Why is it that when some men touch you in the most casual manner you feel like they're ushering their mother into church? When others do, you feel like you're being invited onto cloud nine? Might be a good story. I'll have to call a few psychologists for the show.

Last P.S. Mom told me the most interesting
story today. She always talks about Dad on holi-
days. I know she must miss him terribly, but she
so seldom lets on, it surprised me. She didn't exactly like Dad when she first met him. He had the
first motorcycle in Kassel, Germany. She thought
he was a rake. My dear, darling, quiet father a
rake! Funny, I missed him, too, today, even
though he hasn't been with us for a long, long
time.

Chapter Four

"They accepted? That's fantastic!" Amelia could hardly contain her excitement as she listened to the real estate agent. "You mean they're not going to counteroffer? I went in a good twelve thousand dollars less than they were asking." She listened again, her smile creeping farther across her flushed face.

"Well, yes, I guess if you're transferred there isn't much you can do about it. I can sympathize, but I've got to tell you I'm not overly upset that they didn't have time to wait for a better offer. Thanks again, Sally. Yeah, start escrow. My credit has already been approved, so the loan should be in the bag. Bye-bye."

Amelia put down the phone and sat back, swiveling slightly in her chair. The little house on the beach was hers. It was the first bit of good news she had had in the last two weeks.

Ever since her lunch with Scott Alexander, Amelia had felt at sixes and sevens, unable to put her finger on the problem. It certainly wasn't the Windsurfer king who caused her to feel that way. She didn't deny that he was charming, and more handsome than most, but rationally she knew they hadn't known each other long enough for him to have that kind of impact on her.

She had been, thankfully, immune to him after her written outburst in her log.

No, it was something else. She was on a plateau. Her career had been on a fast track for so long that she was suddenly dissatisfied because she knew her job so well. Local personalities and stories left her flat, wishing for more substance. Her apartment, once a haven where she could rest after her long, exciting days, now seemed cold and lacking in personality.

Her friends were busy with their lives. The women she knew were having babies. Babies! All those women who had been so dedicated to their careers were now cooing about their child's newest tooth. It wasn't that Amelia was bored with such talk; she simply felt left out.

Only thoughts of the little house on the beach seemed to make her perk up. As she did with everything else in her life, Amelia had decided to live with the idea of buying it for a while, checking out all the angles before committing herself to it. Then, quite suddenly, she had been gripped by the sudden urge to own the little house.

She had picked up the phone and called Sally, a friend who continued to work despite her growing brood, and asked Sally to help her make an offer. For three days Amelia immersed herself in the frenzy of filing for lines of credit to insure that she would qualify for a loan, driving by the house to make sure the For Sale sign was still up, dreaming about how she would arrange her furniture once the house was hers. Then, as quickly as the urge to buy it had gripped her it was gone again, and her days were once again filled with interviews and editing, staff meetings and planning sessions with her crew. Apathy had taken hold once more. Until this morning. Now the house was hers, and Amelia felt a surge of excitement so overwhelming she wanted to shout.

And, as she contemplated the oddity that the purchase of a house should cause her to feel so wonderfully alive, Scott Alexander's face rose in her mind's eye. For an instant she allowed herself to wonder if she bought the house in the hopes of "accidentally" running into him again.

That was silly. It had been two weeks since she had heard from him, long enough for him to have contacted her if he was interested, which he obviously wasn't. Amelia felt a pang somewhere in the vicinity of her heart as she realized that she would have liked him to call her. Oh, they weren't suited for any long-term romance, but certainly they could have been friends. He was interesting and lovely to look at. It was just as well he hadn't tried to get in touch with her, though. He was an insistent man and he would never have understood that they might have been friends. No, he was the type that would want it all. Fast and furious was how he would play it. They would be lovers for a while and then his interest would roam elsewhere. This Amelia knew. Despite the fact that she had found a certain amount of respect for him, she still believed they were far too different to carry on any kind of real relationship. Yet, if she lived in Redondo they might see each other now and again. Still, believing he was insistent, Amelia was bothered by the fact that he hadn't called.

Well, since Scott Alexander was obviously a moot point, Amelia forced her attention back to the house. She loved it and her offer had been accepted. It was hers. She twirled in the chair and picked up the phone once again.

Quickly she dialed, and then tapped her nails on the desk as she waited for her mother to answer.

"Mom, I'm so glad you're home." Amelia began babbling as soon as her mother answered and couldn't stop herself. "Have I got a surprise for you. Can you be ready to go out in about an hour?"

"Amelia!" Her mother's voice, calm with just a hint of a smile, put Amelia's chatter to a stop. "What has gotten into you? You sound as though you've won the lottery."

"Much better than that, Mom." Amelia smiled. Her mother loved surprises, though she would never admit it, and Amelia was not going to spoil this by telling her the news over the phone. "But I'm not going to tell you what it is. I'm going to show you. Now, can you be ready to go out with me in one hour or not?"

"All right. I'll be ready. But I'm not going to get dressed up. I just took a bath and put on a clean housedress...."

"Mom, it's okay, believe me. You don't need to dress up. Just listen for me. I'll honk when I get there. I'm sure you can find something to busy yourself with until then."

"Yes." Her mother sighed, and Amelia almost laughed. She was sure the woman had a hundred and one things still on her list of things to do, but Amelia would put a stop to those plans. If she was going to be free and frivolous, so could her mother. "I'll start dinner, Amelia. How long will we be gone?"

"Too long. Now, listen, Mother. No cooking for you tonight. I'm taking you to dinner. And don't worry," she added quickly, "we won't go anywhere fancy. Just a little celebration...the two of us. See you in an hour."

"But, Amelia, it's barely noon. Where could we be going so long?" Martha protested. She didn't like to have her day broken up like this.

"One hour, Mama!" Amelia replaced the receiver without giving her mother a chance to protest.

The hands of the wall clock were edging toward twelve. Amelia glanced at her desk. The work piled there told her that her day shouldn't end until at least seven. Automatically, she picked up a pencil. Then, thinking again, she tossed it onto the desk. Resolutely, she stood up, put on her jacket, picked up her purse and, with a grin on her face, waltzed out of the office, leaving a string of secretaries to wonder who the man was who could put a smile like that on Amelia Jenkins's face.

"NO ANSWER," Scott said as he, too, hung up a telephone receiver. There was a smile plastered on his face. She was already gone. And for the day, no less.

He glanced up at Sailor, who sat with his feet propped up on a chair. The man looked as if he didn't have a worry in the world. And so he shouldn't. Business was booming and he had first shot at the very best assignments that came in. Then Scott noticed Sailor's fingers drumming on the arms of the chair in which he sat. Well, he had at least one care. Scott had known Sailor for too long not to recognize that small sign of disenchantment. Well, he would wheedle the problem out of Sailor before long, but first, maybe, he should try to contact Amelia at home. Perhaps she was sick. It was hard to believe that the workaholic of KNXT had actually taken a day off just to have fun. He stared at the phone and almost reached for it.

Then his mind swerved off in another direction. He had a much better plan in mind. God, how he wanted to see her again. If nothing else, just to make sure that she was real. She was a beauty, there was no doubt about it. It seemed like forever since he had first laid eyes on her and felt that incredible energy that sparked from her every fiber.

But business was business. The trips to various trade shows he had just made couldn't have been put off for anything, not even for Amelia. Would she, he wondered, be surprised to find that he had just spent two weeks on the road selling and pitching his boards to everyone who would listen? Probably. It seemed that Amelia Jenkins thought his business grew just because he wished it to. Still, there had been that lunch, and he knew for a fact that inroads had been made with the woman. Suddenly Sailor spoke, and Scott Alexander was called back to the present.

"You're wasting your time," Sailor muttered as he watched his fingers drum in unison on the chair arm.

"Well, well, he speaks," Scott answered gaily. He felt so wonderful that even one of Sailor's moods couldn't get him down. It was good to be home.

"Yeah, well, somebody's got to." Sailor glanced at him, then lowered his eyes again.

"And what has 'somebody' got to talk about?" Scott's chair squeaked as he leaned back and laced his fingers behind his head.

"About what a fool you are determined to make of yourself" came the reply. "I've seen that look before. You're getting ready to romance this chick from the TV station and she's bad news. Not for you."

"Thank you, Ann Landers," Scott said, laughing at his friend's concern. "It's nice to know someone is watching out for this poor boy from the sticks."

"Okay, but don't say I didn't warn you." Sailor shrugged and Scott could tell the matter was not being laid to rest.

"I won't. But let's get a few things straight here. First, you haven't exactly seen this look before. This look goes a little deeper than teaching one of our lovely beach girls how to windsurf. And secondly, I don't know where you get off calling her bad news. You didn't even speak to her the other day. You hardly looked at her either here in the office or when we were on the beach."

"Hey, man, I didn't have to look at her. All I needed was to hear the way she talked to you. You think I didn't live with myself long enough to recognize the signs? She's going to take you for a ride, Scott; that is if she even lets you in the car."

Sailor stood up and thrust his hands deep into the pockets of his cutoff jeans. His hairy legs were bowed from years of surfing. His sneakers were without laces. Slowly, like a caged bear, he began to pace the office.

"Scott, man, I just don't want to see you hurt. You got to sail, you know. Like you always told me . . . go with the flow of things. And I'm telling you this lady doesn't know how to do it. There's no flow there, only a spring ready to let go. And I'll tell you one thing. That spring is going to smack you right in the face, then I'm going to have to be the one pulling you out of a hole."

"That might not be such a bad idea. Then you can see how tough it is," Scott shot back.

He immediately regretted his words. It was unfair. He hadn't pulled Sailor out of anything. He had simply been there for a friend when he was needed. He tried not to think about the last time, the worst time, when he found Sailor deep in his grief. The man had been on the verge of suicide but Sailor had pulled himself up. Scott only stood by and encouraged him, just as he had done that night on the ropes. He gave his friend a haven and had been repaid time and again with concern and friendship and caring.

"Hey, I'm sorry," Scott said, leaning forward in his chair. "It's just that I got to know her better the other day. Sure she's uptight. You were too about making it big at one time, as I remember. But look at you now. It was in you all the time to look at life in three dimensions. Amelia Jenkins is that way, too. She's interesting and kind. She's concerned about doing the right thing for her and for the people she meets. I mean, if she wasn't would she have told me it was a no-go? I could tell the lady was interested but she didn't want to hurt my feelings, or hers, by letting anything go on between us. Unfortunately, she doesn't know who she's up against. I want to see her again. I need to, Sailor. If it doesn't work out I'll come and cry on your shoulder, and you can say 'I told you so.' "

"That's just it. I don't want you to have to do that. Haven't you got enough now? Haven't you got this business that's going so great and a thousand chicks ready to fall at your feet any second?"

"Yeah, I guess I do, but you know better than most, it's not the same. I want more, Sailor. I want someone with me for a long time. Maybe I'm getting old. But I don't want a crowd of women around the barbecue. I want to share a bottle of wine at sunset with someone special.''

"Then look around. There are some real special women here that understand your life, that love it. Like Susie . . .''

"Too young.''

"Okay, how about Carla? There's a great-looking girl. . . .''

"Interested in having some man take care of her. Amelia would never settle for that. She's got spirit.''

"Spirit? That's what you want? How about Pippy? That one can take any wave the ocean spits up.''

"And our kids would think that life began and ended at the water's edge. Can you imagine Pippy helping them with their homework?'' Scott raised an eyebrow, and Sailor couldn't help smiling. The image of Pippy pouring over new math was even too much for him. "You know what it is, Sailor. It's that indefinable something that draws you to a person and makes you take a risk even though you know you may be barking up the wrong tree.

"Listen, I'm not going to crumble if this doesn't work out. But I'm old enough to take a chance. I think I can handle it.'' Scott smiled and Sailor grinned back.

"Old buddy, you of all people could handle that one. It's just I hate to see you wasting your time—''

"Fire!''

Sailor's words were snipped off in midsentence as both men heard the cry from the warehouse. Scott pushed himself from his desk, every muscle tensed for action, but Sailor was quicker. He reached for the door before Scott and stood for a second with both hands against it.

"It's not here," he said, and Scott nodded. They had both been in enough situations during the war to know that they had to check for the source of the fire before forging ahead.

"Open it," Scott commanded, and the door burst ahead of them as though it too wanted them to rush to aid whoever was calling.

Both men ran into the large room. They quickly assessed the situation. The back of the warehouse was clear but they could smell the heavy odor of burning resin. A board, if not more, was definitely on fire. They turned on their heels and rounded the corner that led to the great expanse of workroom.

Rolling toward them was a cloud of thick black smoke. It twirled up to the ceiling as it made its way through the concrete warehouse.

"Down," Scott yelled, and Sailor crunched into a ball. Both of them headed toward the front. They could hear frantic movement ahead. Neither spoke. Sailor stood up for a moment and was enveloped by the smoke. But when Scott looked around to check on his friend he saw him once again behind him, now clutching a fire extinguisher, taking deep gulps of air.

"Get that blanket...."

"It's going to spread to those cans...."

Sailor and Scott entered the fray of workmen just as panic was beginning to take over. Luckily, they were on short shift and only three of his regulars were working.

"Out," Scott roared at them, but they simply stopped in their tracks at the sound of his command. "Out, now! Jimmy, get out and call the fire department."

"We'll stay," one of the men cried, and Scott could hear the terror in his voice.

"Damn it, out now, all of you!" Scott shoved the man closest to him and it seemed to bring the rest of them to life.

Frantically, they flew out the door. None of them looked back to see Sailor and Scott approaching the flames, which burned happily on a stack of rags, licking this way and that to find any other surface to play on. Quickly, Scott saw that the resin rags had been left too close to the space heater. Combustion was not just a possibility in that situation, it was a foregone conclusion. One of the boards was already charred by the flames. It was the special order that Scott had taken such care to design.

Scott whipped about, searching for a towel or blanket in the thick smoke. His breath was coming in gasps now. He felt the ungodly heat begin to boil inside him, his chest contracting painfully.

"Now, Sailor!" he hollered, but it was a wasted command. The long-haired man had already raised the extinguisher, and by the time the last word was out of Scott's mouth a spray of foam was covering the rags.

Scott pulled a blanket from under one of the workbenches and began to smother the flames, which had just then caught on the board. For long minutes the two of them worked, frantically beating and spraying until all that could be heard in the cavernous warehouse was the sound of their rasping breath.

They stood together, exhausted. Finally, Scott threw his arm around Sailor's shoulders, and they moved slowly toward the door. The smoke was already beginning to disperse. They could hear the sound of sirens in the distance. Sailor fell against the wall as Scott labored to crank open a window. Soon both breathed deeply of the fresh sea air.

"That was the dumbest thing we've ever done," Sailor croaked.

"Correction," Scott answered between breaths, "that was the dumbest thing *you've* ever done. This is my business. I take the risks. When I said 'out' that meant you, too, buddy."

"Never, my man. Not even if you do something stupid like that again. I'm going to look out for you."

They looked at each other through the clearing air, and then Scott began to laugh. He laughed long and hard, and when he and Sailor finally burst through the front entrance they were falling all over each other like drunks.

In moments, the firemen had them on oxygen, though both of them swore they didn't need it. Behind the clear masks their smiles continued. As Scott watched the firemen check the damage he thought of only one thing: seeing Amelia Jenkins. After all, what was one more life-threatening situation when it involved something, or someone, you cared about? And, if he succumbed to that one, how sweet it would be.

AMELIA WATCHED her mother come down the stairs of the apartment building. Moments like this were rare and she savored every instant. The chance to quietly watch Martha was unusual. At home, she never stopped moving long enough for Amelia to get a good look.

Martha Jenkins was sixty-three and still lovely. Her legs were shapely, her posture perfect. Her dress was perhaps a tad unfashionable, but it was impeccable nonetheless. Amazingly, her hair showed no signs of graying and her skin was laced with only fine signs of aging.

God, I hope I look that good when I'm her age, Amelia thought as her mother looked up, smiled, and walked toward the car. Amelia reached over and unlocked the door.

"I told you this was going to be casual, Mom," Amelia said, smiling as she nodded at her mother's gloves.

"Better safe than sorry," came the curt reply. Then the older woman swiveled in her seat and smiled one of her amazingly wonderful smiles. "Now, daughter of mine, are you going to tell me what this is all about?"

Amelia answered as she started the car and pulled away from the curb. "Not yet. For the next forty minutes you're just going to have to enjoy a little bit of light conversation."

Martha sighed, knowing that any further questioning was useless. Her lovely daughter was as stubborn as she herself was. So she settled back with a smile and filled Amelia in on the details of her very busy day.

By the time Martha had finished telling her that Father Crendly had asked her to help organize a Fourth of July pancake breakfast at the church, Amelia could see the off ramp for the Los Angeles airport and they were stuck firmly in the continuous traffic.

"Damn!" Amelia's open palm hit the steering wheel.

"Amelia!" Martha reprimanded her daughter.

"Sorry, Mom," Amelia apologized. "It's just that I was so excited about this surprise and now it's just not going to be the same. I get so upset in this kind of traffic.''

The car inched ahead and then came to a stop once again.

''Amelia,'' her mother said, shaking her head in mock dismay. ''My daughter, who was out of line when the good Lord handed out patience. I thought after all these years someone would have taught it to you along the way.''

''I have patience,'' Amelia objected, ''with the important things in life. After all, I waited a long time to get where I am today. Don't you think that took patience?''

''No. That took hard work. Patience is another matter altogether. If you don't have it, then you'll never have a peaceful heart, and life will never be what you want it to be.'' Martha finished her sentence solidly and crossed her arms over her chest.

''Oh, you're a philosopher in your old age?'' Amelia bantered with a chuckle.

''No. Just realistic. After all, I had to have the patience of a saint to raise you, didn't I?'' Her mother raised an eyebrow.

''I wouldn't say that. I never gave you cause to worry.'' Amelia defended herself knowing full well her mother was pulling her leg. She had become used to Martha's sense of humor years ago and it never ceased to delight her.

''No, you didn't. At least not when you were young.''

''Oh, you mean now I make you worry?'' Amelia watched the traffic ahead of her. It was beginning to move. She pressed the accelerator, swerving into the right lane.

"An accident," she said, pointing to the left of the freeway. Her mother's eyes followed.

"I hope no one was hurt," Martha muttered and crossed herself.

"So do I. They have most of it cleaned up, but it looks like it was bad. Maybe I should stop. There might be a story."

"Amelia, you keep driving. First of all, those poor people don't need to be harassed by a reporter, and second, you promised me a surprise. Sometimes I think all you think about is work, work, work."

"Like mother like daughter, Mom," Amelia answered with a smile. The car picked up speed and the wreck was left behind on the freeway. But Amelia kept the scene in sight in her rearview mirror and tucked away the thought that she must watch the news tonight to find out if there was a human-interest story in there somewhere. When they were once again flying down the road, Martha picked up her dissertation on pancake breakfasts as though there had never been an interruption.

By the time she had finished, Amelia was looking for a parking space on the street that was soon to become her own. Martha was looking about her now with undisguised curiosity. Her face was impassive but her eyes were darting about, trying to discern the meaning of this odd trip. Finally, Amelia pulled her Toyota next to the curb.

"This is it." She turned off the ignition and began to open the car door.

"So, you've taken me to the beach just like when you were little. I was expecting more of a surprise."

"You don't fool me for an instant, Mom. You're just trying to get me to show my hand. Well, forget it.

Now, hop out of the car and come with me.'' In an instant Amelia was around the car, and the two women fell into step.

"Okay, just one block and we're there.'' The excitement was beginning to build again.

"Mom," Amelia said as she came to a stop, "take a look at my new home.''

"Oh, Amelia, you have finally done it.'' Martha's face shone with pleasure as she perused the little house with a critical eye. Then she smiled. "Yes, it's perfect. So much like you. So pretty and gentle, nestled here above the beach.''

"Pretty and gentle! Mother, don't let anyone at the station hear you say that. They all think I'm hard as nails.'' Amelia laughed airily, actually enjoying the adjectives her mother used.

"That's because you don't let them see underneath your facade," Martha said, sniffing. "But I know you. You are pretty and gentle and sweet. The house is perfect. I wish we could go inside. When will you move in? Has the loan been approved yet? I can help you paint and wallpaper—''

"Mom, slow down. I can move in in a few weeks. Yes, the loan has been approved and no, you won't help me paint and paper. It's perfect the way it is.'' Amelia laughed at her mother's excitement. It was good to be with someone who shared her mood. "As for going in . . . why not give it a try? I'm sure they won't mind. And if they do, we'll run around peeking in the windows.'' Amelia laughed as she went up the walk and rang the doorbell.

Amelia tipped her head. She heard "I'll get it'' and the sound of running feet. The door was flung open by one of the smallest women she had ever seen. At first she thought it was a young girl, but on closer inspection Amelia saw that the youthful appearance came from the sheer radiance of the woman's face.

"Hello?" Bright eyes turned from Amelia to Martha and back again.

"Hi," Amelia answered, knowing now that she had not been wrong to intrude. "I'm Amelia Jenkins. I'm buying this house and this is my mother." Amelia nodded over her shoulder. "I know this is an imposition, but we were wondering if we might come in for a moment. I'm so excited about the house that I wanted my mom to see it. I should have known we wouldn't be happy just looking at the outside."

"Who is it, hon?" A man's voice drifted through the living room followed almost immediately by the man himself. Their hostess held out a hand to him.

"It's the lady who's buying the house, John." Her arm snaked around his waist as he came to a stop before Amelia. Amelia almost sighed. They were a good-looking couple and obviously very much in love. Newlyweds, she decided.

"Hi," John said, holding out his hand to Amelia. As he shook it his eyes narrowed, then his face lit up. "Aren't you . . . ?"

"Yes," Amelia answered, her embarrassment evident.

"My goodness. A real-live celebrity is going to be living in our house, Judy." He laughed without self-consciousness.

"I thought you looked familiar. I've seen you on the news. Well, this is exciting," the woman exclaimed. "And where are my manners? Of course, come in and look around." She held the door open for Amelia and Martha, who both thanked her as they entered. "I just hope you'll excuse the mess. Everything is happening so fast that if we don't get the packing done now you're going to own a furnished house."

"We should be the ones apologizing," Amelia retorted immediately. "I should have known better, but you know how it is with your first house."

"Boy, do we. This was our first house...right after we were married. Nine years ago. I can hardly believe it." John had moved ahead into the living room as he spoke. He knelt beside a large carton. "You don't mind if I go ahead, do you? Judy can answer any questions you have."

"Not at all." Martha spoke for the first time. "Packing is a miserable job."

"No kidding. You wouldn't like to help, would you?" the man joked. If Amelia were to close her eyes and only hear his voice and its inflections, she knew that Scott's face would be before her. She looked at Judy. Was this the kind of woman Scott would eventually settle down with? Someone so totally different from Amelia? Easy, carefree, happy with the world. She snapped her attention back to John, banishing her thoughts of Scott completely. It didn't matter what Scott Alexander did or didn't do, wanted or didn't want.

"Don't tempt her." Amelia moved to stand beside her mother. "Once she starts she never stops. If she helps you pack she'll insist on going with you to unpack at the other end."

Amelia touched her mother's arm as their hosts laughed. Judy walked along with them as they looked into each room, graciously accepting all of Martha's compliments as she poked about.

"The wallpaper is wonderful," Martha said as they entered the kitchen. "And, Amelia, what a view you'll have."

"Oh, yes, you'll love it on summer evenings. The breeze is fantastic. You and your honey will have many a romantic dinner out there, I promise." Judy looked longingly out into the backyard as though remembering each and every moment she and her husband had spent there. In that moment Amelia felt so lonely she thought she might cry. Somehow everything seemed a little sad just then. She stared into the yard and out toward the ocean, trying to imagine herself there with Tom. No, it wouldn't be the kind of evening Judy was thinking about. Barbecuing with her mother was an even sadder thought. But with someone like Scott . . . well, maybe then she would know what Judy was talking about.

"Well," Martha said, sensing her daughter's uneasiness, "I think we better be going. I know you two have a lot to do. We appreciate this so much and I'm sure my daughter will be very happy here."

"Oh, I'm sorry. I didn't mean to be rude. It's just that we've spent such happy times here. I guess I'm getting a little sentimental. I think if they told us we had two months instead of two weeks to move I never would."

Judy had turned her beautiful, liquid brown eyes toward them. Then she shrugged her shoulders and the moment was gone.

"I'm really so happy you decided to come up. It's nice to know that someone bought this house because they loved it. I was so worried it would be bought by one of those awful developers who would tear it down and smash six condominiums onto this lot."

"No need to worry on that account," Amelia said, forcing her sadness away. "I doubt that I'll ever leave this place. I promise to take good care of it."

The women made small talk as they walked slowly back through the house. John rose from his task long enough to say goodbye, and then Amelia and Martha took their leave.

"Such a nice couple, weren't they, Amelia?" Martha asked the moment the door had closed.

"Yes, they are," Amelia answered, looking over her shoulder just in time to see Judy kiss the top of her husband's head. She made a mental note to put heavy drapes across the front window. It was so easy to see in. But then, what would someone see if they were to look in on her? Certainly not a scene such as one she just witnessed.

"It is a little small though," Martha commented.

"For one person?" Amelia cried in disbelief.

"No, for one it's all right. I'm just wondering where you're going to put my grandchildren," Martha chided.

"Oh, Mom!" Amelia threw up her hands in mock disgust. "Why don't we worry about a husband first?"

"I have been," her mother retorted. The two women laughed all the way to the car. Martha never pointed out that Amelia's laugh had an edge to it that said more than any words could.

IT WAS STILL EARLY when Amelia arrived back home. They had eaten an early supper, and having declined her mother's offer of coffee because she had so much to do, Amelia now couldn't remember what all those tasks were. The creeping sense of dissatisfaction she had felt earlier was upon her again, the trip to the house having been only a temporary balm.

In her bedroom she undressed, dropping her red and white jacket and print dress in a heap in the corner. The scene she had witnessed at her soon-to-be home floated about in her mind.

Nine years of marriage. Was that the key to youth? Judy and John would have seemed more real if they had been unpacking wedding presents rather than packing up the belongings people gather after nine years of marriage.

In the shower, Amelia let the water course over her as she considered the evening. She tried to identify and label those things she was feeling. Certainly not apathy. This was an active dissatisfaction. Was it jealousy of two people she didn't even know? Or maybe it was her mother's comments. All evening Martha had been alluding to her daughter's life-style, and Amelia had laughed off every single quip or comment. After all, she had heard them for years. But tonight they seemed to hit home. Her mother was becoming anxious for Amelia to follow in her footsteps—settle down, have a family. She had obviously forgotten that a few years ago she preached something very different.

How was she to keep up with what her mother wanted? Amelia was quite suddenly angered, and she flipped off the faucets, shaking her long wet hair. She thought her mother would be proud of her. After all, she'd been the one who taught Amelia to be so self-sufficient.

Amelia pushed the shower door open with a bang and immediately regretted both her action and her thoughts. It was all so silly. She had a touch of the

blues and nothing to cure it. The last thing she should
do was blame it on people she didn't know or on her
mother, whom she loved so dearly.

Allowing her ingrained resolve to come to the forefront, she toweled herself quickly, ran a comb through
her hair and stepped into her lounging outfit.

"If the guys at the station could see me now," she
muttered wryly to herself as she buttoned up the long
dress that was designed to look like an oversized foot-
ball jersey. It was hardly the image her public had of
her, she was sure. But on screen the image had to be
right; off screen, she could be herself. And herself
liked old, worn and comfortable.

There was actually a spring in her step as she left the
bathroom. Stopping long enough to pick up her discarded clothes and put them in the basket for the
cleaner, Amelia then went to the kitchen. Humming
while the water heated for tea, she searched for a pen
and a pad of paper, determined not to let the excitement of the last few hours leave her again.

Now, sitting at the dining room table, she sipped the
orange-flavored liquid and began to sketch. Her
memory was explicit and served her well as she drew
the floor plan of her new home. Soon her fingers were
flying and the little house was there in all its one-
dimensional glory.

Sitting back, Amelia considered her furniture.
Then, carefully, she started to draw the pieces on the
paper. Rectangles and circles and squares became her
real furniture, and soon she could almost feel how it
would be to walk into her new home. Over and over
again she rearranged the blocks, made notes and considered her work as the evening melted into late night.

Just as she was drawing the large rectangle that represented her king-size bed the doorbell rang.

Putting the last leg on her drawing, Amelia laid down the pencil and went to the door. She peeked through the spy hole but the hallway was empty. Her brow furrowed and she put her ear against the door as she called "Hello? Who's there?" but all was quiet. Quickly she put the chain in its holder, and then slowly opened the door a crack. No one was there. But just as she was about to close the door again, she noticed something on the floor. It was a note.

Amelia took off the chain, opened the door wide and picked up the piece of paper. It was a three-by-five index card with a string attached to it. Curiously she read the words that had been hurriedly scrawled there.

There are better things to do than sit alone in your apartment. Follow me and find out what.

Wary, but consumed by curiosity, Amelia hesitated only a moment before letting the string slip through her fingers. After all, her neighbors were home and she had an excellent set of lungs. If it was someone who wished her harm, he would probably be more frightened of her scream than she would be of him. And she could never let a mystery pass her by. What kind of reporter would she be?

A few feet away the string was attached to a bottle of wine. She hadn't noticed it at first because it was sitting against the wall. Another note was attached.

A fine bottle of wine is a good start!

It *was* a fine bottle of wine. Mouton Cadet. She

clutched it to her and went on. Just before the hall turned she found a rose with another note.

And, what would an evening be without flowers?

Amelia laughed outright. Any misgivings she had had were gone. It had to be Tom, but she had never known him to be so outrageous...so romantic. Where was he? Lurking around the corner, no doubt, for that was where the string led.

A grin came to her lips and she pulled on the string.

"Okay, Tom, the joke's over. This is wonderful but it's late—" The rest of the sentence was never uttered. It wasn't Tom who was pulled around the corner. Attached to the end of the string was a strong, callused hand and it was attached to Scott Alexander.

Chapter Five

"You!" Amelia couldn't contain her surprise. He was the last person she expected to see, but from the palpitations of her heart it was obvious that some part of her was thrilled that it was him.

"I figured as much," Scott answered her with a grin. Then, a look of mock surprise dancing in his eyes, he plucked at a card pinned to his open-necked shirt. "Oh, you forgot the last one."

Scott's long fingers pushed the card toward her. With a reaction as natural as pushing a strand of hair from her eyes Amelia leaned forward, her eyes narrowing. Five words were scrawled in the now-unmistakable hand:

Don't spend the night alone.

Amelia straightened, her eyes still firmly fixed on the card, her face contemplative. Scott watched with amusement, wondering what would happen next. He knew he should put his money on anger, or at least a terse word of dismissal, which would force him to summon up all the charm he possessed to counteract her. The laws of probability were against a delighted reaction but at least he could hope.

Little did he know that at that moment Amelia Jenkins was not trying to decide how to handle the situation at hand. Her eyes were not riveted to the card on his shirt. Rather, her brow was furrowed against the fact that she found the smooth, tan skin exposed by the open neck of his shirt quite lovely.

His chest was almost hairless. It was the color of pecans and as smooth as an almond. He shifted under her gaze, impatient since she had made no response at all, and Amelia noted the ripple of muscle. Again she was seized with an almost uncontrollable desire to touch him, but his movement banished the feeling and she looked into his face.

He grinned. So did she.

"That wasn't what I expected, Amelia, but let me tell you I'm certainly glad to see that beautiful smile of yours." His fingers deftly removed the pin that held the card to his shirt and Amelia thought that, for an instant, she saw a flash of embarrassment flicker across his face. It made her smile widen to think that even Scott Alexander, the man behind this elaborate wooing, could be made to feel uncomfortable.

"It seems as if you expected a less than happy welcome?" Amelia queried, raising her brow theatrically.

"Well, you could say that," he admitted, as he stuffed the note into his breast pocket. "I didn't know if you liked surprises."

Deftly, Amelia reached out and plucked the note away from him. Her fingers brushed his chest and she could feel that she had been right. Mr. Alexander was all muscle. She shuddered slightly but drew his atten-

tion away from her physical reaction with her next
words.

"I usually don't, but in this case—" she pulled at
the string she still held, surprising herself, and gripped
the bottle of wine and the rose closer to her "—I think
I'll make an exception."

"Thank God. I simply can't deal with rejection!"
Scott wailed to the ceiling, his beautiful white teeth
glinting under the hall lamp.

"I'll just bet you can't," Amelia countered knowingly, the slight tease evident in her tone. "And since
you've gone to so much trouble to make this work, I
won't reject you. Come on." She tugged on the string,
still connected to his wrist. "I can at least be gracious
enough to offer you a glass of wine. Besides, I don't
want you to make any more of a fuss. What if my
neighbors were to step out into the hall and see you
trussed up like this?"

"They'd certainly think you were hard up if you had
to lasso a man," he said, laughing.

"Don't be absurd," Amelia quipped back. "I
would never be so gauche as to lasso a man. Usually,
I simply dig a hole out front and wait for someone to
fall in."

So surprised was Scott at her free and easy manner
that his smile faltered and then widened again. He had
thought for certain that it would take than a little prank to melt his ice queen. But he was not going
to tempt fate by asking questions. Instead, he followed her happily down the hall.

In moments they were in her apartment. Once the
door closed and Amelia turned to look at her unexpected guest, she thought she must be crazy. She
should be mad as hell. His stunt was definitely high

school, but he had carried it off with such aplomb, such finesse, that he had won her over without her giving a second thought to the situation. It had been the same way at the restaurant two weeks ago. She wanted to convince herself that she couldn't be attracted to him physically, but her body kept denying all arguments. Now, though, she was sure that she was attracted to him as an amusing, intelligent person with a quick wit. She had felt stirrings of it at the restaurant and now those feelings were full-grown. Two weeks ago she never— Then it hit her. Two weeks! How rude he was!

Scott immediately saw the change in her as he finally untied the piece of string from his wrist. He moved toward her, capturing her shoulders in his strong hands.

"I note a change of heart, my dear celebrity," he chided her. "Don't tell me you're going to get rid of me just when you've given me hope?"

"I can't imagine what you're talking about," she answered drolly, raising her chin defiantly.

"Neither can I. I thought you found my entrance charming." One hand attempted to tip up her chin, but Amelia moved her head petulantly.

"Perhaps the surprise of it made me think I did." Amelia shook off the restraining hands and went to the kitchen, leaving him standing, confused, in the living room.

Her words kept coming but he could hardly hear her. He only caught bits and pieces of her one-sided conversation. "You know, you're always surprising me. Popping up at the studio, now here. Don't you plan your life any better than that, Mr. Alexander? Or do you have so many women to choose from that you wait until the last minute to decide who will have the pleasure of your company?''

"Wait a minute. What did I do?" He hurried after her. His words were confused but sincere, and when Amelia glanced over her shoulder she saw a face flushed with excitement, a happy smile, a man totally in control.

Well, if he didn't know…didn't understand… No, she would tell him. And this time he wouldn't miss one word. Amelia literally turned on her heel, her feet bare. He stopped in his tracks and backed up as she came toward him. Her hair was almost dry now and formed a golden halo around her head and shoulders. He thought she looked intimidatingly lovely but he also knew now was not the time to say so.

"I don't know who you think you're dealing with, Scott Alexander. I must tell you that I may have been taken in by this little prank of yours for a moment, but do you know it's been two full weeks since I've spoken to you? Any normal human being, if he were interested in seeing another person, as he had indicated at their last meeting, would have had the decency to call, even if it was just to say hello, so the other person wouldn't be surprised when that person just showed up on her doorstep."

Amelia had run out of breath and had backed Scott up against the wall. To her chagrin she actually found herself shaking one beautifully manicured finger at him. She realized she was making an utter fool of herself, but she couldn't help it. This man made her crazy; he popped up in her mind's eye more often than she could count; he drew her toward him without even trying. Then, just when she had decided she would never see him again, up he popped again. That's what made her mad, this lack of control when it came to Scott.

She took a deep breath in order to continue, but before another word came from her mouth he grabbed her around the waist and pulled her toward him.

Amelia gasped in surprise. His arms were strong and she felt almost diminutive in his embrace despite her willowy height. Then his lips were on hers, warm, sensitive. His kiss was gentle, shocking her into silence. She melted into him, completely forgetting her tirade. No one had ever treated her like this. No one had ever calmed her fury or stirred her from apathy. Now, Scott Alexander had done both. Then, carefully, he pushed her to arm's length. He held onto her and looked into her deep blue eyes.

"Are you finished?" he asked warily. When she didn't answer he continued. "Good. Now, if I may answer the charges: first, I was out of town until this morning. I was going to tell you when you left the car but you seemed determined to leave without another word. Second, today was my first day back in the shop. I was trying to call you but you had already left the office. Then there was a small fire at the plant and there were more than a few things to take care of. Ergo, the lateness of the hour. And, third—" he moved toward her, his face close and inviting "—if I recall, the last time we met you made it almost clear that there really was no future for us. So, like any other red-blooded male, I had to gather up my courage before I approached you again. Now, any other questions?"

Amelia shook her head. What a shrew he must think she was! Why did she always think that the world should revolve around her timetable? And he was right. She had not given him much encouragement the last time she saw him. But it wasn't until a moment ago that she realized how much she had wanted to see him. And the thought that he had spent the last two weeks sunning and funning at the beach—and working, of course—was almost too much to bear. She had thought he could have at least picked up the phone.

"Well," she said contritely, "there is one question: was anyone hurt in the fire?"

Scott threw back his head and laughed. He released her and Amelia immediately felt the loss. He drew one hand through his blond hair, stuffing the other one into the pocket of his well-fitting khakis, and took a few steps into the living room. Then he turned and faced her, both hands now in his pockets.

"Amelia Jenkins, you are a wonder! I can't figure you out for the life of me. One instant you're the most desirable, charming woman, the next you're a hard-nosed reporter or a woman very reminiscent of my mother telling me to clean up my room. God, but you are unbelievable."

"Not really. I think I'm very normal, thank you." Amelia pouted and returned to the kitchen. As she found a vase and opened the wine she looked over the counter and watched him move toward her. He leaned his elbows on the white Formica.

"I suppose you think so. But that spring of yours does pop at the strangest times." He watched her reach for the glasses and noted the fine full line of her breasts underneath her shapeless dress. She might be an intense woman, he decided, but she was definitely all woman. He shook his head and forced his eyes to look at the delicate features of her face while she poured the sparkling red liquid.

"However, I do appreciate your asking about the plant. No one was hurt, thank God." He took the glass she offered, then continued. "But we did lose two beautiful boards. It was a small loss compared to what it might have been. We have so much flammable material at the plant that it could have been a disaster."

"I'm sorry," Amelia answered contritely. She was sorry about her outburst, but his assessment of her had hit too close to home to make her comfortable. First her mother wondering if she was a woman with normal drives and now him. Her shoulders sagged for a moment, then she looked up at him.

In his eyes she saw nothing more than a man delighted to be with her. Despite his characterization of her he seemed to genuinely like her. She smiled, relaxed, grabbed the bottle of wine and went around the counter to meet him.

He moved with her into the living room and sat in one of the deep white chairs. Leaning back, he watched her sit on the matching sofa and tuck her feet under her.

"Look, Scott, that was ridiculous of me. I've had an awfully long day and I guess I'm not very good at handling surprises. I like to know exactly what's going to happen so I don't do things like I just did." She shrugged her shoulders. It was as close to an apology as she was going to get.

"That's okay, it's part of your charm. I think." He chuckled and she laughed along with him. Another surprise: she was laughing at herself. It had been a long time since she had done so. Perhaps that was part of his charm—his ability to throw her off balance. He was a challenge.

"So," he said, breaking into her thoughts, "what horrendous story did you have to cover today that's got you so wound up?"

"I know you're going to find this hard to believe, but it wasn't work." Scott cocked his head, a small, questioning smile playing on his lips. He sipped his wine to hide the grin that was about to claim his face. He could hardly believe his ears. Amelia Jenkins actually did something other than work.

"It must have been a corker, then. I wasn't sure anything but your work excited you," he answered as the glass left his lips. Amelia blushed. She was so transparent.

"Well, believe it. I've just bought a house and I took my mother out to see it this afternoon." Scott allowed himself to grin now. There was so much of a young girl in her open excitement that it touched him.

"Really? That's great. The first one is always scary though. Have you gone out on much of a financial limb?" He leaned forward, his face taking on a seriousness that Amelia found quite appealing.

"Not really," Amelia answered, anxious now to tell him about her house. She forgot everything except the fact that she was sharing her excitement with someone who seemed truly interested. Even his sensuality was forgotten as he listened contentedly to her talk.

"No, not at all. It's not big and I don't expect to get much of a tax break, but it's everything I've always wanted. It overlooks the beach near—" She hesitated. The next words would sound so horrible, but she plunged ahead. "Actually, it's very near your plant."

She expected to see him puff up like a peacock. He would no doubt decide she just couldn't stay away from him. But all she saw was his concentration as he paid close attention to her. It made her so happy, this reaction that seemed so out of character for him. Now, she wasn't so sure.

"Anyway, it's got a beautiful view of the beach and just enough room for me. Here..." She jumped up from the couch. "Let me show you. In minutes she rejoined him, having collected her papers from the table. She spread them out on the chocolate-colored carpeting and knelt over them, her hair falling onto the paper.

Scott eased himself from his chair and knelt beside her, listening to her explain how each and every piece of furniture would fit into her new home. She talked about the pieces she would still need to get, the housewarming she planned. Then, unable to resist, he reached out and drew her long hair back, tucking it over her ear.

Her chatter stopped immediately and she sat up straighter at his touch.

"I'm sorry," he said quietly. "I couldn't see the drawing."

Amelia turned her head to look into his eyes. She felt, and almost saw, the electricity dance between them. Her lashes lowered, not from any false sense of shyness, but simply to cut the current and steel herself against what she hoped was not an inevitability.

"It doesn't matter," she finally said. "I was done anyway. I think I've probably gone over everything twice as it is."

Amelia leaned over once more, grateful that her wayward locks would not stay in place. Her hands moved quickly as she stacked the papers together. She put her hand out to steady herself as she rose, but his reached out and covered hers, keeping her in her place.

"There's no need to get up," he commanded gently. "Sit here with me for a while."

Strangely, Amelia found herself sitting back down as he had asked. The papers were still clutched in her hands, and when he reached for them, they slipped through her fingers as though she had no control over her muscles. Carefully, he laid the drawings on the table, then turned back to her.

"I hope you'll let me help you warm your new house." This was hardly a question and Amelia looked up into his eyes. "When do you move in?"

"I can start moving things week after next . . ." she answered, words failing her as she fell under the spell of his gaze.

"I'll get Sailor and a few of the guys to help. We'll have you in in no time . . . just name the day." His voice was warm, lulling her like the last licks of a fire.

"Thank you. I appreciate it, but it's really not necessary. I was going to have a moving company do it. I'm at the office so late, you understand."

"Oh, no, you don't," he insisted quickly, his hands capturing hers and bringing them to his lips. The warmth of them on her fingertips was like cinders dancing over her skin, but she was powerless to pull away. "You're going to take a few days off to move into your new house. Any fool could see how much this means to you. I'm sure the station can get by for a day or two."

Amelia opened her mouth to protest but nothing came out. She couldn't possibly take time off. Could she?

"I'll take that to be an affirmative," Scott went on as he scooted closer to her. "Therefore I'll expect you to tell me what day you want me and my crew here. And I'll expect that information soon."

"But you'll be taking people away from your plant." Amelia made an effort to protest. It just wasn't right, either of them ditching work to move.

"That's all right. Really. Work isn't everything, you know." Amelia felt her cheeks color, knowing this statement was directed at her, the thoughts she now felt he could read. "Friends do this kind of thing all the time. But I want us to be more than friends, Amelia. Much more."

With that, Scott's hands freed hers only to wind themselves through her hair and pull her face close to his. His lips found hers and Amelia melted into him. Gently, cradling her head as though she were an infant, he lowered her onto the carpeting, his lips never leaving hers.

For an instant Amelia thought of stopping him. For a minute she wanted to tell him that he couldn't close the plant and she couldn't possibly get off work to move. But then the moment passed, as she was gently ushered into a world that existed only for the two of them and only for that night.

Scott leaned closer, his legs moving over hers. She felt her gown riding up so that her legs were free. As his kisses became insistent, his body rolled gently until he was lying almost on top of her.

Amelia shuddered, a sigh of desire bubbling from her lips as she realized how much she wanted him. Her hands came alive, fluttering over his back, feeling the muscles there constrict at her touch. He breathed a whisper of delight, and she felt his warm breath over her cheek, her neck, as he buried his face in the mass of golden tresses.

"Amelia." She heard the word as though it were a breeze through the autumn trees, and she quivered like the leaves destined to fall from those trees.

Then he rolled away from her, one of his hands still entangled in her hair, the other running through his own as he lay on his back, his eyes closed. Stunned, Amelia lifted herself on her elbow and looked down at him, not knowing what she expected to see. Mirth, because he could tell she was reacting like a girl on her first date? Boredom? No. What she saw was his lovely face, calm, content. His lips were curled in a gentle smile, his brow was slightly furrowed. She leaned down to kiss the creases on his forehead and his eyes opened, showering her with a look that came close to love.

"Is everything all right?" she whispered, not caring that the future might not be theirs, only wanting the moment to be right.

"Oh, Amelia." He reached out and pulled her on top of him. "Better than all right. I want you. I want you so badly."

She understood. He was questioning her, asking her if she, too, felt the same way. Amelia lowered her face, pressing her cheek against his broad chest. Yes, she wanted him. She wanted him more than anything. She wanted to feel him, to know him, to love him. The thoughts she had been having could become realities there in the dim light of the living room.

She raised her head and looked at him once again. Why not? This relationship could be anything she wanted it to be. He had made no demands. Neither would she. Just this once she would not think of where she would be in two days, two weeks or two years. Tonight she would only think of where she would be in two hours—in his arms.

She moved away from him and rose. Looking down, she saw the flitting sorrow of loss move over his face. *She's gone,* he thought. But then she surprised him. Her hand moved and she held it out for him to take. Scott smiled and grasped it, tentatively, then more firmly. With the grace of an athlete he came to his feet, and slipping his arm over her shoulders, led her into the bedroom.

The room was dark, but light from the street bathed the bed and its coral-colored quilt. Even in the dim light Scott could see that it was old. And the bed was an antique four-poster. He felt his heart swell at this intimate look into Amelia Jenkins—hard as nails on the air and in her interviews, but all woman at heart. If only she understood that the two personae could co-exist so beautifully.

Turning toward her, he cupped her chin and kissed the tip of her nose. Then, ever so gently, his hands slid to the alabaster column that was her neck and traveled on to play with the buttons of her jersey. His fingers lingered. He waited for any sign of hesitation, but there was none. No fear, no waning desire. The top button opened, then the next and the next. Scott felt Amelia quiver, saw her eyes flutter shut and open again. They shone with honest desire and utter willingness. And, as he slipped the gown from her, he was overwhelmed by her beauty.

Carefully, he led her to the bed and lay her down. The shadows played over her. Her breasts were full and high, rounded, her stomach flat, her hips smooth and her legs long and inviting.

As she watched, Scott removed his shirt. Amelia heard the starched cotton crinkle in the quiet. He turned slightly as his slacks fell from his body and she smiled at this bit of shyness. Then he was beside her and his skin was warm and smooth. She could restrain herself no longer.

Instantly her hands began to explore. Their arms were around each other, their lips hungry. There came a blending and a meeting that surprised Amelia with its force and sincerity, and she fell under its spell. As he moved on top of her, his legs naturally falling in place between hers, Amelia Jenkins forgot everything but the man to whom she was so willingly giving herself. She would not remember work or house or ambitions until later... much, much later. Finally spent, Amelia fell asleep in Scott's arms, wishing that the morning would never come.

But come it did, and when she woke she was alone. She rolled over, clutching the pillow where Scott's head had lain, but it was cold. Had he left so early? Shame and remorse flooded over her, her fear that she would be a one-night stand seemed to have become a reality. She raised her fist and smashed it into the pillow. The apartment was deathly quiet. He had gone like a thief in the night.

Then she heard a noise. Pulling the sheets up around her nakedness, she listened. As she reached for her robe, realizing she was not alone, the door to the bedroom opened and Scott Alexander stood in the doorway, grinning from ear to ear.

"Don't you ever eat? The only thing I could find in the refrigerator was a stalk of celery that's seen better days, butter, Gatorade and nail polish." He advanced into the room, bringing with him as he chattered a light greater than that of the day outside. "I did manage, however, to find coffee. I didn't know if you took it black but I figured you did. Any self-respecting professional should take it black." He lowered himself onto the bed, handing her a mug as he did so. The bed squeaked under his weight.

"Now, tell me," he went on, "what in the hell is nail polish doing in your refrigerator?"

Amelia had accepted the mug and brought it quickly to her lips so that he wouldn't see that her smile was not only one of happiness but also one of relief. Surreptitiously, she glanced at him. He had slipped into his slacks but his chest was bare, beautifully smooth and tanned and muscled. When she finally regained her composure, Amelia relaxed into the pillows and looked up at him.

"It keeps it fresh," she said matter-of-factly.

"I see. Well, I'll have to stock in a few bottles of Pink Starlight...just in case. Besides, it will add color to my refrigerator." He glanced at her, hoping to see her smile in understanding. But her eyes were hooded by her long, dark lashes. He couldn't possibly know that her stomach had contracted and her heart had skipped a beat in relief when he spoke those words. The night's promises were being delivered, and she had never felt more content.

"I'd be happy to lend you a bottle of my own so you don't have to go out and buy some," Amelia answered coquettishly. She raised her lashes and looked into his eyes.

"I was hoping you would say that." Scott leaned over, holding his mug away from the bed, and lightly kissed her. He started to raise his head, then thinking again, lowered his lips once more, giving her a good-morning kiss that she was sure would last until the afternoon.

"That's better than any breakfast I could have found in the refrigerator," he said when they finally parted.

"It is a nice way to start the morning," Amelia agreed, sipping her coffee once more. "How long have you been up?"

"Since seven." Scott sat back on the bed, curling his legs underneath him.

"Seven?" Amelia shook her head slightly. The alarm should have gone off. She bolted upright in bed and grabbed the clock. The sheet had fallen away and her breasts were even more beautiful in the light of morning. Scott reached out but thought better of offering a caress when he saw her eyes widen in horror.

"Scott! It's already eight-thirty. I had to be in the office by eight." She quickly put the mug on the bed-side table and threw the covers from her, unashamed of her nakedness in her hurry.

Just as quickly Scott put his mug down and pulled her back onto the bed. His body rolled atop hers, and he felt her give and then stiffen again.

"Did you miss an interview?" His question showed sincere concern despite the odd situation in which it was asked, so Amelia took the time to explain.

"No. But I'm always in the office by eight. That way I can get all my memos to the secretary before she gets in, write notes to Tom..."

"Amelia," Scott said, as he laughed and sat up, pulling her with him and reveling in the feel of her satiny skin, "you mean you're upset because you won't be in the office before everyone else?"

"I'm upset because I have a certain way of conducting business and I like to keep to that schedule." Her tone was aloof and she pulled away from him, trying to reach around him for the robe she had so hurriedly discarded the night before.

Scott let his hands fall from her. He held them out to his sides, leaning back as she grabbed for the garment.

"Okay, okay," he said instantly, serious for the moment. Such a beautiful workaholic. "I'm sorry. I didn't mean to laugh. It's just that you are allowed to keep normal hours, you know."

"I never do just what I'm allowed to do, Scott, and you might as well understand that right now," Amelia answered, finally capturing her gown. She continued as she held it up, trying to get the sleeves right side out. "I set very high standards for myself and I intend to keep to them, no matter what."

"No matter what?" Scott said, pulling down the dress and running his hand over her shoulders. He felt her tense and then melt under his touch.

"All right. I'm sorry. But last night was kind of special and I hate to have you run away from me in such a state. Just this once, Amelia, for me, couldn't you slow down a minute and say good morning?"

Amelia looked at him. His attractiveness was not lessened, despite her concern with getting to work. No, he was as wonderfully sensuous in the light of day as he had been in the shadows of night.

"Good morning," she said sweetly, allowing herself to grin. Quickly, she planted a kiss on his lips, sat back, then said, "Now may I go?"

"Yes," he teased, "but don't think I'm going to let you rush off like this every morning."

Amelia hopped from the bed. "That sounds like you're going to be here every morning."

He followed her into the bathroom and lounged against the door as she stepped into the shower.

"No. Sometimes you'll be at my place," he hollered above the roar of the water. Amelia smiled behind the glass of the shower door.

"Aren't you assuming a bit too much?" she called. Then she tipped her head, waiting for his answer. Instead of words, though, the response was that the door slid open and Scott slipped into the shower with her. His hands found her waist, slippery and silky from the soap, and he pulled her to him.

"I don't think so, Amelia. Do you?"

She let her fingers touch his cheek and outline his lips. Then she smiled.

"No, I don't. But," she said, bending down to find the soap as the water coursed over both of them, "you are going to have to realize that I'm very dedicated to my work. So you can wash my back while I do my hair."

The soap flew into the air, forcing Scott to release her and grab for it as it fell back down. Shaking his head as she turned to face the spray of water, Scott wondered how long it would be before Amelia would have to face the fact that work was not the be all and end all of a person's existence. Lathering up his hands and putting them on her beautiful back, he hoped he would be around when it finally dawned on her.

He was toweling himself dry when Amelia reentered the bathroom.

"I've got to go now," she said to his back, and when he turned, she was greeted with a look of surprise.

"How do you do that?" he asked.

"What?"

"Look so gorgeous no matter what you're wearing . . . or what you're not wearing," Scott answered, winding the towel around his slender waist as he advanced on her.

"No, you don't!" Amelia backed away with a laugh. "I'm already very late as it is. Besides, you're still wet, and water spots on silk never come out."

"All right, you're safe for now," Scott warned, stopping in his tracks. "But tonight I won't promise."

"Tonight?" Amelia raised an eyebrow in question.

"I was hoping you'd let me buy you dinner."

"I think that could be arranged as long as you promise no hanky-panky."

"And why not, may I ask?"

"Because tonight's a school night." Amelia watched him, enjoying his look of confusion. "Didn't your mother ever tell you you couldn't stay out late on a school night?"

"I vaguely remember something like that, but I didn't pay attention then and I'm not in school now." The banter amused Scott. Amelia seemed to have discarded her earlier worries about the hour, and he was glad.

"Well, when you grow up, a school night simply translates into a work night. No matter how much I adored our evening together I have no intention of replaying this morning."

"What if I promise to set six alarm clocks around the bed?" Scott offered. "Amelia, you can't be telling me that I'll have to wake up alone the rest of the week."

"That's exactly what I'm telling you," she answered crisply, knowing full well that she had no intention of keeping that promise.

"Well, then, there's only one thing to do about it," Scott said as he moved toward her and rested his arm against the door.

"Yes?" Amelia tipped her head and raised her eyes to his, a smile hovering at the corners of her mouth. Scott Alexander seemed to bring out every feminine wile she possessed and she loved it.

"I'll have to marry you. Then you'd be forced to spend all your nights with me."

Amelia looked into his eyes, a laugh already on her lips. But when she saw his seriousness, the firm set of his jaw, she was no longer sure that he was joking. For a moment she simply looked at him. Then, gently, she kissed him. Her fingertips traced the outline of his jaw as she considered him for a moment longer. Then she spoke.

"Well, we'll have to see about that. I'll talk to you tonight." Amelia looked at him one more time, then turned and left the apartment. She couldn't leave the thought of Scott and his strange proposal behind, though, no matter how hard she tried.

AND, IF THE TRUTH BE TOLD, Amelia didn't try very hard to push the memory of Scott's proposal, or Scott himself, from her mind. He was far too delicious a diversion, or so she had told herself initially. But soon she wasn't lying anymore. He was much more than a diversion. Scott Alexander had become a part of her life, a welcome part, a much-loved part.

The idea of seeing him every night after work, waking with him in the morning, made the days fly by.

No longer was there that laconic attack on her professional chores. It wasn't that the station offered her any more challenging outlets for her creative energy than she had been used to; her work load remained the same. But no longer were her days centered around the office and the next interview.

Instead, they were spent analyzing and storing everything she found out about Scott Alexander. He was, indeed, everything she had first thought him to be: easygoing, boyish and fun-loving. Yet, he was also so much more. A true friend, one willing to lend a helping hand when it was needed. A gentleman who enjoyed pleasing a woman as much as he enjoyed being pleased by her. And an astute businessman. It was the last that truly amazed her, and Amelia remembered well their conversation over a dinner of sushi and wine.

"We're not a high-volume business." Scott had wiggled his chopsticks at her as he spoke, and Amelia couldn't resist the urge to snap playfully at the piece of raw salmon that dangled from them. "Boy, a guy tries to get serious and all you can think about is food. I thought I was the one who was supposed to be the frivolous part of this act."

"Sorry." Amelia shrugged in apology. "I just couldn't help myself. You've been wiggling that tasty morsel for over two minutes now. If you're going to talk, don't tempt me."

"Okay." He laid down the chopsticks and crossed his arms on the table. "Now, where was I?"

"High-volume business..." Amelia reminded him, still eyeing the sushi on his plate. She hated people who could nonchalantly keep the best for last. She always rushed ahead and ate the best first.

"Oh, yes. Well, it's tough to get a bank loan for something that specialized. You see, a marketing plan couldn't forecast a great enough volume to convince the banks that the loan would be secured. Anyway, that's why I went to my father. Now, you've got to remember, Dad's rolling in dough. But the one thing he always taught me is business is business, so I didn't expect any special treatment.

"He made me do a cash-flow analysis as well as outline my strategy for contacting those segments of the marketplace that would be my best bet for sales. Then, once he was satisfied it would work, he lent me the money at ten and a half percent interest.... That's about one point below the going rate."

"How rude!" Amelia immediately retorted.

"What?"

"Charging you interest on a family loan. If your father is that well off, why didn't he just give you the money?"

"Nothing rude about it. He's always made me learn from everything I do. Never has he put down any idea I've had, but he's always helped me to thrash them out. If I went ahead with them despite his advice then I was liable for the outcome. Sometimes my schemes worked and sometimes they didn't. But each time, I understood in greater depth what he was trying to do. He was trying to make me think, be responsible. I don't think that's rude. I think it's smart and a damn good way to teach children."

Scott leaned back, thoroughly pleased with both his explanation and the look of utter shock on Amelia's face. He was all too aware of her reservations, and he enjoyed knocking down the walls one by one.

That night had been only the first of many such lessons she was to learn from Scott Alexander about his business and his ethics.

The second lesson came on a Sunday morning during the first weekend they spent together. Scott had effectively dissuaded Amelia from working until at least mid-afternoon.

"Scott," Amelia protested as they lay in her bed together, "you'll just never understand how important this job is. I mean it's not like painting a Windsurfer and letting it sit to dry. This is think work."

"Think work!" Scott leaped from under the covers, grabbed his pillow and playfully batted at Amelia, who immediately dove for cover. "Painting? Drying? How could you even say such a thing? After all this time and our interview I thought you had a bit more respect than that for my calling."

"I do, I do...." Amelia giggled, out of control. "I'm sorry. Please stop with the pillow."

"Okay," Scott conceded as he burrowed under the covers to find her. "But I'm not letting you off so easily. You're getting dressed and coming with me."

"Where are we going?"

"To the plant, where I should have been since six-thirty this morning. But, because of you, I shirked my responsibilities. Well, missy, it's time for a lesson. You help me work this morning, then I'll let you do your think work this afternoon."

Scott fairly dragged Amelia out of the bed, twirling her naked body to his just long enough for a kiss. Then he unceremoniously dug through her closet. Soon she was dressed in her oldest jeans and a sweatshirt that had seen better days.

Kindly, Scott stopped for coffee and donuts before driving to the plant. And from the moment they got back into the car he talked about Windsurfers: the different kinds, the weight considerations, the wave and wind considerations. Amelia's head was reeling with facts and figures by the time they got to the warehouse.

"All right, Ms Jenkins," Scott said as he peeled his light jacket off and threw it into a corner, "what kind of board would you use for a high-speed, high-wind situation?"

Amelia stood on the cold concrete and stared at Scott. He had to be kidding! If he thought she had caught even a portion of that instant lesson on windsurfing he was crazy. She was still considering the explanation of the sport itself. There had been no time to listen closely to the explanation of the many types of boards and sails.

"No answer?" Scott asked gaily as he pulled up a stool for each of them.

"I know," Amelia said, figuring that a stab at the right answer was better than no answer at all. She wasn't going to let him get her goat, good-natured or no. "It's the small board where the rider has to actually hold on to the sail and pull himself from the water onto the board because the board is so small and light it can't take the extra weight and get its momentum up. . . ."

"You got it. Now it's called a . . ."

"I can't remember. . . ."

"A surfing and jumping board. It's not used for calm-water sailing; it's for launching off waves or outrunning them. And it's usually how long?"

"Seven feet? Eight feet?"

Scott continued to shake his head as Amelia laughed out her answers. "It's eight feet six inches. I don't think I'll even ask you about the Transition Board or the Regatta. No, anyone can see you're not ready for the 'thinking' end of this business. We better start you on something easier. Think you can handle it?"

"Anything but this," Amelia wailed and collapsed onto her stool. She smiled as she watched Scott move to a workbench that was covered with colorful paints and sheets of fiberglass.

"Let's see if you can handle the mechanical end of the business. Now," he turned back to her holding out some sheets of what appeared to be paper, "this is 320-, 400- and 600-grit sandpaper. This is a board that needs wet sanding before we can rub it out and give it a final polish. Do you think you could handle that?"

"No doubt about it, Mr. Alexander, sir." Amelia leapt to her feet and offered him an outrageous salute. This was going to be a breeze. She'd be home working in no time. Although she had to admit that the thought of preparing an interview was definitely less appealing than it had been that morning. Scott always managed to bring a smile to her face, and she hated the thought of being without him even for an evening.

"Just tell me which one to use, sir." Amelia played her part to the hilt as he took her shoulders and helped her kneel down on the cold concrete in front of the board. "I'll have this job down in record time."

"Oh, you will, will you?" Scott chuckled and leaned down closer to her ear. "Then, to answer your question, the paper you use is 320-, 400- *and* 600-grit."

"All of them?" Amelia gulped.

"All of them," Scott answered before he kissed her ear and disappeared into the back room.

Amelia watched him go, her eyes blazing with anger. A lesson was a lesson, but this was ridiculous. Well, she would show the Windsurfer king a thing or two. She would sand this board to perfection, then she would flounce into his office, drop the used paper on his desk and demand to be taken home to work. How long could it take? With an ungodly vigor she attacked the board, and with each swipe of 320-grit paper she wiped the self-satisfied grin off Scott's face.

Three hours later, though, when she looked up, Scott stood before her, that same grin firmly in place. Amelia's resolve was firmly shaken.

"Had enough?"

"Just about," Amelia answered as she sat back on her heels and pushed a strand of hair from her eyes. She was so tired she thought she might cry. And she was only half finished.

"Are you ever again going to think that my business should take a back seat to yours?" Scott asked gently. Amelia shook her head in defeat. If she had to do that every day for a living she would simply die. "Thank you," he said. His arms encircled her shoulders and he raised her up to lean against him. "It's only one o'clock. I'm going to take you home so you can work."

"All right." Amelia threw the used sheets of sandpaper onto the board and turned toward the exit.

"How about next weekend I teach you how to use one of those things?" Scott asked.

"Don't be absurd." Amelia yawned. "I don't care if I never see one again in my life."

Scott laughed heartily as he eased his exhausted lover into the car. It was the last sound she heard until Scott woke her to tell her she was home. Once upstairs, he took matters in hand. He laid Amelia on her bed and went to run a hot bath for her. By morning, he knew, her arm would feel as if it had been disconnected if she didn't soak it now. But when he went to fetch her he found her fast asleep, clutching a pad and pencil she had heroically taken from the bedside table.

"No more work for you today, my love," he whispered as he took away the tools of her trade. "Someone has to save you from yourself."

Covering her with a light blanket, Scott left her to sleep the afternoon away, returning that same evening to massage her hurt muscles with ointment and her hurt pride with kisses.

They wove themselves closer and closer together as the days passed until Amelia was sure she never wanted to be free of Scott Alexander again. In fact, it was on a rather normal working morning that she chose to consider the question of when she should introduce Scott to her mother. Normal, that is, until she stepped out of the elevator doors and into KNXT's lobby.

Chapter Six

"Hey, Amelia!"

The call came from Diane, the receptionist, just as Amelia slipped by three people headed the opposite way.

"I almost didn't see you in that crunch," Diane said as Amelia turned back to the front desk. "It's a good thing you're not a Munchkin like me."

"I'd hardly call you a Munchkin." Amelia laughed as she rested her arms on the high desk. "Petite is much more in vogue, you know. Whatcha got?"

"A message from somebody in New York." The slip of paper was duly handed over, and Amelia knit her brow as she looked at the name.

"Jan Dickerson? I don't know any Jan Dickerson in New York." Amelia raised her eyes in a silent query, but Diane only shrugged. "She didn't leave a message?" Amelia asked.

"Nope, sorry. I asked, but she just said it was too involved to explain over the phone and would you please call her the moment you got in. Which, by the way, I told her would be an hour ago."

"You know the office doesn't open until nine, Diane," Amelia quipped, pocketing the message before

she went on her way. "And believe it or not," she
called over her shoulder just before she disappeared
into the labyrinth of hallways, "I just found that out
myself."

"Was that Amelia Jenkins?" Diane turned to the
secretary who stopped to chat just as Amelia made her
exit.

"Yeah, can you believe it?" Diane said, chuckling.
"Either she's lost her senses, found a new job or some
guy's got her on the string."

"I hope it's the latter. I think I'd feel more comfortable around her if she was that breezy all the time.
Not that I don't like her anyway. But, God, is she intense."

"I know what you mean. Well," Diane shrugged as
she picked up the telephone to answer an incoming
call, "whatever it is, it would be nice for her if it never
ended."

The other secretary nodded, gathered the mail that
was waiting at the reception desk and left the lobby.

"Amelia." This time it was Tom who hailed her just
before she ducked into her office.

"Morning, Tom." Amelia smiled. All was right
with the world and she felt wonderful. Diane was not
the only one to notice. Tom saw the difference the
moment he took the chair opposite her.

"I was here early and I was starting to worry. Did
you have car trouble?"

"Nope."

His curiosity piqued, Tom leaned forward and went
on. "Just slept late, then?"

"You might say that," Amelia answered enigmati-
cally. Then, seeing Tom's interest, and for the first
time understanding it, she went on more sympatheti-

cally. After all, she did sort of owe him some sort of explanation.

"I had a visitor last night who stayed rather late and—"

"Oh, hey, I'm sorry," Tom interjected, his face coloring as he realized fully what the situation was.

"No need, Tom, but I thought you should know," Amelia answered delicately. As casual as she may have thought their relationship was, she knew Tom didn't share the same feelings.

"Sure, of course. Anyone I know?"

Amelia looked Tom straight in the eye. She saw curiosity and caring, but there was no indication that he was dreadfully hurt. A good sign. Tom always did have a good head on his shoulders, and that was part of his charm. But, Amelia knew now, there could be so much more to charm. So much more... She shook her head. Scott would have to be relegated to his proper corner if she was going to get anything done.

"Actually you do in a way," she admitted. "It's Scott Alexander."

Tom appeared at a loss. Then his face opened and he smiled. Thankfully, he didn't laugh. "Not the Windsurfer king?"

"Yes, what of it?" Amelia asked defensively. For the first time in a long while she again felt the twinges of insecurity that had plagued her whenever she had considered a relationship with Scott.

"Well, it's just that..." Tom shrugged. "I didn't think you thought that much of him."

"I didn't at first, but he really is quite an unusual man. He's well read, well traveled—" Amelia stopped. There was no need to defend him to Tom.

Or was she defending him to herself? Whatever the situation, it didn't matter. In that instant she realized that she was willing to play their relationship to its end. Yes, even she deserved to indulge herself now and again. And if Scott Alexander brought her happiness and contentment, that was great. They were both rational adults with a lot in common. That was enough.

"Well, that's nice, Amelia." Tom cut in on the silence that had strung itself out between them.

"Yes, it is," Amelia said. Then she started to look through the papers on her desk. "Were you looking for me for anything special?"

"No, it doesn't matter now," Tom answered. Amelia glanced up, but her friend's face remained unreadably open.

"Okay." She reached into her pocket and withdrew the message Diane had given her. "By the way, do you know a Jan Dickerson in New York?"

"Nope, can't say that I do. Why?"

"No special reason. I got this message to call her immediately and I just thought you might have a clue."

"Sorry, I can't help you." Tom rose and stuck his hands into his pockets. "Why don't you give her a call right now, because we're going to be out most of the day."

"Good idea. I'll see you in about an hour, right?" Amelia picked up the telephone receiver.

"We'll be ready." With that, Tom was gone, and Amelia hummed as she dialed the number in New York.

The phone rang six times and Amelia almost hung up. Then the ringing stopped and the greeting came, stopping Amelia's heart along with it.

"ABC, New York, may I help you?"

"Yes, I'm sorry," Amelia stammered. This was not at all what she had expected. She pulled her jacket straighter and sat up. "I'd like to speak to Jan Dickerson, please."

"Just one moment."

Amelia waited as the phone rang a second time. She tried to control her anticipation. This call could be nothing, but then again, it could be everything to her.

"Ms Dickerson's office, may I help you?" This time the voice was warm and inviting. Amelia could almost see the secretary. Highly paid, well dressed, impeccably trained. She recognized the mannerisms even over the phone.

"Yes, I would like to speak to Ms Dickerson, please." Amelia answered in her most professional manner.

"And may I say who is calling?"

"This is Amelia Jenkins in Los Angeles. Ms Dickerson asked that I return her call."

"Oh, yes, Ms Jenkins. Ms Dickerson has been waiting," the secretary answered, making Amelia feel as though all of New York had been waiting for her to return the call. "I'll put you through."

"Hello." Before Amelia could catch her breath a third voice was speaking to her. This one was gravelly, hurried. Amelia could feel the power of the woman, because her tone also held a kindness. "This is Jan Dickerson, and I am so pleased to speak with you, Ms Jenkins."

"I'm afraid you have me at a disadvantage, Ms Dickerson," Amelia answered politely, wondering all the while if the woman could hear her heart beating.

"Of course I do, my dear. Let me introduce myself. I'm executive vice president in charge of programming and I'm in receipt of a tape of yours. We're losing one of our hosts on *Meet America* and we would very much like to test you for the spot."

Amelia's quick intake of breath was not lost on Jan Dickerson, and the woman laughed in a marvelously warm way.

"I know this must come as some kind of a shock to you, since you didn't send us the tape. Someone who obviously thinks quite highly of you...a Tom...I can't quite make out the last name on the letter...sent it to us. I tried to find your agent, but I gather you don't have one."

"No, no, I don't. And I do know Tom. He's head of my crew here in Los Angeles...." Amelia began to explain, then she, too, chuckled. "Ms Dickerson, you must forgive me. I'm just so taken aback. I can't tell you what an honor this is."

"Well, don't tell me about honor, tell me if you're interested in coming to talk to us. If you're serious about your career, you couldn't do better than *Meet America*."

"I know that. And if I may say so, I am very serious about my career," Amelia answered without blinking an eye, and for that moment even thoughts of her night with Scott were put out of her mind.

Chapter Seven

"Tom, could I see you in my office for a minute?" Amelia asked quietly as the tired crew filed into the station. It had been a very long but fruitful day. Although it had been almost impossible for Amelia not to speak of her conversation with Jan Dickerson during the day, she had managed to control her excitement. It wasn't time to let anyone but Tom know of the offer.

"Sure thing. Be with you as soon as I get the equipment locked up," Tom answered brightly. Like Amelia, he never seemed to tire. He loved his work and he loved the people he worked with.

In her office, Amelia poured two cups of coffee. She put one on the desk and held the other to her lips as she moved to her chair and let her fingers ruffle through the messages and mail that lay atop the already cluttered surface. The leather chair breathed under her weight just as the door opened and Tom walked in.

"Could you close the door, please?" Amelia asked.

"Oh-oh, this sounds dreadful." Tom smiled as the door clicked shut.

"On the contrary. I think I have something to thank you for," Amelia answered as he sat down across from her.

"I can't imagine what."

"Jan Dickerson still doesn't ring a bell?" Amelia queried.

"Nope." Tom's brow knit as he considered the name, and Amelia could tell that he was truly at a loss.

"Did you send one of my tapes to New York? To *Meet America*?" Amelia attempted to jog his memory. It worked. Tom's face lit up in surprise.

"You're kidding!" Tom nearly jumped out of his seat with excitement. "You mean that's what that call was about? Geez, Amelia, it was just a shot in the dark. I mean, I thought you'd be perfect for that show so I sent it in blind. That's why I didn't know the name."

"Tom, calm down." Amelia laughed, enjoying the fact that he was as thrilled as she. "You'd think you were the one going to New York."

"I feel like I am. Amelia, I can't tell you how excited I am for you. But why did you wait all day to tell me?" He plopped down in his chair again but leaned forward expectantly, his elbows on his knees.

"I almost told you a thousand times today but I wanted to kind of live with this for a little bit before I shared it with you."

What she didn't say was that throughout the day she, Amelia Jenkins, fast-track newslady, had experienced some pricks of misgiving. Scott and his lovemaking and his wit and his friendship loomed fresh in her mind, stayed close to her heart, and a small bit of her didn't even want to consider the other job. Then the old Amelia took over and she began to plan—what she would wear, how she would act, where she would live once she got the job. It was everything she had ever wanted...wasn't it?

"That's understandable."

"What isn't understandable is what possessed you to do such a thing," Amelia said, hardly able to contain her feelings.

"I did it because I believe in you. I believe that you are one of the brightest, most talented women on the air today and, I think, you've been feeling like you're at a dead end here. You've got the drive to make something like this work. You've got the looks, the personality, the intelligence, the—"

"Hold on!" Amelia laughed, ignoring the underlying sadness in his tone. It was somehow hard to hear how determined she was to work her way to the top. It was easier to live with it as a given. "I appreciate the vote of confidence, but enough is enough."

"I can't help it. I've never met anyone who deserves a break like this more. When do you start?"

Amelia grinned. That's what she loved about Tom: any victory that came to her was a foregone conclusion.

"I don't think it's as simple as that," Amelia answered, thinking back over the itinerary Jan Dickerson had outlined. "First I go to New York to meet with the brass at the station for interviews, that kind of thing. Then there'll be a screen test with the type of material they use on the show. In the middle of this there's a cocktail party—I guess they want to see how I react in social situations—and there are bound to be lots of public appearances."

"Well, I just know you're going to do great. These are all preliminaries. I have no doubt you're going to get the job."

"There are three other people up for the job, you know," Amelia answered, her voice rising, unable to control her confidence any longer. "But, Tom, I really feel that this is it. You know how your bones tell you things? Well, mine are just tingling. The trip is next week. I'm going to have to put in for vacation. There's a million things to do. The house is closing escrow." Amelia rambled on, her excitement growing by the minute. "Oh, my God, the house! I just bought my dream house and now I may have to leave it!"

"Think positively, Amelia. Think you *will* have to leave it." Tom laughed. Amelia did, too, as she watched him. She almost expected him to get up and dance a jig. Well, if this was his reaction to her moving on, he couldn't be too much in love with her. The thought that perhaps she had always counted on Tom as someone to fall back on pricked her, but it was gone as soon as it was acknowledged.

"I guess I can always rent it. Besides, it's better not to count your chickens before they're hatched, right?" Amelia raised an eyebrow, not believing for a moment that this little chick wouldn't hatch for her.

"That's the spirit!" Tom leaned forward, as excited as she. "Now, how about if we celebrate..." Tom began, but the ringing of the phone interrupted him.

Amelia held up a finger to silence him and picked up the receiver, plucking off her earring as she put the receiver to her ear.

"Amelia Jenkins," she said. "Oh, Scott, I almost forgot about dinner. I'm so happy you called. Have I got news for you...."

Tom got up quietly. He stood before the desk for just an instant, then let himself silently out the door while Amelia swiveled in her chair chatting with Scott.

He had seen the beautiful color rise to her cheeks when she heard his voice. He had seen her eyes sparkle with excitement as she began to tell him her news. He also realized that she had never had those same reactions to him. But it was all right. He'd known for a long time that he just didn't inspire Amelia the way she needed to be inspired. He wasn't a challenge. She needed to work for what she loved. It still hurt, but it hurt less this way. Besides, Scott Alexander wouldn't last, either. Not with this New York job looming in the very near future. And, from what Tom had seen, Scott lacked the intensity to capture Amelia for good. That was, at least, a little consolation.

AMELIA PICKED UP HER LOG and looked at it for a moment. Then she looked at the clock. There really wasn't time to put her racing thoughts into words. Besides, her desire to see Scott was growing by the minute. That inexplicable something he had had worked its magic on her. She wanted to share her excitement with him; she wanted to be in his arms, in his bed.

Amelia, you're becoming quite the romantic, she thought to herself. But it was nothing to laugh at. It was a wonderful new experience. Perhaps she should have told her mother about Scott at the same time as she told her about the job. Maybe that would have softened Martha just a bit.

It wasn't that her mother wasn't pleased for her, but Amelia had detected something under the surface of Martha's congratulations. Something was lacking, like real sincerity. Well, she would deal with her mother later and get to the bottom of things. Tonight she was going to celebrate properly. She had the whole thing planned. She would meet Scott at the plant. They would have a romantic little dinner at some fine restaurant, maybe a walk on the beach, then... Yes, everything was planned.

Amelia put her log back into the top drawer of her desk, checked the contents of her purse and glanced in the mirror one last time. She nodded as she noted the fall of her red silk dress. The cut was understated, skimming her knees, falling in one fluid line from the wide, Joan Crawford shoulders. The color added gaiety. It wasn't her usual style, but then she was headed to New York.

Moments later she was in her car, breezing down the San Diego freeway toward Redondo Beach. The usual Easter rains had miraculously never appeared, and the night was clear and warm. As she drove, Amelia admired the sprawl of the city, the twinkling stars and the black, wild ocean she saw as she pulled to a stop in front of Scott's plant.

Yes, there were things she would miss about this wonderful city. But New York was where her professional destiny was, and no real estate could keep her from it. No love could, either, she thought, knowing it would be hard to leave Scott. But then, as whimsical as he was, he would probably simply flit back and forth to see her. Yes, that was what he would do.

Amelia swung her long legs from the car and looked toward the plant. She had been surprised when Scott told her this was his home. She had been even more surprised when he told her that he had sold a beauti-

ful house in the Hollywood Hills to get the rest of the
cash he needed to open the plant.

The lights were burning brightly. He must be finishing up the day's work. Her high heels clicked on the
bike path that ran in front of the building. It was so
beautifully quiet at the beach that she could hear the
lapping of the waves on the white sands a hundred
yards away. Amelia breathed deeply, then pushed
away the longing once again as she opened the door to
Scott.

The front of the large workroom was empty save for
the brightly colored sails and fiberglass sheets. Toward the back Amelia heard music. Classical. She
smiled. It was nice of Scott to put on something other
than that sixties rock. She moved toward the sound.
Walking through a plant that was devoid of people,
with haunting music drawing her farther through the
building, Amelia felt as though she were in a dream.

She was conscious of the silk dress moving against
her body. She felt confident going to a man who
wanted her, knowing that she was soon to accomplish
everything she had worked for. It was, perhaps, a
feeling of power, a feeling of completion. She could
think no further than the moment. She allowed no
sadness at the thought of leaving Scott behind. For
her, the world was bright, and she longed to share her
good fortune with him.

She saw a small enclosure to her left. The music was
coming from there. She smiled and ran her hand
through her hair, fanning it out for fullness. Amelia
licked her lips. Her eyes already shone with anticipation of the celebration that was before her. Swiftly, she
rounded the corner, her fingers itching to wrap themselves around Scott. A word of greeting froze on her

lips, though, as she saw another figure hunched over the board. It was Sailor. She faltered, her heel skidding on the concrete, and he turned his head to look at her.

Their eyes met for a moment. He seemed to assess her, make his decision and discard her all in the flick of an eye. Amelia blushed with embarrassment. This rude man had dismissed her as though she were a bothersome street urchin. Anger flared where only sweet anticipation had been moments before. She heard the scraping of the sandpaper as he continued to work. It seemed to sand away her skin, until her nerve endings were naked.

"Excuse me." Amelia controlled herself as she spoke. The silence was becoming unendurable. Still, the man did not turn to her. She spoke louder. "Pardon me."

"Yeah?" Thank God he spoke, even though he didn't turn to look at her.

"I was supposed to meet Scott here," Amelia explained politely.

"Yeah, he told me."

"Well?" Her patience was wearing thin. Even this man must hear it.

"Well, what?" he growled back, still not having the courtesy to look at her.

"Could you just tell me where he is?" Her anger bubbled hazardously close to the surface.

"I don't know. He went out and told me to tell you to wait," he answered without skipping a beat in his work.

"Why didn't you say so?" Amelia demanded.

"I figured you would figure it out. Aren't you the one who's got the world on a string?" He finally put down the sandpaper and turned to her. He rested one long, muscled arm on his knee. Amelia shuddered. He looked like a Darwinian model with all that long hair on his head and all that curling dark hair on his arms and legs. She felt threatened by him, although she was sure there was no logic to such feelings.

"Look, I'm not psychic," Amelia complained, "and it's only simple courtesy to pass along a message."

"So, I'm not courteous," he said. His eyes looked her up and down. She could almost hear him scoff at the luxury of her outfit and it enraged her. But before she spoke again he turned away.

Amelia felt challenged. She took four quick steps to his side and, hands on hips, looked down at him.

"Look. I don't know what your problem is, but I was invited here. There's no need to pick a fight. All you had to do was tell me where to wait and I would have done so." Amelia had intended this to sound like a rational explanation of the situation but instead it was almost a hysterical cry for him to acknowledge her.

"Look, lady, I'm not pickin' a fight. I'm sorry, okay?" His apology had all the sincerity of a slap in the face. "You can wait in the office. It's over there." He jerked his head toward a small glass-enclosed room and went back to his work. Intrigued by his attitude and her own anger, Amelia couldn't let it go.

"What have you got against me, Sailor? After all, we've only met a few times. We've only spoken a few words. Yet you treat me as if I had an incurable disease."

"As far as I'm concerned you do, Ms Jenkins." He drew her name out as though he found it distasteful.

Amelia was shocked into silence for an instant. Her hands fell from her hips; her purse dangled from fingers that seemed to have lost all feeling.

"What . . . what?" She stammered in disbelief.

"Look, why don't you just go sit in the office and forget I said anything." Sailor waved her away with his words, looking askance at her as he did so.

Amelia was crouched beside him in an instant. She couldn't believe this was the man Scott had defended so adamantly. "Are you kidding? Listen, buster, I don't let someone talk to me like that without an explanation. How can you presume to make assumptions about me?"

Sailor's sandpaper made one last sweep over the board on which he worked. Then, with a great show of deliberation, he sat back on his heels and looked closely at her. Amelia's eyes faltered under his glare, but she would not give him the satisfaction of lowering them. Then he spoke.

"I'm not making assumptions. I knew who you were and what you were from the first minute you breezed in here like a queen bee. You and that crew of yours. Everyone kowtowing to you so that you could look good, make your mark. Lady, you're out to get the brass ring and no one and nothing is going to stand in your way. You don't have a string pulling you up by the bootstraps, you got a God damn hoist and—"

Amelia could listen no longer without defending herself.

"And there's something wrong with that? Just because I want to work hard and make something of myself? You're right," she went on, "I do work hard. And if that's a reason for disdain, then I'm glad I earned yours. But not everyone seems to agree with your assessment."

"You're right, and it's the saddest thing I've ever seen. Scott deserves—"

"The best he can get. Just as I do, and even you have that prerogative. But some people don't want to work for it. Some people are willing to just sit back and—"

"You don't know what I've got. All right, maybe I was wrong laying into you. Maybe you've got more on the ball than just work, work and more work. That's fine. Maybe I don't know all about you. But you sure as hell haven't got a clue about me."

The exchange was heating up; Amelia was warming to the fight. Without knowing why, it was important that she make this man understand that her goals were worth going after, that she would not hurt Scott or herself. Perhaps it was because Scott seemed so completely enamored with this friend of his. More than likely it was because Amelia hated injustice, especially when it was directed at her. But before she could continue, Scott surprised them both.

"Ah-ha! Sailor, I knew I shouldn't have left you alone. You're working your incredible magic on my lady, aren't you?" Scott swooped into the room. The paper bag he held with his left arm crackled as he gathered Amelia's shoulders in his other arm and planted a kiss atop her head.

Amelia rose into his embrace, but her eyes remained riveted on Sailor.

"Yeah, sure, boss," Sailor mumbled. He turned back to his work without further comment.

Amelia watched as Scott's eyes glassed over with concern. Then, thinking better of pursuing the conversation, he turned his attention to Amelia.

"I'm sorry I wasn't here when you arrived. But I see that you're none the worse for wear. Were you waiting long?" His smile was hesitant, then grew brighter as he looked into her blue eyes.

"No, no," Amelia answered distractedly. Her attention was still on the strange confrontation she had had with Sailor. Every reporter's instinct in her was on alert. There was a story here. She could feel it. But the man was not going to open up to her that night. Maybe he never would. She felt Scott gently urge her forward and she found they were walking farther back into the plant.

"You look wonderful," he whispered in her hair. She leaned into his lips, loving the warmth of his breath.

"Thanks. I hope I won't be too dressed up for wherever we're going," Amelia answered, now giving her full attention to the man beside her.

"Not on your life, since we're going right here." Scott released his hold on her and reached for the knob on the door in front of them. It swung open to reveal a cozily appointed room. In one corner was a couch, in another a small dinette and kitchen. Colorful posters of windsurfers decorated the walls. There was an easy chair and a television.

"Welcome to my home," Scott said as he ushered her in.

"But I thought... I assumed..." Amelia stammered. She had so convinced herself that her plans for the evening were theirs that this change surprised her.

"You assumed what, my lovely lady in red?" Scott asked as he deposited his bag on the kitchen counter. He began to remove groceries: a steak, a bottle of wine, a head of lettuce.

"Well, I just assumed we would be going out," Amelia said, recovering some of her confidence.

"I'm sorry, Amelia. After all, this is a celebration for you. I guess I just assumed you wouldn't want a hassle with a crowd of people who might recognize you," he apologized sheepishly. "I thought a more private celebration was in order. We do seem to think differently, don't we?"

"Oh, Scott, what a sweet thought," Amelia said, ashamed now that she had simply expected him to follow a game plan he hadn't even heard of. "Of course this is great. I guess sometimes I just get so used to calling the shots at work I forget other people have opinions, too."

"That's okay. And I'm glad you're finally learning how to leave the office behind," he said as he returned to his task. "Now, how do you like your steak? Rare, medium, well done or in the refrigerator?"

"In the refrigerator?" Amelia asked as she joined him in the kitchen.

"That's my specialty. We put it in the refrigerator and leave it there until tomorrow, after we've got the more important things out of the way." His arms were around her waist as he spoke and his lips began to explore every inch of her face. Amelia stiffened in his embrace.

"Is this a typical entrepreneurial ploy?" Amelia could have bitten her tongue as soon as the words were out. His arms dropped from her waist, and she longed to reach out and capture his hands in hers. But she could see he was hurt by her accusation. When was she going to learn to take things at face value and not dig beneath the surface?

"No, it's not. I simply have been thinking about you all day and I needed to be with you. But obviously you're a bit wound up after your exciting day and your head isn't really here."

"Scott, that's not true," Amelia admonished. She didn't dare tell him about Sailor's accusation. "I guess I'm just tired. It has been a long, exciting day, and then, when you weren't here when I arrived, I was disappointed. You can understand that, can't you?"

"Yes, I can. If it's the truth," Scott said, tearing the plastic wrap off the large steak. "It is the truth, isn't it?"

Amelia looked deeply into his eyes, seeing the need in them. He was, in so many ways, vulnerable. It was not an unattractive feature.

"Yes, it is." Amelia moved toward him and took his face into her hands. With a bit of shyness that surprised her, Amelia lowered her lips to his and offered him an apology that eased his uncertainty.

"That's better. Damn it, Amelia. You're so single-minded you make me crazy!" He laughed and brushed her hair behind her ears. "If I had any brains in my head I'd fix you dinner, show you out and really go find myself a beach bunny... one who's going to stay around Los Angeles."

"Thank goodness you don't have any brains," Amelia said. She chuckled, wanting to start the evening all over again. "Let's begin again, shall we? Now, what can I do? I'm not much of a cook but I certainly can make a salad."

"You got it. With the way you work, this salad will probably be perfection." He picked up the head of lettuce and pitched it toward her. She caught it in midair, ignoring the flicks of water that splattered onto her silk dress.

"So, tell me. Are you really leaving me for New York and the big time?" Scott said in all seriousness as she busied herself with the salad. The tone of his voice made her hesitate before answering.

"I don't know. This is only the interview stage. I've got a lot to go through before they decide, you know. Would you mind so much if I did go?"

"You know I would," Scott answered, abandoning the salt and pepper shakers to turn and look at her. "Look, Amelia, I know we haven't known each other long, but we're so good together. Couldn't you...?"

"What?" Amelia turned to meet his gaze.

"Nothing. I'm really happy for you." Scott covered his disappointment. Actually, he *was* thrilled. Amelia was a talented woman and deserved to make it to the top. But he wished she would understand that there was more to life than the top job. So much more. And he could be the one to show her. He would simply have to bide his time. He hoped he had the patience. It would be a shame to lose what they had now, when they were so close to winning.

"Thanks. It's really an honor. You know, Tom was the one who sent in my tape. I just can't believe he went to all that trouble." Amelia attempted to right the conversation, pulling it back to the particular rather than the personal.

"He obviously cares about you a lot and thinks highly of your abilities," Scott said as he put the finishing spices on the steak and turned on the broiler.

"I guess he does. You know, Scott, I don't think I've ever wanted anything in my life as much as I want this job. It's everything I've been working for all these years. It'll mean security, professional respect. I want to do so well," Amelia said wistfully, sharing with him her deepest desires. It felt good. She did it with so few people.

"You will, Amelia. You will. I just hope you know what you're getting into. It means long hours, no social life, no time to share a life with someone else."

"It sounds like you've been there." Amelia cocked her head toward him, handing him the salad bowl as she did so.

"Kind of," Scott admitted. "And the result wasn't as rosy as you would tend to believe."

"Do you want to talk about it?"

"No. It's not my place. It happened to someone else. But it was close enough to home to make me realize that it wasn't something I wanted." Scott handed her a glass of wine and invited her into the sitting room.

"I see," Amelia said, more out of politeness than understanding. It was hard for her to realize that the top job, position, wasn't what everyone craved. It was simply opting out of what people were put on earth for—to work. But she didn't want to spoil the evening by pointing this out. Scott settled himself in the easy chair, Amelia on the couch.

"Where does all this leave us, Amelia?" Scott asked. When she looked at him she realized that he was asking the question without any rancor but with a deep longing. She could almost feel him willing the commitment from her. Unfortunately, the situation wasn't cut-and-dried in her mind.

"I don't really know, Scott. I would be traveling a lot. I would hope you could come to New York and see me and I could come here to you if we both wanted to try and make this work," she answered gently after thinking a moment.

"You make it sound like an employment contract," Scott said. He gazed thoughtfully at her. Such a beautiful woman. He had such deep feelings for her, for the woman she didn't yet know she was, that it surprised him and even frightened him a little bit. But he had to give her her head and let her find out if it was him she wanted or a fleeting position on top of the corporate world.

"Not at all." She defended herself quietly, a little hurt. "I didn't mean for it to sound like that. It's just that what we have needs time to grow. I think you'll even admit that." Scott nodded. "But this opportunity in New York won't wait. I have to try. If nothing else, I must try."

Amelia felt as though she were pleading with Scott for understanding. And, she had to admit, she was. She didn't want to lose him, but neither could she pass up this opportunity. If he couldn't understand that then there was no future for them anyway.

"Of course you do." He rose and came toward her, giving her a semblance of peace with his answer. As he loomed over her in the indirect lighting, Amelia felt diminished in his presence. He exuded a strength that she had thought she possessed. Yet, now she realized that her power and strength were on the surface. His came from some sort of wisdom deep inside of him. But if she reached her goal, got this job, she would feel the same strength inside her. All it took was work.

"Now, if I don't see to that steak your celebration dinner is going to be ruined." He smiled a smile that lit up the room as if it were a low-wattage bulb: beautiful but subdued by a tinge of sadness. Scott went into the kitchen. "You, my dear, can set the table."

She set out dishes and glasses, forks and knives, and the mood lightened. Amelia found herself chattering away as she went about her task.

"You know, we're allowed to bring our spouses for the reception the contenders will be attending. And since I don't have a spouse I wonder if you'd like to come with me."

"When is it?" Scott asked as he set the steak on the table and cut a piece of steaming meat. Amelia watched the knife slice through the steak. It was charred on the outside, rare inside. Perfect. Like Scott. Perfection done so easily. He had barely paid attention to the steak, yet it was cooked exactly as it should have been.

"Next week...Thursday," Amelia said, tearing her eyes from her meal and putting her thoughts of Scott's easy manner behind her.

"Weren't you planning on moving in next week?" He took his seat across from her and picked up his fork.

"Well, actually, yes. I don't think I can now. I don't know what I'm going to do. I've given my notice on the apartment. But I just can't miss this opportunity, house or not."

"When do you actually leave?" Scott queried.

"I leave on Tuesday. The interview process is Wednesday and Thursday, then the party is Thursday night." Amelia's litany was succinct. Always to the point, Scott thought.

"Well, then, I have a wonderful idea. What would you say if my crew and I moved your things while you were gone and then I met you in New York for the party?"

"Oh, would you?" Amelia sighed with relief. That was one less worry.

"Of course. Now, I can't promise everything will be as you want it, but I think we can manage. The only problem is you'll have to pack up before you go. That only gives you four days," Scott said. Then he reached out and took her hands in his. "But I'd be happy to help with that too—day and night."

"I think that's one of those offers I simply can't refuse," Amelia said quietly, her smile telling him she knew exactly what he meant.

"Amelia, if you got this job, when would you be moving?" His hand tightened around hers and brought her fingertips to his lips. For a moment Amelia couldn't think of anything but the warmth that shot through her body, the tingling of every nerve, the man who loved her.

"I don't know. We didn't discuss that. But," she said, leaning into him, her lips parting for a kiss, "I can tell you that I would hold it off as long as possible."

"What if I asked you not to go at all?" Scott murmured, his lips accepting her invitation.

It was an eternity before he released her, but Amelia's mind whirled with conflicting thoughts. The feel of him made her want to tell him she would stay within the confines of that very room if he asked her, but the stronger pull of her lifetime of striving won out. She couldn't do what he asked, if he truly asked. It would be like giving up on everything her mother taught her.

She would not, could not, abandon the objectives she had held close to her heart for so many years. Still, he was here with her. She felt herself loving him and wanting him more with each passing minute.

"I would say," Amelia answered when they finally parted, "that your food is getting cold." She nodded toward his plate, her eyes lowered for fear that one look into his would mean that all would be lost.

"Amelia," Scott called gently as he tipped her chin with his finger, "don't dodge the question. I'm not joking now. I need to know. We're not so different. We both want success. We both want to be wanted and don't deny it. I can feel it in every fiber of your body."

"I won't deny it. Of course I want to be wanted. But there are things I must do before I can commit to a lifetime with someone. And—" she hesitated, pulling her chin away from his touch "—I'm not sure we're enough alike to make it last. I'm not saying that I don't care for you deeply. I do. And that in itself surprises me more and more every time I think about it. You are a kind and sensitive and intelligent man. But there still is something...lacking."

It was the only word she could think of. But "lacking" was a poor adjective. She would never judge him as she had the first time they met. What she realized was simply that he chose to rank his priorities differently than she. There was no right or wrong in that. But it did mean that there was a basic difference in them that could ruin what they had if they relied on each other too much.

"Lacking?" Scott asked as though reading her mind. "Or is it that I'm not the way you've always imagined your Prince Charming to be? Someone who's on the same never-ending treadmill that you've put yourself on?''

"You make it sound so horrible." Amelia raised her eyes to his in defiance without conviction.

"It is horrible in a way." He picked up his napkin and put it on the table, then rose and came toward her. Amelia watched as he hunched down on the balls of his feet, his eyes boring into hers. "Don't you see what you've given up all these years, what you've buried inside you?" He reached out and gently touched the place over her heart.

"Oh, Amelia, there is so much inside you, such great gentleness and such an ability to give of yourself. But you hide it in a shell. You're like a torpedo shot into the world. Your only goal is to make it to your target. But have you ever thought about what the target is? What the top is?

"I mean," he continued urgently, "by many standards I'm at the top. I have money, I have freedom, I enjoy myself. But what you're shooting for is nothing unless your goal is notoriety or money. That's all you'll have. You'll work your tail off every day and most nights, and fifteen years from now you'll still be going home to an empty apartment."

Scott heaved a sigh, rose and turned away from her. He had given it his best shot. Damn that woman. There were a thousand like her in every city of every state in the country. And there were a thousand more who would be happy just being with him, a wife with a ton of children. So why did he have to fall for her? That nameless something in her had him roped like a calf, and he was powerless to simply let her go or think of her as a casual fling.

He half turned to look at her. Amelia sat with her hands in her lap. Gone was the confident news reporter. Instead, Scott saw a lovely, vulnerable woman deep in thought. Slowly she raised her eyes to his, locking them there for just a moment.

"I don't know about fifteen years from now. Fifteen minutes from now all I want is to be with you. Fifteen days from now, I want to be told I'm the newest anchor on *Meet America*. And a year from now I still want to be that, but I want to be seeing you, too."

"You can't have it both ways, Amelia—not when we're on separate sides of the country," he explained patiently, tenderly.

"I can try, can't I? If I work hard enough it will be all right, I just know it." Amelia rose and moved toward him. She snaked her arms around his waist and lay her head against his back. She would have to make him see that it could all happen for them.

He turned slowly in her arms and wrapped his own arms around her shoulders. The cool, crisp cotton of his shirt felt wonderful against her cheek. She breathed deeply, smelling the starch mingled with the clean, fresh scent of his after-shave. For a long while they stood like that, Scott's lips buried in her hair. Neither of them spoke. Then, just as Amelia lifted her head and opened her mouth to reassure him, there was a short knock and the door to the room flew open.

"Sorry..." Sailor entered the room and both of them started, pulling away from one another like teenagers surprised by their parents.

"It's okay, come on in," Scott said, a sheepish grin on his face. Amelia looked at Sailor, noting the scowl on his face. He didn't return her look. She reclaimed her seat at the table and began to eat.

"I'm having trouble with that board for John Simmons. I thought you might be able to spare a few minutes to look at it."

"Oh, sure," Scott said, "if you don't mind, Amelia."

She put down her fork and looked at the two men. The animosity flowing from Sailor was almost too much to bear. She tried to ignore it but it wormed under her skin like an itch.

"No, of course not." She shook her head and pushed back her chair. "Actually, I'm kind of tired and I think I'll just head on home, if that's all right with you."

"But, dinner..." Scott objected, his unfinished sentence implying so much more. He wanted to finish the conversation. He wanted to hold her in his arms and make love to her. But the spell was broken, the tenderness vanishing with Sailor's presence.

"I have a feeling you wouldn't be joining me anyway," Amelia answered, glancing at Sailor. "So why don't we take a rain check." Amelia picked up her purse and gave Scott a dazzling smile she didn't feel. She moved close to him, unwilling to leave him with sadness or anger. "I'll see you tomorrow night? To help me pack?"

"Wild horses couldn't keep me away." Scott answered softly and kissed her lightly. He held her only an instant longer than she thought he would, and it eased the confusion in her soul. He loved her no matter what. Of that she was sure.

"Good night, Sailor," Amelia said as she slipped by him and out the door. He didn't answer, and she walked toward the front of the building deep in thought.

AMELIA'S LOG

April 16

Sorry, it's late. There won't be much tonight. I know I skipped last night but I definitely had better things to do.

Scott stayed over. He's a wonderful lover. A surprising suitor. He led me down the yellow brick road with wine and flowers. I loved it. One would think I'm turning into a soft touch. Why not? I'm allowed to stray now and then. The only problem is, it would be so easy to stray and stay. He could make me want to give it all up and follow him to the ends of the earth. Luckily, morning comes and I remember there are other things in my life.

Other things . . . I can't believe they're happening to me. New York called. They called me. I didn't have to go begging for the job. Well, not really. Tom took care of that. Still, they liked what they saw and now I have a chance to make it big. *Meet America*. Will I look back on this entry a month from now and realize that it isn't a wish anymore? Will I be the co-anchor on the show?

My God, the thought of it is amazing. I can't seem to write any other adjective for it. There is a large part of me that can't get excited about it. I know it's not really me. It's only the excitement, the first rush of loving Scott. Or "amazement" is the right word, because I'm not there yet. I'm an outsider looking in. Once I reach New York, once I'm on that set, then I'll think in terms of "thrilling," "deserved," "right." Yes, I'll know it's right. I just have to get there and away from Scott so that I can concentrate. He has the damnedest way of making me forget where I'm going to.

Still, knowing he cares makes the day go faster. I seem to want to call him every fifteen minutes. I restrain myself, of course. New York, Scott. Why after all these years am I faced with two things I want? And why must I make a choice?

Tonight we met for a celebration dinner. What else is there to say? It wasn't much of a celebration. Not with the horrendous hulk lurking around the corner and Scott making things harder by showing me how much he loves me, wants me to be with him. Well, after New York, when things are settled, everything will work itself out. God, I'm tired. Too much is happening.

Oh, I forgot, the house offer was accepted. I got that call just before the one about interviewing for *Meet America*. Amazing...a wonderful man appears on my doorstep, the house of my dreams is mine and now this. Why is it that the job must take me away from the other two? Well, in time I'll settle into what's meant to be. Mom always says things happen for a reason.

New York. Funny, the more I write it the less enamored I am with the job. Tonight my bed looks awfully big. Is it colder this April than last?

This was longer than I thought it would be. If nothing else, Scott has given me more to write about. I'll miss him tonight. How long will I miss him when I'm in New York?

Chapter Eight

The week flew by. Amelia raced around the station, completing her interview and explaining for the hundredth time to the station manager that there was a personal reason why she had to take her vacation time on such short notice. He didn't seem to believe her. He, too, had noticed the change in her. Reluctantly, he signed her vacation chit with the provision that she have enough tape in the can to fill the week she would be gone. It was a strain, but she managed to do it.

The nights were wonderful, though. Scott dutifully appeared bearing take-out Chinese or chicken, wine and flowers. One night, as they packed box after box, he dropped a single flower into each. That way, he told her, she would remember the night when they were opened. He closed the box that held the last flower, taped it and reached for her, calling a halt to the work. He had said she looked tired, yet he kept her up for three more hours, loving her, teasing her and holding her until she fell contentedly asleep. That night she dreamed of her mother and the stories she used to tell. Amelia had been only a young girl then, but her memories were as vivid as if it had happened yesterday.

"Mom," Amelia had said just before her thirteenth Christmas, "do you miss Daddy?"

Martha laid down the ornament she was holding. She placed it carefully on the carpet. It was very old and she had brought it all the way from Germany.

"What a question!" her mother said, furrowing her brow even though she smiled gently. "Of course I do. Your father was a wonderful man."

"Because he took care of us?" Amelia persisted.

"More than that, little one. He loved us more than anything in the world. He worked very hard, but the best thing was that he always made us laugh. Don't you remember just a little bit? It wasn't so long ago, only two years. But it was when you were very little that, maybe, he was the most carefree."

Her mother picked up the ornament and turned toward the tree. Amelia thought it was because there was work to do if they were going to finish the decorating in time for Santa—Martha insisted on holding on to the myth for her daughter despite the fact that Amelia had known by the time she was eight that there was no Santa Claus. She couldn't see the tears of remembrance floating in her mother's eyes or the smile on her face deepen with longing.

"Maybe I remember a little," Amelia answered, knowing full well that she didn't. "Tell me what he used to do."

Martha picked up another ornament while Amelia dutifully unpacked the lights from the box. "Well, when your father would come home from work he would first give us both a big kiss. For you a kiss that smacked on your cheek, and you would giggle and giggle. For me a very nice kiss that said how much he had missed me. Then he would whirl me around in a silly dance and you would laugh some more."

"It's funny I don't remember that," Amelia mused aloud.

"Not really. The last years were hard. He was sick. He worried about us and worked very hard, even though he really shouldn't have. I suppose he just forgot how to dance during those last years. But, Amelia, he never stopped loving us. I know you remember that." Martha turned to her daughter, and for the first time Amelia saw that Martha, too, needed reassurance.

"Yes, Mama," she answered quietly, "I remember that."

They worked in silence for a while longer, each lost in her own thoughts. Amelia closed her eyes for a minute, and she could almost feel her father's presence. Not the way he had been before he died: quiet, anxious, sad to leave them. But she thought she remembered the way he had been when she was small. She wanted to remember it.

"I wish Daddy was here now," Amelia said, her fingers struggling with one very stubborn knot.

"So do I, Amelia," her mother answered quietly.

Amelia thought of that Christmas as she and Scott walked along the beach near her new home. She was breathing hard and she had doubled up, holding on to her sides, which ached from laughing so hard.

Scott had chased her down the beach, determined to exact a kiss from her. Coquettishly, she had eluded him and raced away, listening to his loving threats of what he would do to her once she was caught. And when she had started to laugh, realizing the absurdity of it all, she stopped and he caught her, whisking her

into his arms and kissing every inch of her face until
they both collapsed on the sand, rolling about, laughing hysterically.

As they lay together on that blustery but sunny
Sunday letting their laughter subside, Amelia wondered if this was how her father had made her mother
laugh. Had they been this much in love? For surely
this must be what love was—working side by side but
still making the time to explore each other's minds and
bodies and souls. It was a wonderful feeling, safe and
perfect. How her mother must still miss her husband.

Throughout the week Scott had not repeated his
questions about her leaving, nor had he brought up the
subject of New York in general. Amelia had no way of
knowing that he hoped she would call the trip off. He
seemed so content to help her with the house, the
packing. He talked and talked about her new home,
the plant, the latest board he had designed, which
would skim the water like a smooth stone.

She had joked and laughed and listened as he
talked. She loved the sound of his voice whether it was
raised in laughter or hushed in talk of love. Sometimes she even found that she had forgotten about
New York, and that alone surprised her more than her
ever-deepening feelings for the man who was now her
constant companion.

Now, though, New York was what each of them
thought about as they lay holding each other on the
deserted stretch of beach. Scott's fingers combed her
hair until it fanned out on the sand beneath her.

"You know, your hair is the same color as the sand
today," he whispered as he watched his fingers work.
"It always amazes me that it changes color with the
light. It's beautiful . . . so beautiful."

Amelia watched him, memorizing the planes of his face, then closed her eyes as though they might print his image indelibly on her mind. Opening her eyes once more, she reached up to frame his face with her hands, then slowly raised her head and kissed him gently.

A moment later he rolled away from her and lay with his shoulder just touching hers. Confused, Amelia raised herself on her elbow, her sandy hair falling over the down vest she wore over her beige sweater.

Scott's eyes were closed and she took in everything about him. The shoulders and chest she knew so well were encased in a worn fisherman's knit sweater. The long legs that entwined with hers in the night were stretched out now, the faded denim of his jeans protecting him from the cold. On his feet were worn Topsiders. He wore no socks. His hair was disheveled from the wind, making him look young and vulnerable. Even in these clothes, which had seen better days, there was a sophistication, a completeness, a confidence in him that she admired and wished to emulate. But his face was worried—or sad, she couldn't tell which.

"Scott?" Amelia whispered. "You're not going to sleep, are you?"

"Of course not. Just thinking." He answered without opening his eyes.

"About what?" Amelia lowered her head to his chest and wrapped her arms about his waist. She could feel the gentle rise of his chest as he breathed, and it was comforting.

"About your leaving," he answered almost perfunctorily.

"I've been thinking about it, too," Amelia quietly admitted. She waited to see if he would continue.

"What have you been thinking?" he asked. Though he didn't think it was evident, Amelia could feel the waiting in his body. There was a tenseness, as though he were steeling himself against the pain of rejection.

"I've been thinking that I'm going to do well, Scott. I'm going to do very well. Not because I don't want to be with you. Not necessarily because I want to leave Los Angeles. This is my home, after all. But because that is the only way I know how to do things. To be the best I can possibly be. And because I want this chance. I want it...so much." Amelia had almost said "more than anything else in the world" but she caught herself. She wasn't afraid it would hurt Scott but it wasn't necessarily true anymore. She wanted him just as much, but on a different plane, in a different part of her.

"Oh, Amelia, I don't begrudge you this chance. Truly I don't." His hand once again began to caress her long hair; his head swiveled so that he could look at her.

"I know." It was such a simple thing to say but so true.

"No, you don't. I love you, Amelia. There is simply no two ways about it. I love you and I want you here. Here in that house up the beach. Not in New York where we'll have to try to schedule times to see each other. People who love each other can't live like that." His voice was strained with the depth of emotion he felt, and Amelia's heart lurched.

"Yes, they can. You hear about it all the time. Why, we even did a segment on people who have long-distance relationships..." Amelia began, but never finished, her sentence. Scott grabbed her shoulders and roughly pulled her up so that he could look into her eyes. For a moment he searched her face. She sensed his hurt and anger and frustration. She felt his fingers digging into her shoulders.

"They don't love each other, Amelia!" His words were rough as he strove to make her understand. "You talked to people who were on television. It's not the same for everyday people. I love you. And I know you love me, no matter how hard you fight against the commitment that love brings with it. Doesn't that mean anything?"

"Yes, darling, of course it does. Believe it or not, it means everything," she answered as she moved from his grasp. Amelia sat up and rubbed the sand from her hands while she considered her next words. Then, pulling her legs up to her chest, she wrapped her arms around them and looked out to sea. She began to speak quietly. The day and his emotion seemed to call for it.

"I know it's hard for you to understand. Since we've been together I think we've both learned a lot. I know that you work very hard. I was wrong to assume that everything has simply been handed to you. Oh, success does come easier to you than to most, but you are a good businessman, a kind man and very loving. I couldn't care as much as I do if you weren't." Amelia sighed, took a breath and continued to watch the waves she loved so much roll in to caress the sand. Scott had not moved except to lean his weight on one hand.

"And, hopefully, you've realized that I've changed my ways a bit since we met...." She glanced at him, but his eyes were closed as he listened. "But, Scott,

I'm still the same person deep down inside that I've always been. I couldn't live with you if I didn't give this my best shot. It's what I've always wanted, what I've worked for. It offers the security I need for myself, my mother. I need it for my self-respect. If there is one thing I learned at my mother's knee, it's that we all have to work hard, take the opportunities life offers us. Do you understand?''

"No. I don't understand that security and self-respect can't come from someone who loves you. I can't believe that you wouldn't want me and a job right here, because those two things would make a better and far bigger whole than just the one. And I can't believe the woman who gave birth to you would not understand that, either." Scott sat up abruptly, and Amelia was forced to look at him. "Okay, I've never met her, but she simply can't be that single-minded. Look at all the other qualities she instilled in you. Even if you won't admit them, there is gentleness, caring, energy, the ability to give and receive love. That's what I see, Amelia. I respect everything else, but that's the you that's real to me."

Scott pushed himself up from the sand and stuffed his hands into his pockets. He looked so tall staring down at her. A chilly breeze picked up his hair and blew a lock of it over his forehead. He didn't push it back.

"I think you've just picked up on one of the things she taught you and have never given the others a chance...until now. And now you're willing to throw it all away. Amelia, it's no disgrace to choose to be a big fish in a small pond if there's a good reason. If you turn down this job, it will be because you know there

can be more than work in your life—me and my love
for you.

"If you truly want this job, then I say go for it. But
don't tell me you love me. Don't give me that hope.
Please. I would rather be a lifelong friend—and lover,
when we can be—when you're on *Meet America*, but
I don't want either of us to think that we could be
more. Not on a part-time basis. You've got to make a
choice."

Scott was breathing hard. He had spoken at great
length. Amelia remained silent, watching him as he
walked to the edge of the ocean. He kicked at the
white froth that scurried to meet him; then he turned,
looked at her and came back. Amelia looked up. His
hand was outstretched in a peace offering. She laid her
hand in his and it closed about hers. Gently he lifted
her into an embrace and whispered against her hair.

"Ah, Amelia. Hell, you make me crazy. I'm sorry.
I really am. Give it your best shot. I'm happy for you.
Maybe it's just selfishness. I just found you and now
I'm going to lose you." He held her tighter, exuding
something that felt almost like resignation.

"No, you're not. I promise," she insisted, her voice
muffled against the yarn of his sweater.

"You can't tell me I'm going to be able to hold this
gorgeous body every night. Even you can't make me
believe that." He laughed sadly.

"No, but I promise it will be as often as possible."
Her lips kissed the tender skin behind his ear, and his
head moved into the caress.

"Just know that I'm rooting for you. If this is what
you want, what you need, then you should have it.
You deserve it. And I'm sure it will be clear sailing for

you. Like an open channel, your sailing will be smooth.''

He tipped her head up and in an instant his lips found hers. Amelia lost herself in his kiss, wrapping her arms around him so tightly that she knew she never wanted to let go. But she also knew that she had to recapture her momentum. Thank goodness they wouldn't be seeing each other again before she left. She would spend Monday night with her mother and leave for the airport the next day. Yes, a day away from him would allow her to concentrate. She had to put him out of her mind if she was going to get this job. It would be the hardest thing she had ever done.

"Let's go home," Scott whispered intensely. "There isn't much time left. An afternoon and a night. It isn't much, and I need so much from you, Amelia."

She nodded against his chest and, arms wrapped about each other, they made their way up the beach. When they reached the car, which they had parked outside her new home, they hesitated for a moment. Both looked at the little house, now empty, waiting for its new owner.

"Do you have the key?" Scott asked.

"Yes, I got it yesterday," she answered without question.

They hesitated no longer. Wordlessly they walked to the front door, and Amelia tried the key. The lock gave easily beneath her fingers and they stepped into the living room. It was spotless and so quiet. She took a few steps and realized how right it felt to be there. To be there with Scott. Amelia turned as she heard the door close.

"I think we should warm this house properly, don't you?" He advanced on her carefully, as though waiting for her to turn and run. But she didn't; she stayed her ground. The sadness she had seen in his eyes earlier was gone, replaced by a look of such deep longing it took her breath away.

Gently, he slipped her vest from her shoulders. He let his finger trace the dip of her cheek and wander down the length of her neck. For a moment he toyed with the soft sweater she wore. Then he continued his exploration, his fingers tracing the sweater's V-shaped neck until he found the cleft of her trembling breasts.

Amelia did not move. She was aware of the now-familiar feeling inching up through her body—a warmth in her legs, a tightening in her stomach, a burning in her mind. She knew that the explosion would come sooner or later like Fourth of July fireworks as Scott launched her on the path to ecstasy. Instinctively she reached out, and her hands found his slim waist. She slipped them under his sweater and felt the warmth of his skin. She shuddered against the sensation.

Slowly, gracefully, their bodies moved in a dance of love and desire until they knelt before each other. Then, as though their lovemaking were choreographed, their hands left each other and they leaned forward to offer first one kiss, then another, their heads turning in slow synchronization. Soon Scott could restrain himself no longer. He needed to show her how great was his caring, and he knew no better way than to give her all of himself.

Carefully he rolled her sweater up, his knuckles brushing her porcelain skin, sending shivers of desire shooting through her. Amelia raised her arms as Scott peeled the sweater from her body.

Reverently, Scott ran his hands over her shoulders and down her sides to her waist. Amelia's eyes closed and her head fell back. She could feel her thick tresses brush the small of her back. Scott hesitated, and Amelia could actually feel him looking at her. Then his fingers were teasing the lacy fabric of her bra as his lips found the gentle swell of her breast. She heard a snap and the fabric fell away from her body. Amelia caught her breath, holding it against the pain of utter delight that threatened to claim her too soon.

Scott's hands captured her, squeezing against her ribs. Then, ever so gently, he lowered her farther and farther until she lay on the floor, curled in a ball of anticipation. When he did not immediately join her, Amelia lazily opened her eyes. She watched through lowered lashes as he disrobed. First his sweater came off, his muscles flexing as he crossed his arms and pulled it over his head. Then his jeans peeled easily away. She smiled softly, noting that he wore no underwear. Then he, too, was lying on the soft carpeting, raised on one elbow looking at her.

He ran his hand over her carefully until it rested on the waistband of her slacks. His fingers curled and snapped the fastener. The zipper grated open, and Amelia's hips instinctively rose to meet the cool air.

Moments later the luxury of their lovemaking was left behind and the passion each felt swept over them, crashing, like a tidal wave assaulting an unsuspecting beach. Finally, like the wave, their desire subsided, leaving behind two hearts full of wonder and two bodies swept clean of need . . . for the moment.

The last thing Amelia remembered before sleep claimed her was Scott draping her sweater over her nakedness and his arms gathering her to him. She wished that she had her log. There were things about that moment she never wanted to forget. But then, it really didn't matter. She had no words to describe her happiness, her contentment. And she was sure she would never forget the night of her private house-warming. She slept contentedly with the man she loved beside her.

Amelia woke before dawn crept through the windows of the little house. She began to stretch, then realized that Scott still slept soundly beside her. Not wishing to disturb him, she pulled her arms back toward her and didn't bend to kiss his forehead before she rose and slipped into her clothes.

She thought she watched him as she dressed in order to make sure she didn't wake him. But, in reality, Amelia simply could not tear her eyes away from Scott's sleeping figure. He looked so young and, despite the strength of his body, vulnerable. It was as if she were looking at a living piece of sculpture or all the goodness that was in him come to the surface as living, breathing flesh.

She checked her watch. It was four in the morning. They had slept so long. It had been only a little after dark when they entered the house the night before. But, she realized, their lovemaking had seemed to last forever, so maybe their rest hadn't been as long as she imagined.

Amelia finally looked around. The house was completely empty. John and Judy had left nothing but the paper on the walls to indicate that they had ever been there. The house was spotlessly clean. Still, the little structure exuded a warmth that no empty house should have. Perhaps the cause of that was the lush carpeting, the sheen of the wood floors beyond, the cheery wallpaper. Perhaps it was the happiness of the previous occupants, left there as a present for her. Or maybe it was that she and Scott shared the house. Without his presence would it be a place where she wanted to live? She looked down at him once more, then turned away and began to walk through the rooms.

It didn't matter what would and wouldn't be. She was on her way in three days to "The Big Apple." How silly that the thought of it should make her nervous. New York was only a city, tall where Los Angeles was sprawling. It was filled with people just like her. Yes, more like her than many she had met in her hometown. People who moved fast toward the top of their professions. They had purpose, drive. But...

She stood in the bedroom and looked through the French doors at the garden and beyond that the beach. Her feet moved. She reached out and touched the glass panes. They were cool. Then, moving closer, she lay her cheek against them and closed her eyes. Those people were everything she had always thought herself to be, the kind of people she wanted to be around. But they weren't Scott. He had changed everything and she didn't want it to be changed. She wouldn't let it. She couldn't let him ruin everything.

Amelia pushed herself away from the door. No house, no man, nothing could keep her from doing what she was meant to do. Moments later Amelia was back in the living room. Her heart lurched as she saw that Scott had turned on his side and curled up like a child. His arm was outstretched and his brow was furrowed as though, in sleep, he was wondering where she was. But she fought against going to him as a lover. She gathered up his clothes quickly, then knelt beside him. She reached out and touched his shoulder.

"Scott," she said gently. He sighed and rolled toward her. She pushed him back. "Scott, it's time to get up. We've got to get going."

His eyes opened. They were bleary with sleep, but the happiness she saw there could not be disguised. To her surprise, his reactions were quick. He reached up and pulled her on top of him, then rolled her over onto her back so that he had her pinned to the ground.

"Good morning," he drawled, his voice heavy with sleep. And he smiled just before his lips descended to hers.

Amelia felt herself begin to respond. Her arms almost went around him. Instead, the palms of her hands met his chest and she pushed him gently but firmly away.

"Scott!" There was a false laugh in her voice. "Not now. It's time to go. We've got a ton of things to do today."

"We've got plenty of time." Scott glanced toward the window. "The sun hasn't even risen yet. My men are hard workers, but they're not gluttons for punishment." Once again he bent to kiss her, but she rolled from underneath him.

"I'm not kidding," she said. She turned away from him so that he wouldn't see that she was confused. It would be harder than she had anticipated to stick to her resolve.

"I see," Scott said quietly.

"I'm glad." Amelia's reply was overly curt, but she could think of nothing else to say. Then she took a deep breath and turned back to him, a wide smile on her face. "You better get dressed. We can't have you going about in the buff, can we?"

"No, I guess not." Scott looked at her a moment longer, then bent to retrieve his jeans and sweater. The silence between them was almost unendurable. She could almost feel his clothing grating against his skin the way their unspoken words grated against their minds. Finally, he broke the silence.

"Funny thing, Amelia…" Scott began. "I feel like we're meeting all over again."

"What do you mean?"

"Oh, it seems that a good night's sleep has brought back the woman who first walked into my plant. You've pulled inside again. Worried about the interview?"

"No, actually, I'm not," Amelia answered as she ran her hand over the windowsill, then sat upon it.

"Good. I was worried that you might be losing your confidence." Scott turned to her just as he snapped his jeans, leaving her to wonder if it was sarcasm she had heard. "What worries me is that sometime between last night and this morning you've decided that I just don't fit into the scenario you've planned for yourself."

His eyes bore into her and Amelia had to avert her own. He knew her very well after such a short time. What could she say to his accusation? Nothing. Nothing except that he was right. She had pulled inside herself like a fighter just before entering the ring. It was the one thing she couldn't share with him, since he didn't have the capacity to understand that kind of determination. So she remained silent as Scott approached.

"Is it true?" He stood before her but didn't touch her. Yet the force of his words was like a slap in the face.

"No, it's not true that I wouldn't want you to be part of it if I get this job. But it is true that I don't think it will work. You were right yesterday on the beach. Long-distance relationships are impossible...." Her words trailed off. She couldn't look at him because he would see that she herself wasn't sure that this was what she wanted.

"Amelia." This time his voice was gentle and concerned. "I think you've just got a case of the jitters. You're worried about this house. You're worried about us. I spoke out of turn when I put those thoughts in your mind. I don't want it to end like this. I'm sorry for my part in your confusion. You're not even sure you're going to get the job. Not that I don't think you will." He chuckled and touched her face. "How could they possibly reject you?"

Scott moved closer and gathered her into his arms, forcing her to look into his face.

"No, I know what I have to do.... You didn't do anything to facilitate the change...."

Amelia began to protest, trying to remain cool.

"Look, I don't care what you think at this point. I just want you to know that I love you and that I'll be waiting if it doesn't work out. And if it does—" he hesitated "—well, we'll cross that bridge when we come to it. Please, Amelia. Our lovemaking last night was so beautiful. Let's hang on to that for now. Please."

Amelia nodded and lowered her cheek to rest on his chest. In her mind she knew that she couldn't accept his proposition. It would be better to make a clean break. But what did her heart feel? Well, she tried to ignore the longing there, but gave in for one last moment.

"Now," Scott said, holding her away from him. The grin she had come to adore was on his lips. "You'll go to New York in a few days and knock 'em dead. Worry about it Tuesday. Meanwhile, back at the old homestead, let's move your things into this charming abode. Then I'll fly east to be with you for the party with all those bigwigs. And sooner than you know, we'll both be back here, anxiously awaiting word about the newest anchor on *Meet America*. How does that sound?"

"Wonderful," Amelia said, forcing a smile to her lips. "But, Scott, I think maybe we ought to wait on moving my things. After all, if I get the job..." She hesitated, then plunged ahead. "Well, I won't be living here and I would just have to move everything out for the renters. You do see, don't you?"

"Of course." His hands dropped to his sides and his smile faltered slightly. Then it brightened again. "Instead of renting, wouldn't it be better to move your things in? Just in case everything doesn't work out, it'll be ready for you. And if you do get the job, then maybe your mother would like to move in. Sort of keep the home fires burning for you. You said she loved the beach and her apartment is furnished. How does that sound?"

"Actually, I already discussed that with her," Amelia answered. "But when I brought it up she just waved the idea away. I don't know if it's because she doesn't think I'll get the job or because she doesn't want to leave her friends, her church groups and everything. You know, I really wish I had introduced you two before I left. You'd like her.''

"I know I would," Scott replied, heading toward the door. "And there'll be plenty of time for us to get to know each other. Especially if you're in New York half the time. I'll need someone to watch out for me. So, shall we find someplace for breakfast and then go collect Sailor and the crew? We'll have your stuff in this place in no time."

"I'm not sure Sailor wants to touch my things." Amelia's wry statement was not lost on Scott.

"Amelia, you're just going to have to take him as he is. I'm sorry if he hasn't been the friendliest toward you...."

"Hah!" Amelia scoffed. "That's the understatement of the year."

"Well, be that as it may, he has a heart of gold. The man's just been hurt." Scott began to explain but went no further.

"Is that any reason to take it out on the world?" Amelia queried, stepping through the door Scott now held open for her.

"In his case I would say yes." Scott stepped out behind her, jiggled the doorknob to make sure it was locked and took her arm. "You have to know Sailor a long time to earn his respect and friendship. Then, and only then, he explains himself. And when he does, you wish you'd never cared to find out. Believe me. Leave that reporter's curiosity behind where Sailor is concerned."

They had arrived at the end of the walk and both turned toward the car. They were silent as they settled themselves in, Scott starting the car for the drive to her apartment in the valley.

While Amelia's curiosity was piqued by his assessment of Sailor, she put the other man out of her mind and concentrated on the drive. Each inch of ground they covered brought their relationship closer to an end, although Scott wouldn't admit it.

Amelia closed her eyes. Sunrise on the freeway was not exactly a beautiful sight. She knew she would get the job. There was no doubt in her mind. She wanted it, she needed it and she would work for it. The people in New York wouldn't be able to miss the fact that she would work harder than anyone else for a spot on their show. Then she and Scott would try to keep up their long-distance romance, but it would fail in the end. He was right. If she knew nothing else about him she did understand his need to have someone to himself, someone to care for him. That she couldn't deny him. She would sever the strings and he would find a new lady love.

She sighed quietly and moved in the seat. The leather gave under her. He was a lot to give up. But she had given up things before because of her ambition. This would be different only because she would miss him for such a very long, long time.

Amelia turned her head again and looked at his profile. His eyes were intent on the road. How beautiful he was. He looked at her and smiled sweetly. She could feel his love for her. If she was anyone else she would say that a world of riches sat beside her. But her world demanded more. And if Scott Alexander couldn't see it, she could.

"Scott," Amelia said quietly, "I don't think you should come to New York with me."

His hand covered hers and a small sad silence descended upon them.

"All right, Amelia. We'll get your things moved and we'll talk about it later."

"There's nothing to talk about!" Amelia cried in exasperation. Why was he making this harder than it was? "It's the right thing to do."

"Okay." Scott's hand found the steering wheel again and suddenly he was bubbling, full of good cheer.

"What's wrong with you?" Amelia demanded, tears of frustration stinging her eyes. He seemed to be taking this so lightly.

"Nothing is wrong with me. I'm just not going to let you do this. You can mope around and be sad if you want to, but I have you for two more days. In those two days I'm going to love you and watch you and help you. I'm going to pretend that it's both of us who are moving into that little house. And when all is done, I'll ask you to tell me again what it is you want. So, Amelia, like the song says, nothing's going to rain on my parade, or some such thing."

Amelia listened openmouthed as he spoke. She saw the fine laugh lines crinkle about his eyes. She saw the glint of white as he grinned at the oncoming traffic. She couldn't figure it out. Had she hurt him so much that he was covering the hurt? Or did he truly believe that two days would make a difference?

Well, either way his determination to ignore the situation was obvious, so Amelia sat back. She, too, could pretend for a day or two more, pretend that the inevitable wouldn't happen. She closed her eyes. Letting a dream last a bit longer was a wonderful thing, even if the dreamer knew she would have to wake sooner or later.

All right, my love, she thought as the car sped along the freeway. Because I love you. Two more days just for you.

TRUE TO HER PROMISE, Amelia acted as though nothing had ever passed between them. She accepted his kisses as he went by with his hands full of clothes or boxes. She stopped to rub his shoulders, knowing full well they would ache in the morning despite the fact that windsurfing had built up his muscles.

She ran for pizza and set up a picnic for the crew in the backyard. Even Sailor offered what passed as a smile as she handed out cold beer, soft drinks and thick slices of steaming pepperoni pizza. Then they were all back at work again.

The day had disappeared behind them, and by the time Sailor and the other two men took their leave, Amelia was exhausted both physically and mentally. She felt cruel playacting as she had all day. The little lie that everything was as it had been played havoc with her heart and her soul. As Scott walked the men out to the truck she lay down on her unmade bed and closed her eyes, knowing she would have to be ready to continue the sham the moment Scott returned. Her heart longed for him, but she also knew it was time to end this.

"Oh, no, you don't, sleepyhead," Scott called from the doorway just before he pounced on the mattress. He nuzzled into Amelia's neck, forcing her back to wakefulness.

"Oh, I wasn't going to sleep, honestly," she mumbled as she curled tighter into a ball. She didn't want to be touched. His loving ministrations only reminded her of how wrong this all was.

"Of course you weren't," Scott whispered. "But the day is almost gone and there are still things to do."

"I can finish unpacking tomorrow," Amelia complained. "There's nothing absolutely necessary that has to be put away right now and I'm tired."

"Cranky, aren't we?" Scott teased, and began to tickle her.

"Scott, cut it out!" Amelia yelled, springing away from him. "Is everything fun and games with you? I'm tired, I told you."

Amelia's eyes blazed. She regretted her harsh words but she had had enough of game playing. It had been hard pretending all day. She wasn't one to act and Scott had forced her into it. Now she wanted him to understand that what had been said that morning was the truth and that the rest of the day had been a sham. She had felt as though she were taking advantage of him. But he had seemed very happy, so she tried harder. Now the strain of the lie had become too much.

"Sorry, Amelia," Scott said as he moved off the bed. "I just thought you'd be happy to be alone with me for a while. I guess I was wrong. I suppose you were right this morning."

He moved to the door. Amelia watched his graceful body walk, sway, turn and then lean against the doorjamb. She turned her eyes away from him. If she looked into those eyes she would be in those arms.

"I love you, Amelia," he said. He smiled softly before he left her alone in her dream house.

AMELIA'S LOG

April 29

I'm packed. My suitcase is in the corner of my old room. Mom is asleep. I'm left alone with my thoughts on this night, this very important night.

Mom fixed a wonderful dinner... sauerkraut and bratwurst. My favorite ever since I was a little kid. We chatted, just chatted. She didn't ask too much about New York or the interview. I guess she feels it's a foregone conclusion that I've got the job. Actually, she was kind of quiet. There was very little conversation after I suggested she live in the house. I think she's going to miss me more than she's willing to let on.

Miss... to long for. Miss... to wish for. Already I miss Scott. I keep looking at that damn phone. Mr. Bell, I wish you had never invented that stupid thing. It's so hard to resist at moments like this.

I tried not to think of him all evening, all day. I was so stupid Saturday when I blew up like that. I probably shouldn't have told him I didn't want him to come to New York. I didn't really know what I wanted. I was only trying to do the right thing. But I had expected some sort of outburst. To be honest, I wanted it. But he was so sweet, as though he understood all the conflicting things I was feeling. I think that made it worse. I don't want him to understand if I don't!

I'm being silly. I'm a big girl and I don't need anyone now. But can I really do it on my own this time? Mom's always been there before. This time she doesn't seem to want to encourage me. Not that she isn't encouraging, but there isn't that excitement in her about this next step in my life. Scott didn't have it either. At least he had a kind of acceptance, a willingness to go along with the game plan and encourage me. Who am I kidding? I do need him. I'll just have to do without him. I chose it and he respects me enough to stand by my wishes. Thank you, Scott.

My darling, I'm so scared.

Chapter Nine

"Hi, Mom?" Amelia shouted into the phone, knowing full well that she needn't despite the long distance the call covered. Still, the excitement she felt at actually being in New York translated into a few extra decibels in her tone.

"Amelia!" came the surprised greeting, "I didn't expect to hear from you tonight. I thought you'd be exhausted after such a long flight."

"Not at all. Mom, it's fabulous here. I wish you could share this with me. The city looked so, so..." Some reporter, she thought, as she searched for the word to describe how she felt flying over the Statue of Liberty, the Empire State Building. She tried again, "...so spectacular. Almost unreal. Lights were just coming on, you know, it was the end of the workday when I arrived, but people were still hustling all over the place."

"Amelia, how could you tell that from an airplane?" Her mother laughed. Amelia relaxed a bit. It was good to hear her mother joke. She knew she was forcing part of her excitement. It wasn't that she was disappointed in anything so far. The city was spectacular, the road ahead of her thrilling. But she had not forgotten the long hours of her flight, when Scott's face floated before her eyes. At times, as she was reading, she could suddenly feel the sweetness of his kiss, as though his lips were really on hers. He was with her every minute and she didn't want him to be.

"I just could. Don't ask me how. And, Mother..." Amelia went on, anxious to describe her hotel room, the weather, anything to link her back to home just a little while longer.

"I'm sorry, Amelia, but I'm really in a rush. Mr. Lipencott is coming to pick me up. We're going to have dinner at his daughter's house and discuss the rummage sale for the church. I'm happy you called to let me know you arrived safely, but..." There was a silence and Amelia could almost hear her mother cock her head. "*Ach*, he's here. I have to go."

"But, Mom..." Amelia protested, hurt and slightly curious about the excitement Mr. Lipencott obviously created.

"Oh, Amelia, before you hang up..." Martha went on, not having heard Amelia's last words. "Good luck. My heart and thoughts are with you. I'm so proud."

"Thanks, Mom." Amelia sighed. It was a bittersweet good wish. "'Bye."

She listened for the click on the other end of the line before she hung up. Then, slowly, she replaced the receiver and sat on the bed. She felt a bit chilled and all alone. Here in a city of millions she felt a twinge of fright. Amelia shook herself. How silly. She had never minded before when her mother ran off to meetings or fund-raisers or her work. It had been an accepted fact of life and a life-style Amelia had approved of and emulated. Could it be that there was now a bit of jeal-

ousy on Amelia's part because her mother had found
a replacement for her? Mr. Lipencott indeed. Still, her
mother had sounded unnecessarily excited.

Amelia peeled off her suit jacket and tossed it onto
a rose-colored velvet chair that sat beside the bed. Her
eyes lingered on the telephone for a moment. She
really wanted to share all this with someone before it
faded from her memory. She picked up the receiver,
then replaced it again immediately. Even if it killed her
she was not going to call Scott.

Throughout the long flight she had fought with
herself. Despite her surprising request they had parted
sweetly; Scott was still convinced that she would return to him, Amelia was convinced she would not and
neither of them were admitting anything. They had
pretended they would simply wait and see. It amazed
her that Scott still didn't understand the lure of this
opportunity. Perhaps it was because he had always
pursued things he enjoyed and succeeded because of
that. He was content to make his hobbies his work.
That seemed a fair assessment.

But halfway through the movie and right after they
served lunch, and again just before the plane landed,
Amelia was plagued with doubts about her conclusions. Perhaps she was wrong to go after this job with
everything in her. There was no right or wrong answer. Someone was going to lose. Perhaps it would be
Scott; perhaps it would be her. It was a no-win situation.

Anyway, it would do no good to fan the flame she
always felt burning deep inside her for him. One word,
one sound, from his lips and Amelia knew she would
miss him to the point of wanting to be with him . . .
anywhere.

She stood up and flipped the locks on her suitcase, looking around the room all the while. The Helmsley Palace was everything she had been led to believe. Spotlessly clean, it was the height of understated elegance. There was not much furniture, but what there was was opulent, giving a feeling of sophisticated space to the room. The bed was huge, and for an instant she wished Scott was there to share it with her that first night . . . and the second.

"Stop it," Amelia admonished herself. "You're the one who chose this way; he didn't." Then she thought that he could at least have objected. She would more than likely have changed her mind. He should have known she would need his reassurance. She laughed out loud. Just as the night of their "celebratory" dinner. She had expected him to know what was on her mind then, too. For someone fairly intelligent, she decided, she could be rather stupid.

Amelia pulled the first of her new outfits from the suitcase. It was the Albert Nipon dress for the cocktail party Thursday evening. She smiled sadly. Scott wouldn't be there to help her button up the back. Carefully, she lay the hip-tucked beige silk on the bed. It was perfect. She would look wonderful even though she would walk into the party alone.

Next was the suit she intended to wear for her initial interview. Anne Klein. It was trendy in a low-key sort of way, mismatched rather than severely tailored. But the shades of gray and black with the silk apricot-colored blouse would lend her femininity as well as a businesslike appearance. She had carefully thought out her purchases and she was still convinced that they would help her exude the air of a knowledgeable but womanly reporter.

Amelia moved to the lovely armoire that served as a closet. She smiled when she saw real wooden hangers instead of those horrible things that were attached to the closet rods so that no one could steal them. The network certainly knew how to treat its out-of-town guests. She hung up the suit jacket and had just returned to the bed for the skirt when there was a knock on the door.

"Yes?" Amelia called as she approached the door and looked out the peephole.

"Bellman, ma'am," came the reply from the gold-jacketed man who stood in front of the door. Amelia could hardly see him for the flowers he carried.

"Come on in," she said, holding the door open as the man's bald head peeked to the side so he could see where he was going.

"Did you just get married?" he asked as he deposited his load on the table.

"Hardly." Amelia laughed. "I'm here for a job interview."

"Well, I'd say you already got the job," the man answered as he tugged at his jacket.

"I hope you're right." As she handed him a two-dollar tip, her heart soared with anticipation. He bowed slightly and left. Amelia locked the door behind him, then rushed to the table.

This was a bouquet of gargantuan proportions. The sender had obviously spared no expense. Lilies on two-foot stems reached for the ceiling. Peach-colored roses in the perfect state of bloom were interwoven into the bouquet by the dozens. Huge russet-colored flowers with spidery petals added the necessary splash of bright color. Amelia reached for the card and quickly read it.

Welcome to New York. Looking forward to
seeing you tomorrow.

Jan Dickerson, Program Director, ABC

A grin of delight spread across Amelia's face. It was
a good sign. They were going all out to make her visit
a wonderful experience. They were courting her!

She moved the lavish bouquet and looked at the
other items the porter had left. A bottle of wine.
Lovely, Amelia thought. She picked it up to examine
the label and as she did so she noticed there was a
golden string wrapped around the bottle's neck. She
pulled it and a single rose, which also lay on the table,
moved. Curious now, she picked up the rose. There
was a card. She had assumed it was all from Jan. But
this set-up looked all too familiar. Dare she hope . . . ?
As she opened the card and read, her grin faded, to be
replaced with a smile so tender those who knew her
would have been shocked.

My darling,
    This type of offering seems to be my good-luck
charm. I hope it will be yours, too. Best of luck
tomorrow.
Scott

Just then the telephone rang. Amelia rushed to answer it, clutching the bottle and rose to her breast as
she went.

"Hello," she answered breathlessly, knowing full
well that it would be Scott. Her heart burst with the
sweetness inside her and she knew she would ask him
to come to New York, if he still would. But the caller

was not the man she expected, and the love in her heart deflated in disappointment.

"Amelia," Tom said, "it sounds like you ran for the phone. Did you just get in?"

"Yes . . . I mean no . . ." Amelia stuttered. She had been so sure it would be Scott. "Well, in a way. I was just unpacking."

"So how is it there? Are they treating you right?" Tom queried. Amelia could still detect a hint of the old adoration Tom had felt for her, despite his easy acceptance of her relationship with Scott. What a shame, she thought, that no matter what happened someone always managed to get the short end of the stick.

"Oh, yes," she answered with a cheeriness that she hoped hid her disappointment. "They really do things up right."

"Well, I'll let you get back to your unpacking. I just wanted to wish you luck and let you know I'm pulling for you."

"Tom, that's sweet. Thank you. I need all the good wishes I can get," Amelia admitted, knowing that the good wishes of Scott were really all that mattered.

"No, you just need to be yourself and you'll knock 'em dead. Well, that's it. I'll keep the home fires burning. You just be great."

"I'll try, Tom, and thank you," Amelia said sincerely.

"No problem. I hope you get what you want and deserve. Bye." He hung up; the line went dead.

Amelia replaced the receiver, then realized that she was still clutching Scott's present to her. The wine was a very good vintage. She knew that she still would not call him, but with the wine and the flower she felt she almost had him there with her.

Suddenly Amelia was very tired. The exhilaration of the opportunity, the long plane ride and her unruly emotions were getting the best of her. Picking up the phone once again, she dialed room service and ordered a dinner of steak and potatoes, and fruit for dessert. Then, while she waited, she took a leisurely shower, dressed in a gown and robe and was almost finished drying her hair when the food arrived.

The service was excellent, the food outstanding and the wine above reproach. Carefully, Amelia put the tray outside her door, turned on the radio and looked out her window onto Madison Avenue.

She was in New York. This might well be her home in a few months. It didn't look cold and uninviting now. It looked wonderful; it was where she should be. It was a few moments before she realized that her jaw was clenched and her brow furrowed. She decided she must be more tired than she had originally thought. Amelia went back to the table and poured herself another half-glass of wine. It was still too early to sleep, but the bed looked so inviting.

She set down her glass of wine next to her log on the bedside table, removed her robe and climbed under the exquisite cotton sheets. She fluffed the pillows behind her and pulled her journal onto her upraised knees, opening it to a clean page. For a minute she simply stared at it. Then she took a sip of wine, put down the glass and began to write.

AMELIA'S LOG

April 23

I'm really here, I'm really here. Can I do what

I came to do? Am I good enough for a network spot? I'm scared. No one knows it but I am. I wish Scott was here to hold me. Dammit! That is truly what I wish.

Amelia stopped writing and lay her head back on the lush down pillows. She didn't want every word she thought or wrote to be about Scott Alexander. Amelia wanted him out of her mind. No, not just him, but the things he represented, the things he promised to her merely by being. Her eyes closed and it was only the ringing of the telephone that shook the sleep from her.

"Amelia," came the greeting, soft as velvet, "did I wake you?"

Amelia rolled over. The journal slid down the satin coverlet and onto the floor but she didn't care. Her eyes were bleary with sleep and the half-finished glass of wine on the nightstand was a blur of rich burgundy as she fought to wake up properly. But she couldn't. Scott's voice was like a lullabye.

"I was just dozing," she managed to say.

"Then doze on, my love. You have a big day tomorrow. I just wanted to be the one to wish you sweet dreams on such an important night. I love you, Amelia. I want you home but I want you to have everything you dream of, too. Good night, darling."

Amelia smiled. Somehow she put the receiver back on the hook. It was a perfect way to drift back to sleep...with Scott's voice reverberating in her ears. He had such a lovely voice, and she was grateful for his call and his understanding. He did want her to realize her dream. Then sleep claimed her once again and she dozed and dreamed. She dreamed of Scott and the tiny house above the beach.

"AMELIA, SO NICE to meet you."

Jan Dickerson approached like a tidy tornado, the gravelly voice finding Amelia before the outstretched hand. She was a lovely woman of indeterminate age. Her hair was brown but streaked with gray. Her skin was smooth but there were crow's feet just at the corners of her eyes. Her figure was compact but that could have been the effect of her perfectly tailored suit. How was one to know?

Amelia walked past the secretary who held open the door to Jan's office and extended her hand, meeting Jan halfway. Her own grasp was as firm and dry as that of her hostess and possible employer. The first hurdle was passed.

"It's nice to meet you, too. I can't tell you how I've been looking forward to this," Amelia said as Jan casually placed her hand on Amelia's elbow and guided her to a deep chair covered with gray flannel.

"I'm happy to hear it. We think *Meet America* is one of the finest shows on the air and we're looking for people with the same conviction to keep it that way."

"I can easily identify with that. I believe that nothing is more important than doing one's work well—spectacularly, as a matter of fact," Amelia said with deep belief.

Jan took the chair directly across from Amelia, rather than sitting behind the desk. She raised her eyebrow slightly as she listened. Then her face became a pleasant mask once again as she looked directly into Amelia's eyes.

"You must work very hard if you believe that."

"Oh, I do. Sometimes I wonder if it's even worth it to have an apartment. I think that the public has a right to know as much as they can, as soon as they can, about the way this world works today." Jan surreptitiously glanced at Amelia's hands. They were clasped in her lap. The gesture looked normal enough but for the small white dots of pressure at the knuckles.

"That's an admirable attitude. I'm not sure I've met many people with that kind of dedication. But it must be hard on your private life. I know you're not married, but certainly a lovely woman like you must have a gentleman or two waiting in the wings...." Jan was an excellent interviewer. Amelia spoke without really having been asked a direct question, and her answers became more intense as Jan's questions became more subtle.

"Not really. I do, of course, have a social life, but it's not as active as some, I suppose...." Amelia hesitated, thinking of Scott for an instant. How could she possibly call him a "social life"? He had been her life for the last few weeks. But the hesitation was minimal and she went on. "I know that most people still find it hard to believe that some women are willing to forgo family for a profession, but I also know that there are many who feel that way."

"I agree, Amelia, there are, but I know that eventually every woman wishes she had a husband or someone special with whom to share those accomplishments. Don't you agree?" Jan cocked her head to one side. Amelia smiled back. The woman was obviously chatting before getting to the meat of the matter at hand, but it somehow made Amelia uneasy.

"You're right, of course, but the same thing applies to men, does it not?" Amelia answered, not wishing to elaborate any further. This initial phase of the interview was a bit unnerving. She hadn't expected any questions regarding her personal life. But then it dawned on her. Of course, they didn't want to hire someone who had attachments all the way across the country. This realization spurred Amelia on.

"I suppose," she added, "that you must take into account each person's situation. I have worked very hard to get where I am and I intend to work harder. If it is as a host of *Meet America*, all the better. If not, I won't shirk my duties to my current position. If I were to become serious with a man, he would have to understand that. But then, I could protest all day about my commitment to my profession. There is only one way for you to know how deep it runs, and that is to give me a chance."

"Well spoken," Jan answered, but her face didn't light up with delight as Amelia had expected. No matter, really. She knew the network would play it close to the vest. They couldn't possibly tip their hand before everyone had been considered. Still, Amelia felt confident that she had convinced Jan Dickerson of one thing: she was ready for a job like the one on *Meet America*.

"Well, you must be wondering when we're going to get to the real interview." Jan smiled, sitting back in her chair and crossing her legs. Amelia noted the woman's shoes. They were beautiful, expensive and well cared for. This was a woman who appreciated attention to detail. Amelia relaxed and smiled as the interview continued.

"One last question, Amelia, then I'm going to shoot you upstairs to the big boys." Jan had not lost any of her enthusiasm during the hour-long talk, but Amelia already felt drained. She had never worked so hard in her life. "If you could point to one story that you covered that would illustrate what you would consider to be your finest hour, so to speak, on the air, what would it be?"

Amelia leaned forward slightly and uncrossed her legs, then tucked one foot behind the other. Her face became serious and she spoke slowly but very surely.

"I believe that would be the exposé I did on the shameful conditions at a home for unwed mothers. The girls were being mistreated, basically forced to give up their children for adoption, and the home was government-funded. The result of my story was that the home was closed down and the young women residing there were placed elsewhere. I worked on an anonymous tip and had to dig for months to get corroborating evidence. I feel that story was one of my best."

Jan heaved a sigh, smiled and stood up. "Well, Amelia, thanks for answering all my questions so thoughtfully. I'm most impressed with your background."

"Thank you. I hope that you'll find my qualifications fit the job description for the anchor spot."

"Well, they are very impressive. But, as you know, I'm only the tip of the iceberg. Now—" Jan's hand was once again on Amelia's elbow as she steered her out the door "—you're scheduled to see Mr. Willis and Mr. Jensen. I'm sure you'll find them both delightful."

As they walked through the corridor, Amelia noticed every nuance of the network headquarters. The secretaries were busy and impeccably dressed. Young men and women in business suits rushed about. Once Amelia even saw a crew, dressed in much the same casual manner as her own at home, run through the halls, Minicams poised. She already felt at home. She knew that she would fit in here like a hand in a glove.

Four hours later, Amelia was being collected once again by Jan. She had just left a meeting with Mr. Jensen, president of the network. He had proved to be, as Jan had promised, a delightful man to talk to. But Amelia knew that his good-old-boy attitude was only a cover for his very shrewd business-sense. She could see it in his eyes and she knew she must shine.

"How did it go, Amelia?" Jan asked as she escorted the younger woman down in the elevator.

"Fairly well, I think," Amelia replied, not wanting to sound too confident even though she felt on top of the world.

"That's good. Now," Jan said, handing her a file, "here is the background on the imaginary celebrity you are going to interview in your test tomorrow."

Amelia took the thick folder and immediately began to page through it. There was enough reading to last a week, and she had only one night.

"Impressive" was all she could manage to say.

"You mean overwhelming." Jan chuckled. "I know it is, but believe me, it's very close to the real thing for our anchor on *Meet America*. Study it. We'll see you here tomorrow morning at nine o'clock for your test. Good luck. And look on the bright side. Tomorrow night it will all be over and all you'll have to do is enjoy yourself at the party."

With that, Jan Dickerson was gone, and Amelia was left standing alone in the lobby. It was well past two, but people were still rushing back to work from lunch and running out to get a late bite to eat.

"I wonder if people always run in New York," Amelia muttered to herself as she passed the lobby guard.

"If they didn't, they'd get stepped on," the guard said. When Amelia turned to look at him, he smiled knowingly.

"Sounds reasonable," Amelia quipped, then stepped out the door and continued to walk.

She passed stores with merchandise that screamed to be bought, restaurants packed to the door, apartment buildings with elaborate security systems and uniformed doormen. She saw women in fur coats, even though the weather had not yet turned chilly, walking dogs large and small that looked as pampered as their mistresses. There were street people lounging on the benches at the entrances to Central Park and a quartet of musicians playing Mozart on a corner.

Amelia stopped for lunch. A glass of Perrier and a salad was all she felt she could manage. Nerves were finally setting in. She leaned back and took a deep breath as she looked through the window of the restaurant.

New York was so different from Los Angeles. She wondered if people went to the beach. And all that security on apartment doors! It would seem strange to lock herself in that way every night. Would she be able to jog anytime she wanted? Of course, she told herself. On the salary she would be receiving she could well afford to live in a good neighborhood. That wasn't so different from Los Angeles. Every city had its good and bad places. What about her car? Oh, God, she thought, no car. It would be awful. No self-respecting southern Californian was ever without her car. But in this city it would be useless and impractical.

She ate slowly and tried to imagine where she would live, where she would go in the evening, the kind of people she would meet. But it was useless. The only things that came to mind were Scott's smiling face and her little house in Redondo Beach. She knew why. It was because she didn't know New York at all. When she did, she probably wouldn't be able to imagine living anywhere else.

She paid the bill, left the café, hailed a cab and went back to the hotel. There was a lot of work to do.

THE PENCIL IN HER HAND scribbled furiously, almost as if it had a life of its own. Height, weight, likes, dislikes, professional training... On and on went the notes as she delved into the life of the fictional actor/businessman she was going to interview the next day. Amelia wanted to know him from the inside out. It was already seven o'clock and she was just beginning to feel as if she knew him. She still had to come up with some outstanding questions for her fifteen-minute test.

She stood up and stretched her arms high above her head. She heard a joint in some undetermined part of her body crack. Her blouse pulled out of her skirt just as her hair had earlier come loose from the expertly wrapped chignon. Catching a glimpse of herself in the mirror, Amelia laughed. She looked as though she'd pulled an all-nighter as she'd done in college.

She stopped for a minute to order a pot of tea from room service, then went straight to the bathroom and undid her hair. She brushed it out until it fell smooth and golden down her back. Then, flipping it behind her ears, she splashed her face with ice-cold water and reached for one of the towels that hung by the sink.

Just at that moment there was a knock at the door. Eyes tightly shut, she groped for the towel. Her hand was on it and she whipped it from its rack. Scrubbing her face dry as she went, Amelia felt the circulation returning to her entire body. Room service was getting better every day, she thought as she opened the door without looking through the peephole.

But instead of finding the porter with the tea, Amelia found a light-haired man lounging against the door frame, a wide grin of greeting plastered on his face.

"Scott!" Amelia fairly screamed in surprise.

"I thought you'd be surprised," he said happily as he whisked her into his arms and twirled her around, alternating kisses and hugs until there was no breath left in him.

"Surprised is not the word for it," Amelia said breathlessly when her feet finally hit the ground again. "You weren't supposed to be here. I thought we decided that it would be better if you stayed home."

"No, *you* decided it would be better. Oh, I agreed at the time, but that was before I realized how much you needed me, so I caught the first plane out. We moved into your house and, most important, I missed you so dreadfully I couldn't wait another day. So, here I am. Ready and willing to offer moral support and anything else my lady desires."

Amelia tried to hide both her happiness and her disappointment. She had so much work to do that the last thing she needed was a distraction like him! Still, it was hard to deny that nothing could have pleased her more than to see him on her doorstep. "I don't remember telling you—"

"That you needed me? Oh, Amelia, I could hear it in your voice."

"I was asleep," she wailed. "You couldn't have heard any such thing."

"Then let's say I read your mind. Amelia, I needed to see you so much. Cold turkey just isn't for me. Couldn't you pretend that you're happy to see me?"

"Oh, darling, I don't have to pretend," Amelia cried, flinging her arms around his neck, giving in to her happiness. "It's just that . . ."

"Yes?" He kissed her neck, then her cheek, and then he squeezed her tightly.

"But I have a ton of things to do. I've got my test tomorrow and they gave me a file five inches thick." She motioned to the table spread with papers and shrugged her shoulders.

"Not to worry." Scott released her and walked to the table. He picked up her notes and spoke while he scanned them. "Didn't I tell you I was here to help? Well, what if we pretend I'm your interview? Give me fifteen minutes to read this and I'll answer your questions. It'll be great practice."

Amelia instinctively began to shake her head in refusal. It would never work. Then she realized that perhaps it might. She would need longer than fifteen minutes to get her questions in order, but that would give him enough time to shower and study the file. Yes, it might work.

"Only if you promise to take this seriously," Amelia warned. She knew he really had no desire for her to get this job, but she also knew the depth of his caring. He wouldn't sabotage her.

"Scout's honor," he said, standing very straight and flashing three fingers at her. "Besides, I have to make up for this surprise. I wasn't sure if it was the right thing to do. I wasn't sure if maybe this job had changed things so much between us that we could never recapture them. I'm glad I was wrong."

Amelia looked at him for a long while. Their eyes held, saying much more than mere words ever could. He understood everything. She smiled softly, unwilling to think beyond the moment. Their relationship might not work out, but he was here and she was going to be glad for it.

"Okay, then, let's get to it," Amelia answered with renewed vigor. "I'll need an hour and a half to get my questions in order. You shower or unpack and then read the file. No talking, you understand. Then I'll take my best shot."

"*Ja, mein Kommandant,*" Scott said as he turned on his heels and headed toward the bathroom. Then he turned back, clicked his heels together, grabbed her and kissed her hard on the mouth before disappearing into the other room. Amelia laughed at his silliness and then sat down to work.

The work proved to be most difficult. Her mind kept registering every sound Scott made. The shower was running and she could imagine him soaping his body. The shower stopped and she saw, in her mind's eye, the towel running up and down his long legs and over his well-muscled torso. She heard a click and realized he had begun to unpack. Scott, Scott, Scott.

She actually found herself writing his name in the middle of a question. Forcefully she turned her attention back to the interview again and again. And when finally the time was up, she was hopeful that she had not made too many mistakes.

The next two hours were spent deep in concentration. Scott proved to be a quick study. He had learned the material well and answered the questions she fired at him with little or no hesitation. Amelia, on her part, refined and reworded her questions until they were slick and to the point. But at ten-thirty it was Scott who called a halt to the proceedings.

"Enough, Amelia," he said, throwing up his hands.

"No, it isn't. Scott, you promised." She protested vehemently, though her body was taut with exhaustion and anticipation.

"Yes, it is, love." Scott slipped her yellow ruled notepad from her fingers. "You've done a beautiful job. The questions you're going to ask are insightful, your tone is good, you've almost memorized each and every one of them. It's time for a rest."

"I guess you're right, but we'll do it over again in a few minutes."

"No. We're going for a walk," he commanded, moving behind her and placing his strong hands on her shoulders. He began to massage the muscles there and Amelia moved her hair to give him better access. "You're as tight as a drum. Believe me, if you don't lay back a little bit you won't sleep well, you'll get up groggy and you won't do well in this interview."

"I suppose. But I do want to go over the questions once more."

"All right, after our walk, when you're in bed. Reading them again just before you go to sleep will help print those questions in your mind. But, honey, you can't keep this pace up.''

"That's the difference between you and me. You trust chance and I want to head it off at the pass." Amelia laughed tiredly. Two hours ago she never would have joked about their differences, but now her confidence was running high and she realized that there was truth in what he said. Besides, it was nice to have him there; he did bring something she needed desperately—his love.

"I'm glad you're finally able to enjoy our differences rather than hate them," Scott said as he bent down and pecked at the soft skin of her neck. "Better?"

"Much, thanks," Amelia answered. "You know, Scott, maybe we should talk about that...."

"No!" he said adamantly, leaving no room for discussion. "We'll talk about what we're going to do about us after this thing is complete. I just don't want us to make any decisions we'll regret."

"Okay." Amelia held up her hands in defeat. "I give up."

"Good, now grab your jacket. We're going to get some fresh air and then I'm going to tuck you into bed."

"What? Just a tuck?" Amelia teased.

"And maybe a few kisses and one good hug. But that's it. Don't try to take advantage of me, Amelia. I need all my strength for tomorrow night's cocktail party," Scott joked as Amelia slipped into her jacket and took his arm.

She felt so wonderfully free. And, for some reason, her excitement level had built since his arrival. The city looked cleaner, fresher, brighter with him by her side, and Amelia felt that if he didn't hold on to her, she would just fly off into the surprisingly clear night. They stopped for cappuccino and held hands while they looked up at the Empire State Building. Scott told very bad King Kong jokes that made Amelia ache with laughter. And when they finally returned to their hotel, he was true to his word. Carefully, he tucked her into bed and let her read her questions one more time. Then he slipped in beside her, his naked body warming her through her nightgown. He turned out the light, gathered her in his arms and kissed her gently. Cradling her head in the crook of his arm, he smoothed her long tresses until the cadence of the motion lulled her into a deep and contented sleep.

The next morning, before the alarm went off, he simply reversed the process, bringing her awake in the most delightful manner. He didn't try to make love to her, although both of them ached for it. Scott knew that when the time came it would be right. But at that moment Amelia was engrossed in the task ahead. She dressed carefully in the Anne Klein suit she'd bought for the occasion.

Scott insisted that she have something for breakfast, so they went to the dining room, where she nibbled on toast and sipped tea. Then, with plenty of time to spare, he deposited her in front of the network headquarters. He kissed her, wished her luck and closed the door of the cab, leaving Amelia to face the greatest test of her professional career.

Just as Scott's cab pulled into the heart of the diamond district, where he intended to do a bit of shopping, Amelia was being ushered onto a stage. She sat beneath the hot lights, as she had done so often during her career, and waited for the makeup man to finish his last-minute touches. Her hands lay calmly in her lap.

A young man who introduced himself as the fictional businessman to be interviewed sat beside her. He looked tired and just a little bit surly. But Amelia was unflustered. It all felt so right.

The interview began, and for an instant she wished Scott was there to watch. But then she realized that had he been there it might have caused a strain. He would have seen her do her best work ever and he would have known that nothing could keep her from her job. She was a tough and demanding interviewer. Nothing escaped her notice. On and on she went, ending the interview exactly fifiteen minutes after it had begun.

Scott would have seen Amelia thanking the young man, who left the stage shaking his head. Yes, Scott would have seen that she was brilliant, but he would also have seen those in the studio look at one another with slightly puzzled eyes. And he alone would have understood what that meant for Amelia Jenkins.

But he wasn't there. And the only way he had of knowing what transpired during that morning was what Amelia told him when she flew into the hotel room, her eyes sparkling with happiness and confidence.

"I was brilliant. I can feel it, Scott," she said before she even kissed him hello. "It's going to be all right. I can feel it. I just know this job is in the bag!"

"That's great, honey," Scott said, forcing a bright smile to his lips though his heart was sinking. "I knew you'd do well. But did someone say something to give you the impression that you've got the job? That woman . . . what's her name?"

"Jan Dickerson. No, not really. But she's so warm toward me. And she thanked me so profusely. I'm just sure that it's going to be all right." Amelia rushed on as she peeled her jacket from her body and slipped out of her shoes. "Oh, God, look at the time. I didn't realize. I walked back and stopped in a few stores. I just felt such abandon, like the feeling you get after you finish a test in school. Anyway, I'm going to take a hot bath and—"

"Whoa, my dear," Scott said, throwing his legs over the side of the bed and going to her. He wrapped his hands around her shoulders and pulled her toward him, kissing her deeply. But Amelia pulled back. Not in anger, but in surprise.

"Scott," she said, squirming from his embrace, "what are you doing?"

"What does if feel like?"

"You know what I mean!" Amelia retorted. "The day isn't done. There's still the party this evening, and it starts early. I've got a ton of things to do."

"Like what? Improve on perfection?" he shot back sarcastically.

"Don't be absurd. I just want to rest, take a bath, take my time getting ready. You can understand that." She moved away from him, unclipping the hammered-gold earrings she wore and placing them on the bureau. She didn't want to look at him. There was a tightness in her that couldn't be assuaged by a caress or a kiss. She didn't want it to be loved away. She had to be single-minded now, ready for anything at that party. Scott would just have to understand.

"I know a great way to relax." Scott attempted to approach her again, running his hands through her hair as he spoke, but she escaped him once more.

"Look, Scott, you know I love you, but this is important. We have to do this my way. It's the only way I can deal with it. I don't need to be made love to. I need to keep my mind on the right track. Don't you see?" She was getting tired of explaining. He should simply accept what she was saying and leave it at that. She felt like an animal ready to spring, taut and graceful and indestructible. And her mate would have to wait until she was ready to go to him again.

"I see." He turned away angrily and sat down hard on the bed. "What you mean is I'm a nice diversion, but when things get hot you don't need me around."

"I wouldn't go that far," Amelia answered, her patience waning. This was so important to her. She thought he knew that, but obviously he became testy when things didn't go his way. Well, if he wanted to be childish, she wanted no part of it. "I'm just telling you how things have to be right now."

"And what about a year from now?" Scott asked coldly. "If you're on a big story and I fly across the country to see you, will it be the same thing? 'Sorry, buster, but I've got other things on my mind'?"

"Scott, this is ridiculous. Of course it won't be that way. I'll have the job then and—" Amelia started to unzip her skirt and hesitated. Why make things worse? She would undress in the bathroom. So she gathered up her cosmetics and turned toward him.

"And then you'll be worried about the interview. Look, Amelia, I've been waiting for you all morning. It's almost two o'clock. The party isn't until six. We have plenty of time. I know you're keyed up—"

"I'm not keyed up. Well, yes, I am. But I'm not so out of it that I don't know what I'm saying. Believe me, I know what I need to do in situations like this.

And what I need is a hot bath, so if you'll excuse me..."

"No, I won't. You asked me here to be with you, then you changed your mind. Then when I showed up last night you seemed happy to see me. Was I mistaken? Did you want me to be with you, or just on your arm so that you have someone to squire you around at this shindig?"

"Scott! Of course I want you here with me, but I knew how things would work out and that's why I thought it would have been better if you didn't come. And that last crack was hitting below the belt."

"Was it? Being with you doesn't mean sitting around this room while you're psyching yourself up. It means holding you and loving you and encouraging you and—"

"Then encourage me with your acceptance of what I am and how I am!" Amelia snapped. She was tired. The interview had taken more out of her than she had realized. At that moment she couldn't remember why she loved him, even though she knew in her heart that she did. But she couldn't conjure up the feelings of tenderness that had made her wonder if she even wanted to try to get the job on *Meet America*. He still could be quite the child. Things weren't going his way and he didn't like it.

"I don't think I can do that, Amelia. This is supposed to be a give-and-take situation here."

"Well, if you don't like it, then maybe you'd like to make other arrangements." She shot back words as cold as a bullet from a gun.

"Maybe I would," Scott said, glaring at her.

At a loss, Amelia felt her face flush with anger. Her eyes bored into him, but he didn't flinch under her gaze. How could she have ever thought this was a man she might spend her life with?

"Well, you decide what's right for you, Scott. I've got a date with a warm bath." Amelia hesitated a moment before turning toward the bathroom. She hoped, half expected, that he would stop her with an apology. But when he didn't, she shut the door behind her and ran the water, watching the bubbles rise higher and higher.

She was aware of his movements in the other room. He was probably wondering what to do. Amelia knew she had hurt his pride. Well, he had to realize that she had certain ways of getting her through the demands of her profession.

She undressed quickly and stepped into the steaming water. Carefully, she eased herself back until her head rested on the tub edge. She waited for a moment, waited for the tension to ease from her shoulder blades, though she knew it wouldn't. She closed her eyes, knowing that when she stepped from the bath she would go and apologize to Scott. He was right, in a sense; she had given him every reason to believe she was happy he had come. They would talk when she was done.

But just as she began to soap her long, lithe body she heard the door slam and felt her heart lurch. He was angrier than she had realized. Well, he had probably gone to the bar for a drink. He needed to settle down. He did it his way, she hers. There was a compromise point there. He would understand.

Fifteen minutes later she toweled herself and carefully applied her makeup. She felt wonderful, and the tension and excitement had eased a bit. She was ready to meet Scott halfway.

Opening the door, wrapped in her silk kimono, a smile on her face, she stepped into the elegant bedroom. But it was empty. He hadn't returned. She looked at the clock. He had only been gone a half hour. Picking up her nail polish, Amelia sat on the edge of the bed and looked around as she shook it. It was then that she noticed the armoire doors were open. It was then that she realized what had happened.

Slowly she rose from the bed and opened the closet door wider. Her clothes still hung neatly on the left, but the right side was empty. Scott was gone. She knew even then that he was on his way home to the beach, to the quiet way of his life.

She stood for a long while listening to the silence of the room, the click of the digital clock as it marked the minutes. Finally she moved back to the bed and lay down upon it. Was it over just like this? Was this how easily he could leave her? Then so be it.

Amelia buried her face in the pillow. She knew how strong she was. She didn't need Scott Alexander for the party or for her life. She loved him, admired him, but she didn't need him to live. That she did very well on her own. And as she realized that she was left with what was truly important—the dream job of a lifetime—she also realized that the pillow she lay on was wet with her own tears.

Chapter Ten

Amelia steeled herself, stopping momentarily before
she entered the building. She had been back at the
studio for four days and still no word from Jan Dickerson or Scott Alexander. Doing her regular show with
Tom hovering over her, an unasked question in his
eyes, was getting to be too much. Answering everyone's questions about her "vacation" added to the
problem and became almost more than she could bear.
She felt as though she were trying to hang on to a lover
whom she had long since ceased to love but still respected.

Amelia glanced at her watch. She was half an hour
late, but this morning it didn't really bother her. The
reason for her tardiness was nothing she could put her
finger on. She had slowly been unpacking for the last
few days, taking out of boxes things that she knew she
would need until the call from New York came. But
she hadn't stayed up late. She was well rested. Still, she
slept as though she was exhausted.

While she wouldn't admit it to herself, she carried
the remembrance of Scott's leaving like a bruise. And
with every box she unpacked she saw the flower, dried
inside, and she thought of him. They had parted for

good, but everywhere something he had done or some word he had said was waiting to be remembered. And if she was late because of a heavy heart she didn't realize it. She had, after all, given the station six years of nonstop work. Now, as she was getting ready to depart, she felt she could ease up a little bit. Her work wasn't suffering and a few people had actually told her that it was a good thing she was slowing down.

Knowing she could stave off the inevitable no longer, Amelia pushed open the doors to the building and walked through the lobby to the elevators, thinking all the while of Scott. As usual, the small, nagging wondering stayed with her. She couldn't help but think of what he was doing, of whether he was thinking about her. But there was no one to ask. Only Sailor. And she knew that would be like coming up against a stone wall. She had to make herself believe that she and Scott were no longer together. She had to remember the reason for it. But as the days had dragged on with no word from New York, those reasons became more and more obscured.

That morning she forced herself to consider her house, rather than Scott. It pleased her to no end that all her furniture had fit perfectly into the house, and more than once she found herself looking out at the ocean, realizing how much she would miss it.

Her mother had visited and had seen the look in her daughter's eyes, but she never discussed the impending move. Martha neither encouraged nor discouraged her regarding the outcome of the interview in New York. She was interested and listened to Amelia's stories with attention. But, inevitably, all she said was "What will be, will be." Amelia supposed this was her mother's way of dealing with the fact that she might not be near her daughter too much longer. It never crossed Amelia's mind that Martha was trying to save her from her own disappointment if the job didn't come through.

The elevator doors opened and she started to step through them before she realized that there were people who wanted to get out. Stepping back, Amelia realized how absentminded she had become as she waited for news. New York and *Meet America* seemed to be on her mind when Scott wasn't.

The elevator was now free, and Amelia stepped into it. Pressing seven, she leaned back against the wall and watched the numbers light up as the elevator rose. The doors opened and she stepped out. Tom was passing by with a cup of coffee.

"That looks good," Amelia said, surprising him.

"Amelia." Tom put his other hand around the cup. "You shouldn't do that to a man who's half awake and carrying a very hot cup of coffee. I have a hard enough time walking and talking at the same time, not to mention balancing!"

"Come on, Tom. I've seen you do sixteen things at once," Amelia joked as she fell into step beside him. Together they stopped at the reception desk.

"One for Tom. Three for Amelia," the receptionist said as she handed each of them their messages. There was silence for an instant as they looked at the small pieces of paper.

"My insurance man," Tom said, his lips curling into a despairing smile. "I'll bet my rates went up because of that ticket I got when—"

He never finished his sentence. Instead, he looked up and saw Amelia's face drain of all color, then blossom again with a rosiness that lit up the reception area.

"Is that it?" he whispered, coming close to her and turning his back to the woman at the desk.

"Yes," she breathed. Then she quickly took his arm and steered him through the double glass doors, almost running to her office. "Do you want to stick around while I call?"

"God, Amelia, I don't know if I could take the tension." Tom continued to whisper despite the fact that they were safely in her office behind closed doors. "Do you want me to?"

"Yes, of course. You're the one who got me into this, so you should be the first one to congratulate me, right?" Amelia almost giggled with excitement.

"Or hold you up if you didn't get it," Tom warned. He flopped into a chair and sipped his coffee while he watched her dial New York.

The confidence she had exuded since her return had not escaped him, and he was worried. Not that Amelia Jenkins didn't have every reason to feel confident in herself. But this new manner bespoke of more than the simple acknowledgement that she had done the best she could. Amelia was sure she was going to be the next host of *Meet America*.

Perhaps it was because everything else was going so well for her. The house went through escrow without a hitch. Then there was Scott Alexander. Tom fought the disappointment that still welled in him when he thought of Amelia's lover. He had hoped he would be able to occupy that place in her heart. But he wasn't one to dwell on what couldn't be, so he wished them both well. Yet he was sure that relationship had added to her feelings of invincibility. That and the fact that

Amelia believed if you worked hard enough for something there was an unspoken guarantee that it was yours. It was funny, though; Amelia hadn't spoken of Alexander in the past four days. Tom began to wonder if maybe the Windsurfer king was out of the picture.

"It's ringing." Amelia broke into his thoughts, covering the mouthpiece of the telephone with her hand. Tom smiled at her and gripped his coffee mug tightly as he listened.

"Jan," Amelia said cheerily, grinning despite the fact that the other woman couldn't see her, "Amelia Jenkins returning your call."

She listened, then told the woman on the other end that she was fine and had had a wonderful trip back to L.A. Tom felt his gut tighten. Small talk. It wasn't a good sign.

"Jan, I can't help it, I'm dying to know. Should I start looking for an apartment in New York?" Tom raised his eyes to the ceiling. Amelia had lost something since this whole thing started. She had lost her perspective. The reporter he had known and loved wouldn't have been so blatant.

He looked back in time to see Amelia's hand start shaking. The action was so slight he might not have noticed it, except he had been unable to look at her crestfallen face. If a person could look devastated, Amelia Jenkins did. Tom felt the color rise to his own cheeks as her color drained away. His embarrassment was for both of them. He regretted seeing her in such a state. The intimacy the situation created was almost unbearable. He knew she would be unable to look him in the eye, and his feelings were borne out when he heard her thank the woman in New York and gently replace the receiver. The quiet in the office was all-encompassing.

"I didn't get it," she said softly, as she clasped her hands in front of her on the desk and looked at them.

Tom rose, saying nothing, and moved around the desk. Carefully he bent down and kissed the top of her head, squeezed her shoulder and quietly left her alone. When he came back an hour later to tell her the crew was ready to go, he found that she had gone home sick. He was unable to reach her at her house and, after a while, he decided that she just needed to be alone.

Tom had been right. Amelia couldn't believe what she had heard. Oh, she could believe that she didn't get the job. But she couldn't understand the reason she didn't get it. It was beyond her to understand their reasoning. Jan Dickerson had said she was... was too... Even now she couldn't bring herself to say the words, even in her mind.

It was unthinkable, so Amelia knew she needed to shut off. She had to run from the embarrassment of having failed, run from the reason why. It was a slap in the face, even though Jan had couched the rejection in the most professional and tactful way.

The receptionist had accepted without a second thought her explanation of not feeling well. Amelia did look drawn and pale. Diane, even from her seat behind the high desk, could see tears welling in Amelia's blue eyes. It was a sure sign of the flu, Diane thought, and was glad Amelia was taking her germs home.

But it wasn't home that Amelia fled to. The confines of her cheery, wonderful little house would have made the pain worse. Instead, Amelia hurried to her car, head down, shoulders hunched. She didn't want anyone to recognize her; she had no desire to even attempt a happy hello.

She slid behind the wheel of her silver Toyota, slammed the door and lay her head back on the headrest, forcing the tears back, so far back that she knew if she didn't cry now she never would again. Then, sitting up, she started the engine, backed out and drove away. Her mind was on hold, she steered the car as if on automatic pilot and she didn't allow herself one moment to think of everything she had lost. Not the job, not Scott.

As she sat in her car overlooking a bluff in Palos Verdes, where she had finally stopped, she let her mind rest. Her eyes looked nowhere in particular, despite the fact that she had before her one of the most spectacular views in all of the South Bay. Stretching below her were the sea and jagged rocks slowly melding into laces of sandy beach and then into the man-made hills and valleys of houses and high-rise apartment buildings. Like the healing of a wound, the unraveling of her mind was tentative. It had sealed over and now was just beginning to allow the healing. But that process was painful and Amelia let it begin bit by bit, knowing even then she would have to have help.

Somewhere in that mishmash of architecture was her home. In Redondo Beach was the little house that she had claimed and then convinced herself she would be leaving for New York. There was Scott's plant and the little room in the back. And farther, much farther away, was the freeway, a ribbon of asphalt that eventually led to her mother's house.

There were so many choices. Scott, her mother, Tom or simply herself. Where would she go with this defeat? At whose feet would she lay it? How could she face anyone else when she could hardly stand to be alone with herself? Certainly not Scott. Though she knew he wouldn't gloat, there would be a victory of sorts for him in her loss. And he had made it clear after all these days that he could exist very well without her.

God, she couldn't understand how this could happen! She had worked her tail off for this opportunity. Her clothes had been right, her interview impeccable. She had made a wonderful impression at the cocktail party, even Jan had said so. But they had found her too... intense. Oh, that word! It was like a wrecking ball in her mind. With one fell swoop that word had simply obliterated all that she had built up.

Intense! Suddenly the anger exploded in her brain. What did they want? Some cutie who could read off idiot cards? Or someone like her who would dig and dig until the story came to fruition?

There were no answers. She would have to go over and over the interviews a hundred times and sort it all out. What had Jan said?

We are a family show. We give news for living. News for living. Amelia mulled this over for a moment. They had decided on someone they felt exuded not only professionalism but also empathy. Empathy. With what? For whom? She empathized with people when she did a story. She could understand almost every situation, but she was a reporter. It wasn't her job to empathize with anyone on camera. That's what made her what she was: a reporter who really knew how to do her job. Well, if they wanted entertainment, then they had been barking up the wrong tree. Damn! It was all so unfair.

Amelia reached for the key in the ignition. She had been sitting alone too long. There was one person who would understand. She was going to see her mother.

As she drove down the winding streets of the Palos Verdes hills, past the mansions with their red tile roofs, and down into Redondo, Amelia considered stopping to see Scott. The temptation was great. But she couldn't be sure that he would welcome her with open arms and she needed and wanted to be held by him. She didn't want to think that there would be pity or reprimand in that embrace. No, she wouldn't, couldn't, see Scott now. Not until she had reconciled herself to the idea that she would not be the anchor on *Meet America*. Then, perhaps, she would go to him, tell him that they had turned her down. At least she would have her pride if she was the one to let him know that it hadn't worked out. Then they could decide what to do, if anything.

Amelia drove faster, flying over the freeway, fighting back the tears that once again stung her eyes. And with each tear that escaped to course down her cheeks she wished that she could turn around and run to Scott. She wanted to throw herself into his arms, but she couldn't. It would be humiliating.

By the time she reached her mother's apartment, Amelia had dried her eyes and pulled her shoulders straight. She sniffled. Her head felt as bloated as it did at the height of a head cold. Her eyes were small and red-rimmed. Amelia looked into the rearview mirror. Her mascara had run. And the advertisement said it was waterproof! She chuckled lamely. It couldn't be that bad if she was thinking about mascara ads. But it *was* that bad.

She swung her legs out of the car and closed the door behind her. Amelia pulled on her suit jacket. Her mother would be disappointed if she looked too terrible. After all, Martha always told her everything happened for the best. She would have to be strong. The door of the apartment opened before Amelia rang the bell.

"*Liebchen*, what are you doing here at this time of the day?" Her mother stepped out of the door, her brow knit with worry.

"What, Mom?" Amelia countered, trying to keep the quiver from her voice. "I need a special time to come see my own mother?"

"No, of course not. It's just so unlike you to leave work. Everyone knows the world would have to come to an end for you to take off work."

"Is that what everyone knows?" Amelia asked as she walked past her mother and sat down.

She looked around. Furniture polish and glass wax were set out on the coffee table. The vacuum was in the corner. The house was spotless.

"I just started cleaning, Amelia." Martha said, in apology for what she considered to be the messy state of her house. Amelia's laugh was tired.

"Nothing ever changes, does it, Mom?" Amelia said, more to herself than to the woman who sat opposite her.

"Some things do," her mother answered quietly. "Like you. You've changed. I've seen it."

"Now, how would you know? I've hardly seen you in the last two months, what with all your committees and Mr. Lipencott and my work and the—" She stopped just before she mentioned New York, but her mother was wise and could read her daughter like a book.

"And the trip to New York and your new young man. Oh, I know, Amelia, you only mentioned him to me once or twice, but that's more often than you've ever mentioned any man. And as for your interview, you haven't mentioned that at all. So it's one or the other that makes your face look like uncooked dough. Your young man or the job in New York. Which is it?"

Amelia slumped back in the couch. How easily she was read by this uncanny woman.

"Both, I think, Mom," Amelia began. "I didn't get the job and Scott, well, that's a long story. But suffice it to say that he hasn't been in the picture for a while and I don't think he's poised to reenter. And you won't believe what they told me when they called...."

Amelia began to talk and talk and talk. She rose and paced the living room; she perched on top of the dining room table. She became angry, sad, confused, and her mother listened without saying a word. Yet Martha did notice that the color was coming back to her daughter's cheeks, her eyes were flashing. Soon Amelia herself would know it was not the end of the world.

"I mean, I just don't understand it. I've worked all my life for this. I put my heart and soul into it and all they could see was that I was too intense. I have feelings just like everyone else but I know where they belong. Just because I don't wear my emotions on my sleeve like half the bleeding-heart reporters...."

Amelia took a deep, trembling breath. There was nothing else to say, yet she felt the need to speak, defend herself, hear her own voice. She was tired but felt impelled to go on, especially when the silence in the room threatened to crack into a million pieces. Finally, she looked directly at her mother for the first time. Surprisingly, Martha's head was bowed, and Amelia immediately felt as though she had let her mother down more than herself.

"Mom, I'm so sorry. After you worked so hard to get me started. I didn't mean to disappoint you."

"Amelia." Her mother finally raised her head and looked into her daughter's eyes. Amelia was taken aback. There was such pain in Martha's beautiful eyes that she could hardly look into them. They seemed to be a reflection of her own but for a much different, more personal reason. "Amelia, did I go so wrong when I raised you? How could you think that I would be disappointed if you didn't get this job? Don't you dare apologize to me for not getting a job. Because that's all it is. A job, a position, something to pass the time if you don't enjoy it, something to do well if you do, something that must be done if you have to. Of course, we have to work. That's what we were put on this good earth for, otherwise we just grow old. But there is so much in life. How did I teach you that the whole world revolved around something like that?" Martha sighed.

"You sound as as though you've lost everything you are because they don't want you for this one job. Listen to yourself. I know it hurts to be turned away after you've done your best. But things happen because they're meant to happen. Maybe you were meant to stay right here and work at the station. Maybe you're meant to marry your young man."

"But, Mom, you always worked so hard and you didn't need to," Amelia objected. Confused now by what her mother was saying, she slid from the table and knelt by her mother's chair. "Weren't you the one who asked what you would do if you didn't work? Didn't you say all those years that whatever one did it had to be one's best?"

"Of course!" Martha said, leaning forward to grasp her daughter's hands in her own. "But what would you have me say? That I wanted to simply sit back and do nothing! Your father left us some money, but not enough for your college. I had to work that hard so that you could be everything you were meant to be. Without him, I didn't want to have the time to think of how it could have been. When he died, my life seemed over. But I enjoyed what I did and I filled my life with love for you." Martha sat back, sighed and looked carefully at her daughter.

"Amelia, with your father I had such joy. We worked so that we could have a good life here in America. We worked so that we could make something better of ourselves because the opportunity was here. But what was most important was that we loved each other and you. That love was worth more to us than anything we owned. If we had lost everything, the modest things we had gained, we would have worked to gain them again. But without the love it all would have been meaningless." Martha held up her hands as though to reach out to Amelia but then lowered them again without a touch. She feared that any contact might make her next words less forceful, and there was so much she had to make Amelia understand.

"Perhaps I didn't speak enough about love and respect and the part it should play in your life. But, Amelia, that was because I thought you understood that. You know, it was never my way to speak of emotions. Not the hardships before we came here and not the joys once we were established. I suppose that's partly because of the way I am, but it's also because I thought the happiness was self-evident. But then, you were such a little girl when your father died. So small, really. Eleven is not a woman. It is still a child. How could you know what I carried in my heart? You never asked and I never offered to share so much of that with you. I think I just assumed that as you grew you would understand. You seemed to understand so many things."

Amelia hung her head, not because she heard a reprimand in her mother's voice but because she had been so wrong about the lesson she thought her mother was teaching her. All these years wasted. No. She had no regrets or personal recriminations. She had gained things she wanted and needed to make her the full woman that she was.

Certainly, before she met Scott she had been, perhaps, too single-minded. Work was everything, and nothing—no one—stood in her way. They still didn't. She had gone after that job on *Meet America* the same way she tackled a good story in Los Angeles. This time it didn't work out.

The difference was that because she had felt sorry for herself and come to her mother, she found that she was loved not because of what she accomplished or how hard she worked. She was loved as a daughter and a person. In and of herself. Scott had been trying to tell her the same thing, but events had clouded her vision. She was the one who had not understood.

Amelia looked up into her mother's deep blue eyes and realized that it was this woman who would allow her to go to Scott with open arms. Disappointed professionally, of course, but willing to accept his love if he would still give it. Because she knew now that love was what mattered the most. She had fought with the idea too long. She had shoved that love aside as she pursued the job of her dreams. Yet, all the while it had been there, steadfast, waiting for her no matter what the outcome of the interview. Why, even Jan Dickerson had seen what was lacking in her. She had called her intense. A good word. But Jan was a new person in her life and Amelia hadn't truly understood what the woman had been saying. What she had needed was to go to her mother as a little girl with a hurt and listen with an open heart. That state of mind had allowed her to open her heart enough to understand fully the one last lesson from her mother. And now she knew where she must go.

"Amelia, I'm so sorry..." Martha began, but then she smiled when she saw her daughter's face.

"No, Mom, I am. I guess I just didn't listen hard enough when I was young. But you can teach an old dog new tricks, and I intend to prove that to someone."

"That's good, Amelia," her mother said gently, a world of meaning in the small word. "I never wanted to push you. But I always believed you had the kind of heart that needed to love *and* the kind of mind that needed to be challenged. I only ask one thing." Amelia raised an eyebrow in question. "May I meet your Scott before you marry him?"

"Is it that evident?" Amelia laughed. The hurt was already healing. There would be no scar, Amelia could feel it.

"You think after all these years I don't recognize that determined gleam in your eye?" Martha laughed back, happy now that her daughter's determination was directed toward a warm, living human being.

"Then I guess I better let him know. I think he believes Amelia Jenkins is out of his life for good, except on prime-time television. And I'm not even sure he watches television. He's going to be very surprised."

"And disappointed?" Martha queried, wanting to know about this man who had so obviously captured her daughter's heart.

"No, Mom," Amelia answered softly, thinking of Scott, knowing his reaction. "He will be disappointed for me, that I know. But then, that's half the reason I love him. He never tried to push me one way or another. I'll admit I frustrated him, angered him, with this work thing, but I don't think he ever gave up. At least I hope he didn't. I guess that in some ways we're very much alike. It's just that his goals were a little more all-encompassing than mine."

Amelia picked up her purse from the couch and allowed herself to feel the warmth in her mother's apartment. Funny, she had never picked up on it before. The caring and wisdom of the woman who lived there was almost palpable. Amelia hoped a little bit of it had rubbed off on her. She straightened her shoulders, shaking off the nagging worry that perhaps Scott wasn't waiting for her. Perhaps his frustration in New York and the lapse in time had made him indifferent. Well, if it had, she would simply have to change his mind. This time she wouldn't lose.

"Thanks, Mom." She retraced her steps and kissed her mother's cheek, then opened the door and left without another word.

Martha Jenkins sat for a long while, dust cloth in hand, and stared at the door, a small smile on her lips. It wasn't her way to speak so openly with her daughter. But then, it hadn't proved to be such a mistake all these years. After all, Amelia had learned the most prized lesson in the world with very little help from her.

Martha picked up her husband's photo, which sat on the occasional table, and felt the love of so many years ago return in force.

"She is a beautiful young woman, Henry," she whispered, "and soon there will be beautiful little ones all around."

Sighing, she put down the picture and stood up to resume her cleaning. Then, thinking better of it, she put away the polishes and waxes, sat down and turned on a game show.

"Why not?" she mused aloud. "If there are going to be grandchildren, I don't want them to misunderstand me, too."

She laughed a little to herself, very pleased with the way life had of turning itself around when you least expected it.

AMELIA'S CAR FLEW down the freeway. Rush hour was over and the lunchtime traffic had not yet begun. It was that magical half hour in Los Angeles when one could even drive past the airport off ramps without slowing down. But as fast as her car moved, Amelia's heart flew before her. She would not allow herself to imagine that Scott would not be thrilled to see her. There was a newness, an excitement, in her that he would not fail to see. She would tell him she loved him before she even told him about New York. Everything would be fine.

As she exited the freeway and slowed down on the surface streets of Redondo Beach, every stoplight flashed green. There was nothing to impede her progress. It was a sign from heaven. When the streetlights worked so well, everything else just had to fall into place.

Slowing now to a crawl, Amelia picked the pins from her chignon and let her long, long hair cascade over her shoulders and down her back. She shook out the confining feeling just as she spotted a parking space and pulled the little car to a stop.

She tore off her jacket and flung it into the back of the car. She felt free and she wanted to look that way for him...for Scott...for her love. Amelia's heels clicked on the worn and cracked bike path that paralleled the sand. She passed two apartment buildings and a hamburger stand and finally stood in front of the door that led to Scott.

Without hesitation, she pushed it open and stepped inside. The rock music was blaring from the sound system, workmen were bent over their tasks and the smell of resin was heavy in the air. Amelia took it all in, breathing deeply, loving every nuance of the place. This was home, she now knew. It was a part of Scott and she would love it and care for it as he did for her and her work. A man with an extremely long mustache looked up and smiled. Amelia returned the greeting without hesitation, then her eyes scanned the large room.

Scott was nowhere to be seen. He was probably in his makeshift apartment in the back. She moved with only one thought in her mind: Scott's arms around her. Amelia ignored the questioning glances. She turned the corner and threw open the door.

"Scott! Scott!" she called breathlessly. Her cheeks were flushed; her chest heaved with the excitement she felt as she looked expectantly around the room. It seemed empty, and Amelia felt deflated until she heard a sound from the kitchen. Her head whipped toward the sound, a smile on her face, but instead of meeting Scott's loving eyes she discovered that it was Sailor who rounded the corner and stood lounging against the partition between the two rooms.

"Oh...Sailor," Amelia stammered, feeling the old curiosity and discomfort return as she looked away from him but continued to speak. "I was looking for Scott. When will he be back?"

"Don't know," the long-haired giant of a man answered as he sipped on a beer. He seemed more predatory than Amelia had remembered.

"Do you know where he went?" Amelia asked, wishing herself away from the man as soon as possible.

"Yeah" was all he said, and Amelia felt anger replacing her curiosity. But then, when she looked back at him ready to demand an answer, she saw a softness in his face that had never been there before.

"Well," she said biting back the snap in her voice, "would you mind telling me where he is, or am I going to have to comb all of Redondo Beach to find him?"

"That's all I wanted to know...Amelia," Sailor said as he walked toward her with a grin on his face.

"What?" she responded, still wary of this change in him.

"I wanted to know that you really wanted to find him because you wanted to be with him and not because you wanted him to commiserate with you because you didn't get that fancy job in New York." He plopped his large frame on the sofa and smiled at her. Instinctively, Amelia was drawn toward him. She sat on the edge of the chair next to him.

"How did you know about that?" she asked cautiously.

"Scott called your office today. He's been miserable since you two haven't talked. That guy you work with told him about it and—"

"Tom?" Amelia interjected.

"Yeah. Anyway, he thought you might need him. I just couldn't figure out why he'd want to get jerked around again, so I tried to stop him. But—" Sailor shrugged his massive, hairy shoulders and pushed back the sweatband wrapped around his head. "But he went anyway. Doesn't surprise me."

Amelia thought for a second, then she snapped her eyes back to Sailor. "What do you mean 'jerked around again'?"

"Look, it wasn't anything Scott said, if that's what you think. He's not like that. He and I go back a long way. He's a real gentleman, a real friend." Sailor took a sip of his beer. His face had become closed again...almost. Then he looked back at Amelia, leaned forward and put his elbows on his knees.

"The reason I knew he was getting jerked around was because I've been there, lady. You and I, well, four years ago we would have been two of a kind. Only I wasn't as lucky as you. I had to find out the hard way what was right and what wasn't. You know, what was important in life."

"And you don't think I found out the hard way? I just lost a spot on the highest-rated national news show in the country," Amelia objected.

"You don't know what hard is," Sailor shot back as he rose from his seat and paced the room, stopping, then turning back to her.

"Then why don't you tell me about it? Why don't you tell me your hard-luck story, mister? Is it Vietnam?" Amelia snapped. "Scott went through Vietnam and he made out just fine. Or was it something a little more esoteric, such as that you couldn't cut it in the business world and you've been carrying a chip on your shoulder ever since?"

"Okay," Sailor said, his face serious, his eyes glistening, "I deserved that. I haven't exactly treated you like a human being. I'll grant you that. And since it seems that you and Scott may have a future after all, I guess we better get used to each other.

"To answer your question, I made it through Vietnam all right. And I made a big splash in the business world, too. No chip on my shoulder there. I was headed straight for director of marketing at Proctor and Gamble. A big job. Paid a lot of money. Security for my family..."

Amelia raised an eyebrow and sat back in the chair.

"Oh, sure, family and everything. Even a station wagon so we could take the dog with us when we went on picnics. Only we never did." Sailor's breath was shallow, shaking with wavering sighs as he pulled on his long, kinky hair. "Anyway, the job. That was the thing. Carol, that was my wife, she would be happy if the checking account was always full. And Nicki, my kid, he just needed the best schools. And me, I needed the prestige. I never said so. Not once. I worked my tail off.

"Then Nicki got sick. Carol begged me to stay home. I mean begged. But I had to go to Minnesota for a big meeting. 'Take Nicki to the doctor and call me,' I said. Then I got in the car and went to the airport. Well, I got busy. I tried to call her once but the line was busy. I forgot. I had a presentation to make.

"Well, I got home. Real full of myself. Everything went great. I got home ready to tell Carol we were moving to a great new house. I got a promotion and a raise. I got home and no one was there. The phone rang. It was my mother-in-law. Nicki was in intensive care...meningitis. He died four days later. And...the rest is..." Sailor turned away from her, and Amelia sat in silence, feeling the weight of his story pulling her down and down.

Then, suddenly, she felt as though she were glowing with a light everyone could see. Yes, his story was tragic. But hers wouldn't be. She knew now what her priorities should be, would be. She wouldn't make the mistake he had.

"God, I haven't talked that much in ten years." Sailor broke into her thoughts, and she raised her eyes in time to see his hand wiping his eyes. "Anyway, I don't want that to happen to Scott. I can tell you, it ticked me off when he started fallin' for you. I tried to tell him to forget it but, lady, you had your hooks in whether you knew it or not. Whether you cared or not."

"Sailor, I do care. What happened wasn't your fault." Amelia fought the urge to go to him. "Sometimes we just get caught up in what we think life is supposed to be like. What you did wasn't intentional.

It was..." Amelia hesitated. There was no word that could describe what had happened to him and his family. "Well, it won't happen to me and Scott. I promise you, Sailor. I promise not to hurt him. I'm not a changed woman. I still want all those things you did. But not at the expense of him or his love. You have to believe me."

"Funny thing, I do. If I hadn't seen your face when you burst in here, maybe I wouldn't. But I did see it. And I believe you. But one thing: you mess up and I'm personally coming after you." Sailor grinned, the brightness of the tears in his eyes replaced with the glow of friendship. Amelia smiled back.

"Thanks, Sailor. I'll need someone to keep me on the straight and narrow," she answered softly. They were silent for a moment, then she spoke. "Sailor? Now will you tell me where he went?"

First he looked at her blankly, then his eyes crinkled and he threw back his head and laughed. It was then, listening to the purity of that sound, that Amelia could imagine him in a business suit, at a meeting, playing the games. But she could no more envision that as a lifelong commitment for him than she could for herself.

"Sure thing, Amelia. He's at your place. Probably sitting on the stoop and planning to stay there until doomsday."

"Thanks, Sailor," Amelia whispered. She rose and went to him. On tiptoe she kissed his rough cheek. "And thanks for filling me in. I'm sorry about your family. But I'm not sorry it led you to Scott. I'm glad you're his friend. I hope you'll be mine."

"You got it, lady." Sailor smiled down at her. "Now get out of here. I don't want him to catch cold waiting for you."

Without another word Amelia turned and raced out the door. Scott was waiting for her. He wanted her. It was all she needed to know.

Leaving the car where it was, she ripped the high-heeled shoes from her feet and rushed down the bike path and up the steep steps to the street. Her hair flowed behind her and her cheeks were flushed with exertion by the time her house came into view. She quickly replaced her shoes and slowed her pace so that by the time she turned up the walk she looked poised, her face serious and unreadable.

Scott looked up as she approached and threw the rose he was holding into the flowerbed. He brushed his hands together and watched her closely; then he turned away as she sat down beside him. They were so close Amelia almost felt as though she were touching him. How she longed to reach out and feel the firm muscles of his arm, the warmth of his lips—but she didn't. There was too much to say.

"I saw Sailor," Amelia began. All the hours they had been apart rushed over her, making her realize what she almost lost.

"Then you know I know," Scott answered, tentatively.

"Yes. I also know about Sailor. And there's something he knows that you should."

Scott chuckled sadly. He knew what was coming.

"We sound like two kids trying to keep a secret and wanting to tell." He picked up the flower again and moved off the step. Then he turned toward her. "Amelia, I'm sorry about the job. Really I am. I'm sorry about that dumb fight we had. I'm sorry I acted like such a jerk and didn't call you. I'm sorry Sailor's been so mean to you. But can't we take it all back? Start again? Amelia, don't tell me it's over. Don't tell me that. I couldn't accept it. Whether you know it or not, you need me and I need—"

Amelia jumped from her seat on the brick steps and rushed to him, her hand outstretched. Gently she placed it over his lips to silence him.

"And you need me. I know that. Sailor and I discussed it at length. That was exactly what I was coming to tell you. Don't worry about that job. There will be others, I won't lie to you, but they'll be right here. Here, where we can look out the window at night and see the open channel to the ocean. Here, where the sailing will be clear because we'll be together. Here, Scott."

Slowly, she removed her fingertips from his lips and leaned into him. He met her halfway and their kiss sealed a bargain that would never need to be spoken of again. The sea breeze blew against Amelia's back, prodding her to put her arms around Scott's narrow waist, and she knew she was home, where she should be. Never again would there be a temptation to take her from his arms.

He pulled her closer and buried his face in her hair. He understood now how it was possible to want something so badly you were willing to give up everything else in the world. And what he wanted was right there in his arms.

AMELIA'S LOG

March 3, 1988

Henry, it seems I hardly have time to write in my journal anymore! Life has become so hectic. But I love it. It wasn't until you that I felt like writing to a person. I've never been very good at putting my feelings on paper.

It's been such a long year. Such a happy one. Mother, of course, was surprised by it all, but I believe she is awfully pleased with the way things turned out.

You know, I'll have to go back to work in a month or two. But I promise you I'll always be there for you. Someday I hope you read this. Someday I want you to understand all those things I may forget to tell you but want you to know anyway. Like how important love is, and respect. Respect not only for what a person does but for what a person is. I hope that someday you will understand that you must give people the first shot, not things.

I love, you, my darling. You are my pride and joy. Never will I leave you alone to face your problems. I'll always be there to hold you, comfort you, listen to you. I . . .

Oh-oh, your father just brought in the bottle. It's time for your nap. You have no idea how hard it is for me to put you down. Your daddy is already trying to get you on that miniature Windsurfer he made you. I keep telling him it'll be a long time before you're ready for that.

My lovely, beautiful son. I never knew I could love anyone as much as I love your father. But you are a miracle, just as Scott Alexander was a miracle before you.

I adore you both.

Harlequin American Romance

COMING NEXT MONTH

#173 WELCOME THE MORNING by Bobby Hutchinson

To Charlie Cossini and her construction crew, work came first, even when
the job site was in sunny Hawaii. So when surfer playboy Ben Gilmour
wanted her for a playmate, he was forced to devise a plan to lure Charlie
away form her hammers and lathes . . . and into his arms.

#174 THE RUNAWAY HEART by Clare Richmond

Barbara Emerson should have been suspicious of a man as elusive as
private investigator Daniel McGuinn, but instead she hired him to find a
missing person. Sometimes, she thought, you had to gamble on blind
instinct and hope that your instincts were right.

#175 SHOOTING STAR by Barbara Bretton

To staid Bostonian Katie Powers, the advice "Be daring" was difficult to
follow. Until she was stranded in a tiny Japanese village with fellow
American Tom Sagan. Then the unexpected happened: over a spectacular
display of fireworks, Katie fell in love.

#176 THE MALLORY TOUCH by Muriel Jensen

Randy Stanton didn't think much of Matt's famed "Midas touch."
Though he brought prosperity to the quaint Oregon coastal town,
whenever they were together disaster followed close behind. But try as she
might to avoid him, it seemed fate had set them on some kind of bizarre
collision course.

Two exciting genres in one great promotion!

Harlequin Gothic and Regency Romance Specials!

GOTHICS—	REGENCIES—
romance and love growing in the shadow of impending doom...	lighthearted romances set in England's Regency period (1811-1820)

SEPTEMBER TITLES

Gothic Romance	Regency Romance
CASTLE MALICE Marilyn Ross	THE TORPID DUKE Pauline York
LORD OF HIGH CLIFF MANOR Irene M. Pascoe	THE IMPERILED HEIRESS Janice Kay Johnson
THE DEVEREAUX LEGACY Carolyn G. Hart	THE GRAND STYLE Leslie Reid

Be sure not to miss
these new and intriguing stories
...224 pages of wonderful reading!

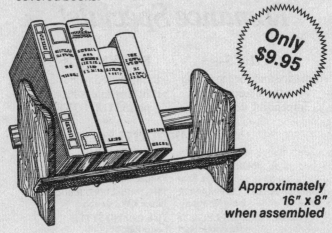

Take 4 books
& a surprise gift
FREE

SPECIAL LIMITED-TIME OFFER

Mail to   **Harlequin Reader Service**®

In the U.S.
901 Fuhrmann Blvd.
P.O. Box 1394
Buffalo, N.Y. 14240-1394

In Canada
P.O. Box 609
Fort Erie, Ontario
L2A 9Z9

YES! Please send me 4 free Harlequin Superromance® novels and my free surprise gift. Then send me 4 brand-new novels every month as they come off the presses. Bill me at the low price of $2.50 each—a 10% saving off the retail price. There are no shipping, handling or other hidden costs. There is no minimum number of books I must purchase. I can always return a shipment and cancel at any time. Even if I never buy another book from Harlequin, the 4 free novels and the surprise gift are mine to keep forever.

154-BPA-BP6F

Name	(PLEASE PRINT)	
Address		Apt. No.
City	State/Prov.	Zip/Postal Code

This offer is limited to one order per household and not valid to present subscribers. Price is subject to change.   DOSR-SUB-1RR

Janet Dailey
Americana

Don't miss a single title from this great collection. The first eight titles have already been published. Complete and mail this coupon today to order books you may have missed.

Harlequin Reader Service

In U.S.A.
901 Fuhrmann Blvd.
P.O. Box 1397
Buffalo, N.Y. 14140

In Canada
P.O. Box 2800
Postal Station A
5170 Yonge Street
Willowdale, Ont. M2N 6J3

Please send me the following titles from the Janet Dailey Americana Collection. I am enclosing a check or money order for $2.75 for each book ordered, plus 75¢ for postage and handling.

_____	ALABAMA	Dangerous Masquerade
_____	ALASKA	Northern Magic
_____	ARIZONA	Sonora Sundown
_____	ARKANSAS	Valley of the Vapours
_____	CALIFORNIA	Fire and Ice
_____	COLORADO	After the Storm
_____	CONNECTICUT	Difficult Decision
_____	DELAWARE	The Matchmakers

Number of titles checked @ $2.75 each = $_____

N.Y. RESIDENTS ADD
   APPROPRIATE SALES TAX $_____

Postage and Handling $___.75___

                        TOTAL $_____

I enclose _____

(Please send check or money order. We cannot be responsible for cash sent through the mail.)

PLEASE PRINT

NAME _____

ADDRESS _____

CITY _____

STATE/PROV. _____

BLJD-A-1